Praise for *The Note*

'An unforgettable love story set in perilous circumstances. It is a reminder that even in the most horrific times love will find a way and ultimately conquer. I can't recommend it enough.'
Heather Morris, bestselling author of *The Tattooist of Auschwitz*

'Gold sets a brisk pace and vividly describes the landscape of war-torn Europe. This WWII love story enthrals.'
Publishers Weekly, USA

'Well-researched and pieced together, the book will appeal to fans of wartime love stories and resistance tales in general . . . A memorable and uplifting work.'
Kirkus Reviews, USA

'The book is sensational – an absolute page turner, full of love but also the grim realities of what war was like for those on the ground.'
The Australian Women's Weekly

'This real-life love story is worthy of a Hollywood blockbuster.'
Brisbane Courier Mail

'The story is gripping and, ultimately, uplifting. *The Note Through the Wire* is an extraordinary tale of survival against unbelievable odds and of the power of love to transcend obstacles, difficulties and boundaries.'
Sunday Star Times

'As World War II non-fiction novels go, it's as gripping as it gets . . . The book is full of brave deeds, betrayals, suspenseful near misses and horrendous atrocities . . .'
North & South

The
Dressmaker
& the
Hidden
Soldier

The
Dressmaker
& the
Hidden
Soldier

Doug Gold

ALLEN&UNWIN
SYDNEY·MELBOURNE·AUCKLAND·LONDON

First published in 2023

Copyright © Doug Gold, 2023

Allen & Unwin
Level 2, 10 College Hill, Freemans Bay
Auckland 1011, New Zealand
Phone: (64 9) 377 3800
Email: auckland@allenandunwin.com
Web: www.allenandunwin.co.nz

83 Alexander Street
Crows Nest NSW 2065, Australia
Phone: (61 2) 8425 0100

A catalogue record for this book is available from
the National Library of New Zealand.

ISBN 978 1 99100 622 6

Cover design by Christabella Designs
Text design by Megan van Staden
Set in Baskerville 12/17
Printed in and bound in Australia by the Opus Group

10 9 8 7 6 5 4 3 2 1

MIX
Paper from
responsible sources
FSC® C001695

The paper in this book is FSC® certified.
FSC® promotes environmentally responsible,
socially beneficial and economically viable
management of the world's forests.

Dedicated to the memory of Peter Blunden and Thalia Christidou, who endured unimaginable hardship, displayed remarkable courage and, ultimately, found love after one of the bloodiest wars in history.

Location of key places and Peter's escape route

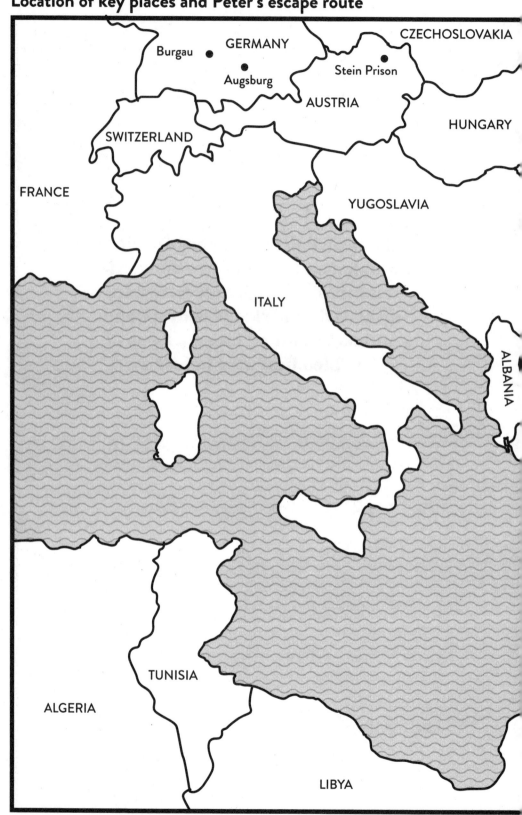

---- Peter's escape route

UKRAINE

MOLDOVA

ROMANIA

BULGARIA

Thessaloniki
Nea Potidea
Saint
Paraskevi

GREECE

Smyrna

TURKEY

Aleppo

Haifa

ISRAEL

SYRIA

EGYPT

Cairo

JORDAN

Chapter
One

Tasoula Paschilidou studied the girl, eyeing her up and down. Wondering if she could be trusted.

'She's very pretty,' she thought, as she looked again at the young woman sitting opposite. The girl was beautiful — bright-eyed with long black curly hair brushed back and tumbling carelessly over her shoulders. But that would make no difference to Tasoula's decision. She had to decide whether she could depend on this girl to keep a secret if she ever learned the truth.

She looked honest and reliable, but that meant nothing in Nazi-occupied Greece. Anyone might be a collaborator: your closest neighbour or your best friend — especially with an extra loaf or two of bread on offer for any information the Germans found useful; more if it led to the arrest of an escaping Allied soldier or a Greek resistance fighter. Tasoula knew better than to rely on instinct, but here she was about to employ a new dressmaking apprentice, someone she might one day have to trust with a secret that could see them both arrested and tortured. Or worse.

Seventeen-year-old Thalia Christidou sensed the uncertainty. The woman was scrutinising her with an intensity that suggested the interview was about more than just her suitability for the job. Thalia noticed the worry lines on the woman's face: she guessed she would be in her late thirties, but it was the face of a much older woman. Thin, mirthless lips, a furrowed forehead and deep creases radiating from the corners of her mouth accentuated her weathered features. What struck Thalia most, though, were the hollowed, charcoal-rimmed eyes — the weary eyes of someone who looked like she was used to facing adversity. Despite her demeanour, though, Thalia suspected she had a kind nature.

Thalia glanced around the room. The furniture was ornate but functional; the house spotless and well cared for. Colourful paintings and family snapshots decorated the walls, all arranged in neat rows. Thalia assumed that the teenage boy standing beside the woman in one photograph was her son. In one series of pictures the woman was surrounded by well-dressed girls, each holding a scroll. Dressmaking certificates, Thalia presumed. Off to one side, she saw the entrance to what looked like the sewing workshop and, opposite where she sat, a closed door, most likely to a spare room.

Thalia averted her eyes to avoid the woman's intense gaze and squirmed in the old rattan chair. She began to fidget, and tried to hide her nervousness by clasping her hands together tightly in a prayer-like grip. It wasn't that she lacked confidence, or self-belief — she had no reason to — but she felt intimidated by this woman and was uncomfortable being subjected to such scrutiny.

The woman eyeballed Thalia again, then spoke.

'What's your name, girl?' The words came out with a harshness that Tasoula didn't intend. She censured herself for being so abrasive.

'Th . . . Thalia.' Thalia struggled to get the word out. 'Thalia Christidou.'

'From where, Thalia?' she asked, softening her tone to make amends for her abruptness. She knew the girl was nervous.

'I was born in Kolindros, ma'am, but I've lived in Thessaloniki most of my life. Very near here. In this district.' Kolindros was a small village around fifty kilometres from Thessaloniki.

'Ah, I see. Kolindros.' Tasoula lingered on the words as if they meant something. Not that they did, but the brief pause gave her time to think.

The woman had a distinct accent. Thalia wondered where she came from. It wasn't a native Greek dialect, not one that Thalia recognised anyway. She couldn't quite place it. Albanian perhaps, or even Turkish? She wasn't sure. She wished she had caught the woman's name when she'd introduced herself earlier, but had been too anxious to concentrate.

Tasoula looked again at the young woman with the dark hair and flawless face. She noted the beautiful eyes — a rich chestnut brown that projected an innocence and sincerity rarely seen in wartime Greece. But these things were not important. Tasoula had a critical decision to make. With jobs so scarce — and unemployment high — Tasoula had no shortage of applicants. Before Thalia she had interviewed several hopefuls, none of whom she deemed suitable. She would have to decide soon.

Tasoula shifted her focus to the apprentice dressmaker's duties.

'Thalia, do you have any dressmaking experience?'

'My favourite aunt is a dressmaker — and her mother was before that — so I have been around dressmaking my whole life. But if you're asking if I have any formal training, the answer's no. I only know what my aunt has taught me. I had always thought I would work for her, but with the war and all that, she can't afford to keep her business going. These days the villagers don't have the money for luxuries like tailored dresses and my aunt earns barely enough from mending clothes to survive.' Thalia was surprised by how much information she had given. She shuffled around on the chair, wondering if she should say more. She decided against it.

Tasoula noted the intricate, hand-sewn bodice and flared dress the girl wore and could tell that her aunt was an expert seamstress.

'I sympathise with your aunt's predicament. Since the Germans invaded, many businesses have suffered. They have a lot to . . .' Tasoula was about to express her views on the Nazi occupation, but thought better of it. Best not to reveal her feelings about the occupiers or hint at her own role in combatting them.

Tasoula and her eighteen-year-old son, Thanasis, were active members of the Greek National Liberation Front, a resistance movement with Communist leanings. They hated the Nazis with a passion bordering on obsession. Tasoula was a key link in a sophisticated escape chain that helped fugitives — most often, escaping Allied soldiers — to safety in Turkey or Syria. Her role was to hide the fugitives until they could be moved, which might be a matter of days or several weeks. Sometimes even months. She passed them over to a Madam Lapper who, in turn, transferred the men to the final link in the chain: a well-funded, British-backed escape organisation that would arrange documentation and passage on a cargo ship. Tasoula also ran a successful dressmaking business — partly as a front to avoid detection, but mostly because she needed the money. She employed twelve dressmakers, and a recent resignation meant that she now had to hire an apprentice. Betrayal, an ever-present threat, would mean a death sentence, which was why the decision about who to employ was such a critical one. If any of 'her girls' ever learned about her resistance work, Tasoula's life would be in their hands.

Tasoula addressed Thalia once more.

'The job doesn't pay much, I'm afraid. Not in these times. Not with the war on,' she said, part of her hoping that the low wages might discourage Thalia and make her decision for her. Tasoula wondered if she might manage with eleven dressmakers. But business was good, and she needed all the work she could get to pay her overheads — and feed the soldiers she sheltered. She had no idea how long the orders would keep flowing in — already, six months after the Germans had marched into the country in April 1941, the war and the deteriorating economy were having an impact — but for the time being she had enough work to keep twelve workers busy.

'We can talk about wages if you get the job, but I have to warn you — I can't afford to pay a lot.'

'I understand. I don't need much. Just enough to get by and help support my family.'

————

A sudden movement caught Thalia's eye, diverting her attention to the window by the door. She glimpsed two thickset men in uniforms walking towards the house. A Greek police officer followed. From nowhere, a tall teenage boy appeared in the doorway — the boy in the photo — gesturing urgently to the woman.

'What do you want, Thanasis?' the woman said, annoyed at the interruption. 'Can't you see I'm . . .' The boy put his finger to his lips, signalling his mother to be quiet, and jerked his head towards the window. The uniformed men were almost at the door.

The woman was startled; Thalia saw the fear in her eyes. She jumped up and strode the few steps to the closed door behind her, turning the handle as if to make sure it was locked. Thalia considered this an odd thing to do. Then the woman rapped once on the door. It sounded to Thalia like a warning to someone inside, but she couldn't be sure if the single knock was deliberate or accidental.

A loud hammering on the front door surprised Thalia, and she heard voices shouting orders. German voices. Thalia spoke good German but didn't understand everything they said; the closed door muffled the words.

The woman looked around the room as though to check on everything before approaching the front door. She seemed a little calmer now. She opened the door and Thalia heard shouting. Someone — the policeman, she presumed — was yelling in Greek. Thalia caught snatches of the exchange: 'Let us in . . . We know . . . We'll . . . if you don't. Step aside or . . . .'

She didn't catch the rest, but had heard enough to realise that the Germans were agitated and must have suspected the woman of some crime or misdemeanour. The woman shouted back, but the policeman screamed at her to shut up and listen.

Thalia watched the drama unfold through the opening.

One soldier shoved the woman backwards and pinned her arms against the wall. The other drew his pistol, poking it in her face. The woman twisted free and pushed the soldier aside. The police officer grabbed her by the shoulders. She was now defiant. 'There's no one here! See for yourself . . . only my . . . and a young . . . Go ahead and . . . find nothing . . . just a dressmaker!' Again Thalia caught only fragments of the confrontation, but she saw one of the men jabbing his finger at the woman and pointing towards the front door.

One soldier shouldered his way past the woman and burst into the living room, knocking over a small table and a glass vase as he pushed the teenage boy to one side. The vase smashed to the floor and the other soldier kicked the table out of the way. The woman followed.

'I told you before — there's no one here but my son and a young girl I'm interviewing for a job. Go ahead, look around. You'll find nothing.' The police officer translated. Thalia thought she detected a note of desperation in the woman's voice, but she showed no outward signs of concern. The soldiers swaggered their way around the room, spilling the contents of drawers, rifling through cupboards and tossing books to the floor. They continued to rummage and ransack until they seemed to lose interest. They ignored the sewing studio, and didn't spot the locked door to the other room, which was hidden by the still-open front door. Thalia thought they were more intent on causing damage than finding anything incriminating.

The policeman watched as the soldiers tore the place apart, but made no attempt to intervene. Thalia wondered how a true Greek could be so subservient that he followed the German bullies like a lowly servant and could be complicit in such mindless destruction. She looked on, horrified. Her heart was thumping.

The two Germans surveyed the room again, then looked at each other, doubtless deciding whether to conduct a more thorough search. One raised his eyebrows as if to say he had seen enough and, without saying a word, they both walked out the door, kicking the table again as they left. The sycophantic Greek policemen followed like a well-trained puppy. Thalia watched them crossing the road towards a house down the street.

The woman gestured to the boy, who dashed outside. Thalia saw him looking left and right to check that the Germans had gone out of sight, then he set about clearing up the mess. The woman was now shaking.

'What . . . what just happened?' Thalia asked, unable to let the incident pass without comment.

'Ahh, nothing,' the woman said, as if it were an everyday occurrence. 'Just another random search. It's not the first time and it won't be the last. They think they'll find evidence of resistance propaganda material or an illicit shortwave radio or some other illegal activity. No chance of that happening, though. Greeks are too smart to get caught that easily. I just tell them they're welcome to look, and they always throw a few things around and then leave. It's the same every time. The Nazis are too lazy to do a proper search, so they'll never find anything.'

'I see,' was all Thalia could find to say, trying to take in what she had just witnessed. The encounter had rattled the woman, and the threatening behaviour of the men suggested that it was anything but a random search. Thalia wondered what the woman had to hide.

Regaining her composure, Tasoula scratched her forehead as she refocused on the interview. 'Now, where were we? Ah yes, wages. As I say, I can't pay much to start with, but if I hire you and you work hard, I may be able to offer a small increase.'

Tasoula explained what the job entailed and outlined the working conditions. She was warming to the young girl. 'Let me show you the workshop, Thalia.' She motioned Thalia to follow. 'By the way, everyone calls me Mrs Tasoula.'

Obediently, Thalia followed Mrs Tasoula into the dress-making studio. A long wooden cutting table dominated the centre of the room, laid out with different types and sizes of scissors, tape measures, tailor's chalk and several flat-irons to smooth out any wrinkles in the fabrics. Long metal rulers were inlaid on both sides of the timber bench, and delicate tissue clothing patterns had been folded and stacked at both ends. Everything had its place. Even the pin cushions and scissor blocks seemed to have their assigned positions.

Around the perimeter, twelve sewing desks, each equipped with a Pfaff treadle sewing machine, lined the walls. Thalia didn't like the fact that it was a German brand — she detested what Germany had done to Greece — but the Pfaff was an excellent machine.

Dozens of reels of different-coloured cotton threads mounted on spindles sat on the desks, behind the sewing machines. What caught Thalia's eye, though, were the large bolts of cloth piled in racks, all stacked according to colour. Row upon row. Cottons, woollens, linens, satins, laces. Reds, greens, blues — a myriad of shades and hues. Some plain, some patterned. Thalia had never seen so many fabrics. Her aunt could afford to buy only one or two rolls at a time, and only when she had firm orders; most of her work was now limited to repairs and alterations.

At one end of the room, dresses, jackets, blouses, coats and suits hung on a long wooden clothes rack attached by chains to the ceiling; some ready to be picked up, others in various stages of completion. A lace-trimmed wedding dress hung on its own beside one of the sewing tables, and Thalia wondered what it would be like to get married during such turbulent times.

Thalia now looked at Tasoula's clothes. She was, as Thalia expected, a skilled dressmaker. Tasoula wore a bright red dress

— Thalia's favourite colour — with a white-trimmed lapel collar and three flower-shaped blue buttons at the top of the bodice. Not a wrinkle or a crease to be seen. Without a doubt, Tasoula was a meticulous person who took care of both her workplace and her appearance.

'What do you think, Thalia?' Tasoula was proud of the studio and the work she did.

'It's wonderful. I've never seen a workshop like this. My aunt has only one machine in a small room at the back of the house. Nothing like this.'

'I've been dressmaking for a very long time, Thalia. I take pride in my work and expect my girls to do the same. Every garment that comes out of this workroom must be perfect — anything less is unacceptable. A tailored dress or coat is a big expense and I want my customers to be happy with what they get.' Thalia sensed that Mrs Tasoula was a woman who paid careful attention to every tiny detail.

They went back into the living room and sat down again. Tasoula asked more questions about Thalia's background, interests and family life, but she wasn't concentrating on the girl's responses; her mind was on other things. Biting her lip, Tasoula ran her manicured fingers through her dark curls. She tilted her head to one side as she weighed up the risks.

'She'll never find out about the soldiers,' she reasoned to herself. 'The others have no idea they're here, so why should this one?' She paused for another few seconds while she deliberated one last time. Then she made up her mind.

'When can you start, Thalia?' she asked, as if she had made the decision much earlier in the conversation and they were now ironing out the details.

'Today if you like. Whenever.' Thalia struggled to contain her excitement. 'I'll work hard, Mrs Tasoula, and I'll do whatever you ask of me.'

Tasoula wondered again if she was making the right decision about the young girl from Kolindros. But it was too late now.

Chapter
Two

Peter Blunden prepared to jump. Patrick Minogue was right behind him; eight others had gone before. Peter looked across at the blurred outline of the trees in the distance — judging by how fast they were flashing past, the train was picking up speed.

He peered down at the ground below and felt disoriented; the rhythmic rattle of iron wheels on metal tracks and the sight of the barren earth hurtling by beneath the train made him feel giddy. He thought he might throw up.

'C'mon Peter, for Christ's sake, jump! It's now or never,' Patrick yelled over the clanging of the train and the noise of the air rushing by. Patrick was right. If he didn't go now, the chance to escape would be lost.

Peter braced himself. He gripped the side of the slatted timber door, took a deep breath and launched himself from the carriage. He leapt as far as he could, reminding himself to relax to cushion the impact when he hit the ground. But he stumbled as he landed, taking his weight first on his left foot and then twisting on to his right. As he turned, his right knee buckled, and he fell. A stabbing pain shot down his lower limb and he screamed in agony. Instinct then kicked in; he rolled away and pulled up several metres from the tracks. He saw Patrick rolling away, too. His friend had also made it.

The piercing clatter of machine-gun fire and the screeching of brakes cut short any elation. The deep-throated growl of Dobermans, attack dogs kept on board to deter escapes or pursue those who tried, rose above the *rat-a-tat* of the Mauser machine guns and the rasping sound of metal on metal as the train wheels locked up. The German guards must have seen the first escapers jump and shouted orders to halt the train. By the time Peter and Patrick hit the ground, the train was slowing. But it was some distance away when it finally stopped and Peter lay still, hoping that his khaki uniform would blend in with the brown earth. Patrick lay a few metres away.

The onslaught from the Mausers was incessant. Bullets whistled by and Peter dared not move. One ricocheted off a small boulder next to his left arm; he could almost feel the heat as it flew past. 'Jesus Christ, that was close,' he thought.

Another shot missed him by inches, and he saw Patrick flinch as a bullet hit the dust above his head. The baying of the snarling Dobermans added to his anxiety. Yet another volley screamed past on Peter's right, close enough to shower him with shards of rock. Peter couldn't tell whether the Germans could see them lying there or were shooting randomly. He prayed that they were firing blindly.

Peter and Patrick were both exposed; if they didn't find cover soon, they would be hit. A lull in the shooting gave Peter the break he needed. He crawled across the dusty earth, elbowing his way towards a large boulder that offered some protection. He gestured for Patrick to follow. Peter was only halfway there when the gunfire opened up again, the repetitive crack of machine guns reverberating around the open terrain. He *had* to get to cover. And fast. He scrambled, half crouching, towards the safety of the large rock, diving the last few metres just as another salvo spat dirt in a wide arc right behind him. His left shoulder struck the hard stone as he dropped to the ground; a burst of pain surged through his arm. Patrick was too slow to move, leaving him stranded in the open. The guards seemed to be zeroing in on their position and Peter was sure that the gunners must now have them in their sights. More shots whizzed past.

Then the guns went silent; Peter heard only the howling of the Dobermans. One of the Germans — an officer by the sound of his assertive tone — barked out an order and everything went quiet; even the dogs were subdued. Holding his breath, Peter lay there expecting the guards and their dogs to rush them on foot and take them back into custody — or, worse, shoot them where they lay. The Germans often shot escaping prisoners on sight. But instead, he heard the familiar clank of the train pulling away. The Germans were either too lackadaisical to chase the fugitives or had decided it was more important to get their human cargo moving than pursue a few recalcitrant POWs, who would doubtless be recaptured by a roving patrol anyway. Peter wondered whether the Germans realised that there were now ten fewer prisoners on board.

'You okay, mate?' Peter called out to Patrick.

'Fine and dandy. As good as gold,' Patrick responded, with the sort of bravado that Peter had come to expect from his friend.

'What about you?'

'Not too bad. Knee's a bit dicky — banged it up when I landed but I think I'll be okay.'

Cautiously, Peter and Patrick stood up, checking that they had no broken bones or serious sprains. Peter tested his knee, gently putting weight on the leg, and declared himself fit and well. Apart from a few scratches and bruises — and Peter's tender knee and sore shoulder — they had both come through unscathed. They dusted themselves off, brushing away grass and dirt with the palms of their hands. The eight other POWs had already scarpered and were nowhere to be seen.

'So here we are,' said Peter, turning towards Patrick. 'What in God's name do we do now?'

Peter and Patrick had both fought in the ill-fated Crete campaign — Peter still had nightmares about it — and were captured amid the carnage of one of the most comprehensive German victories of the war. In a surprise move, Hitler had ordered a Blitzkrieg offensive — lightning air and ground attacks coordinated to inflict maximum damage — and had caught the Allies off guard. The results were devastating. Peter was wounded and taken to a hospital in Athens for treatment before being transferred to the Pentinta transit camp for POWs at Thessaloniki — or Salonika as the soldiers called it. He didn't know Patrick back then.

Patrick had survived the campaign uninjured and was sent straight to Pentinta. Once Peter arrived, the two struck up an immediate friendship. Patrick had already made one spur-of-the-moment escape attempt, sauntering out through the main gate and wandering along the road, but was recaptured after a week on the run — by a Nazi undercover group posing as a British-funded escape organisation. Fortunately, the Greek resistance cell that had passed him on to the imposters had only given him directions to the port and told him to make his own way, so their identities hadn't been revealed. Patrick was determined to escape again, if only to warn the valiant Greeks that Germans, not Greeks, controlled the escape route.

At Pentinta, they hatched a plan to jump from the train that would take them from the transit camp to Stalag 8B in Germany, their permanent POW camp. 'Jumping the rattler', they called it. Eight other prisoners joined them. The ten drew lots to decide who would go first. Patrick drew number three, but Peter was ninth and Patrick gave up his place so he could stay with his friend. The first few to jump would have the greatest chance of escaping, and Peter realised that their odds of a successful getaway were slim. He was disappointed to be almost last in the queue; the escape had been his idea and he had done most of the organising. But the draw for lots was fair and he had no complaints.

Once on the train, Peter had cut through the timber by the carriage door with a keyhole saw he'd stolen from the camp and taped to the inside of his leg to avoid detection. Another prisoner reached through the hole and unlatched the door. Their planning hadn't extended to what to do or where to go once they were off the train. Now they had to decide.

'Well, we can't bloody well stay here, that's for sure', Patrick said after they had tidied themselves up. 'Let's get to Salonika and stay there until we decide what to do next. I have some unfinished business to attend to.' Well aware of Patrick's foiled escape attempt, Peter understood his determination to warn the Greeks about the Nazi infiltration of their escape network. But he disagreed.

'I say we head straight for the port and see if we can get a cargo ship to take us to Turkey. It's worth a shot.'

'Nah,' Patrick said, his mouth tightening. 'Not a chance. We can't just wander around the port asking every Tom, Dick and Harry where we can find a Nazi-hating captain. It would be just our luck to run into a bloody collaborator or a bunch of Krauts. More than likely, we'll end up right back in the clink. We'll need some help from the locals if we're to have any chance of getting on a ship.'

For the first time since they'd met, they were on the verge of an argument. Peter tried to defuse the situation. 'Look, Paddy,' he said, 'let's not have a row over this. I get what you're saying, but we'll have the same problem in Salonika. We have to find somewhere to stay, and we can't bowl up to some stranger's door and ask if they'll put us up for a couple of nights. What if they're Kraut-lovers? Before you know it, we'll be tossed straight back into the cooler.'

'But that's where you're wrong, Peter,' Patrick said with a smug smile. 'I know where we can hole up for a few days. There's a lady in Salonika who runs a safe house: a Mrs Tasoula.'

Chapter
Three

Even from a distance, Peter could see the stooped lady with the straggly grey hair and time-wrinkled face staring at them as they approached the outskirts of the village. She was doubtless wondering whether the two strange uniformed men were friend or foe. Peter gazed back. He was wary; uncertain whether he should trust the woman.

'Whadd'ya reckon, Paddy? She looks harmless enough.'

'We've got to make a move sometime, Peter. Might as well be now.'

Peter signalled his agreement, and they moved forward.

———

After jumping the train, the two men had known they had to ditch their army uniforms and find some civilian clothes. Until then, they could travel only at night. A copse of trees near where they had landed provided some cover: it was out of sight of the railway tracks, and they had lain there until nightfall.

With only the moon to help them navigate, Peter and Patrick then made their way in silence to the nearest road and headed back towards Thessaloniki. They travelled parallel to the road, to avoid any late-night Nazi patrols, and had chanced on this settlement just before dawn. Judging by the sparseness of lights, it was a small village.

The two men now ambled towards the old woman, taking in their surroundings and hoping that their welcome would be a friendly one. A road sign told them they were in Mouries. Several dogs barked ferociously as they approached. People were out and about even at this early hour, and the men quickened their pace, taking care to avoid the dogs.

Peter locked eyes with the elderly peasant woman and nodded at her, raising his eyebrows as he did — querying whether they were welcome. She nodded back. They moved closer.

'Angliki?' she asked, poking her finger at Peter. He didn't understand, but assumed she was asking if they were English.

'Yes, Angliki,' he said, parroting the Greek. 'Me Peter' — pointing at his chest. 'That Patrick,' he continued, motioning towards his friend.

'Ah, Petros,' she said. Peter was about to correct her, but quickly thought better of it.

'What want you Petros?' the old woman asked with an accent so strong that Peter barely recognised the words as English. He glanced at Patrick, wondering again if they should trust the woman. But it was too late for doubt.

'Clothes and shelter,' Peter said, emphasising each syllable in the hope that the woman would understand. But she looked at them quizzically and Peter realised she had no idea what he was saying.

She tried French. 'Parlez-vous français?' she asked, in what sounded like fluent French.

Peter turned to Patrick. 'I learned a bit of the froggie lingo at school, Paddy. I'll try my luck with that.' He turned back to face the elderly woman. 'Oui, oui, oui,' he said, in his best French accent.

'Ah bien. Que recherchez vous·et comment puis je vous aider?' She spoke fast, running the words together so that it was impossible to distinguish one from another.

'Je ne comprend pas,' was the best Peter could manage. He abandoned any further attempt to converse. Resorting again to sign language, he mimicked putting on an imaginary jacket, then clasped his hands together and inclined his head to one side, resting it on his hands to indicate sleep.

'Come,' the old woman said, jerking her head towards a narrow street to their left. Peter and Patrick followed her to a house about a hundred metres along the road. She knocked on the door. Another woman appeared — almost as old, with similarly ruffled hair and yellowed teeth — and motioned them in. Her English was little better, and Peter had to again rely on sign language.

'Ahh', she said when she finally understood, and pointed her gnarled finger towards two chairs in the kitchen.

'Here stay. Plenty Germans.' She raised an open hand, signalling them to remain where they were; then the two women rushed off.

'Whadd'ya make of that, Paddy?' Peter asked.

'I think we're safe for now, but I'm not sure what they're up to. I hope the old girls aren't off to dob us in to the local collaborators.'

The women reappeared half an hour later with a slight, bespectacled man in tow. He wore a frayed tweed jacket with contrasting patches sewn on the elbows, presumably where the fabric had worn through. His trousers, although shiny from constant wear, sported sharp creases. An expertly knotted dark blue tie, slightly stained, hung from the threadbare collar of his light blue shirt. Were it not for the tattered clothes, he might have passed for a distinguished English aristocrat. Peter guessed he was in his early forties.

'He teacher.' The woman beamed, clearly proud of herself for finding someone who was able to communicate with the two strangers.

The teacher introduced himself as Petros Juriss. Peter and Patrick reciprocated.

'Ahh, it seems we have the same Christian name,' the teacher said to Peter. He glanced at the window before ushering the men into an adjoining parlour. Peter explained that they were soldiers on the run looking for clothes and shelter.

'One must be particularly vigilant in this region,' Petros said in impeccable English, with a distinct upper-class accent that wouldn't have been out of place in any of the gentlemen's clubs in Mayfair. 'This area is infested with Germans. Every town within fifty kilometres of here has its detachment of enemy soldiers. They're everywhere.'

His command of the English language impressed Peter.

'Collaborators are everywhere also — not in this village that I'm aware of, but I know there are many in surrounding towns — so extreme caution is necessary. Your sojourn here must be brief, for your own safety and for ours. I'll locate a safe place for you to stay for tonight, but it's imperative that you depart in the morning. I'll return soon with food and clothing and a map.'

The two women remained silent, nodding from time to time as though they had understood something Petros had said.

True to his word, an hour later the teacher arrived back with an old sack — tied top and bottom and slung over his shoulder — and a wicker basket with two brown-crusted loaves of bread and what looked like cheese and salami, partly covered with brown paper. 'There should be some apparel that fits amongst this collection,' he said, opening the bag and emptying its contents onto an old sofa tucked against a wall.

The clothes smelled of sweat and ingrained grime and grease, no doubt the result of many years of hard manual work. Peter and Patrick rummaged through them, Patrick selecting a shirt, trousers and jacket. Peter could find only trousers and a shirt, neither of which fitted well but would have to do. His taller frame meant he wasn't able to find a suitable jacket. The old lady they'd first met crossed herself, removed her own traditional hand-woven tapestry coat, and offered it to him. It was far too small, but the gesture touched him. He bowed his head in gratitude, then shook it to refuse. Peter looked through the clothes again and found a ragged sweater with strands of wool hanging from its ripped seams. It was also too small but he managed to stretch it a bit, although not by enough to reach his wrists or fully cover his midriff. He looked like a lanky schoolboy who had outgrown his regulation jersey.

The teacher then lifted the brown paper from the basket of food. 'Take this,' he said, handing the basket to Peter, 'but conserve some for the next leg of your journey. It's difficult to predict when and where you might be afforded the opportunity to replenish your stocks.' Peter wondered whether the teacher had been educated at some upper-class English public school, but decided not to ask.

'This is too generous,' he said, aware that giving so much to two strangers was a big sacrifice when food was so scarce in Greece and so expensive to buy. 'We must pay you something for your kindness and generosity.' Peter pulled out some of the Greek drachmas he had stolen from a guard at Thessaloniki and pushed them into the teacher's hand.

'No, I cannot take it. It is a privilege for one to help English soldiers in need. I cannot accept any remuneration for my services.'

Rather than argue, Peter grasped his hand and closed it around the money.

'My sincerest thanks for an unnecessary but much appreciated gesture. I expected nothing, but life is difficult for us Greeks, so I will use this to purchase food to distribute to the less fortunate in our community. I must warn you, though, that you need to detour around Miriofyton, which is the next village. There is a large German contingent based near there and collaborators abound in the town.' He produced a map and pointed to the village in question, then traced his finger along the route he recommended they take.

'Thanks for the heads-up,' Peter said. 'We've seen more than enough of Jerry over the last few months, and from now on we'll avoid him like the plague.'

Petros directed the two men to a nearby barn and told them to stay put. He informed them that he would return the following day when it would be safe to move on. He bid them farewell, looking both ways as he exited through the door. Peter and Patrick waved after him, thankful that they could now eat and sleep. They spent the rest of the day relaxing and discussing escape plans.

That night, Peter fell asleep almost straight away, and when he looked at his watch in the morning, it was after 10. Just after midday, Petros burst in, agitated and anxious. 'They're here. You cannot stay.'

'Who's here?' Peter asked. But he already knew the answer.

'Germans,' Petros said, struggling to catch his breath. 'They're everywhere. Searching for you.'

'For us?' Peter asked, surprised. 'How would they know we're here? We've been very careful. Surely no one in the village has betrayed us?'

'No, not the villagers. Apparently, two of your compatriots — the soldiers with whom you escaped — were recaptured by the Germans close to here, so they're scouring the area for any other Allied fugitives. My sources tell me that the Germans shot and killed them both. Bastards!' This was the first time Peter had heard the well-spoken teacher swear.

'Apologies for the profanity, but you must move. They'll be here soon. Who knows what havoc they'll cause? And if they suspect the villagers are implicated in any attempt to conceal your whereabouts, the consequences will be dire. Follow me and I'll take you somewhere safe.'

Peter and Patrick did as he asked, and jogged behind the teacher to the outskirts of the village. He waved towards a vineyard about two hundred metres away. 'Hide yourself in there,' he said. 'The Germans won't bother inspecting this area. I'll let you know when it's okay to come out.'

The pair made their way along the neat rows until they judged they were near the middle of the vineyard. They lay down so that no one would spot them above the vines. And waited. Peter could hear several shots coming from the direction of the village, and he prayed that the Nazis hadn't harmed the townspeople. It would be their fault if the villagers were ill-treated.

———

It was early evening when Petros returned. He told them that the German patrol had terrorised the residents — ransacking three houses, arresting one man who dared to challenge them, and firing several random shots above the crowd that had gathered.

'Fortunately, no one was injured or incapacitated. But it's no longer safe for you here. You can eat in the village and stay overnight in the barn. We'll wait here for another hour to be sure the Germans have dispersed, but you must depart in the morning.'

A sense of relief overwhelmed Peter. He would never have forgiven himself if someone had been killed or injured on their account.

Petros escorted them back to Mouries. The old woman — the one who had offered her jacket — had prepared a meal of moussaka and choriatiki, a tasty Greek salad with tomatoes, cucumber and feta cheese. The language barrier meant that the three of them ate in silence.

'Delicious,' Peter said, pursing his lips and making a flamboyant thumb and forefinger gesture to show appreciation for the excellent food. 'Amen to that,' Patrick added, nodding in agreement.

Petros reappeared at around 8 o'clock with two locals, and the five of them trooped back to the barn.

'I'm not so sure Salonika's such a good idea anymore,' Peter said. 'I know we agreed, but after what just happened, I think we should get out of Greece as quickly as we can and head for Turkey.'

Patrick disagreed. 'No. We stick to the original plan. I must warn Madam Lapper that the Gestapo are double-crossing her. We go to Salonika.'

One of the locals, who spoke some English, intervened. 'No Turkey. Not safe. Away stay. You be . . .' He struggled to find the right word, then looped an imaginary noose around his neck and pointed to a protruding branch on a nearby tree. 'That happen.' He turned to the teacher and explained in rapid-fire Greek what he wanted to say.

'Ahh. My friend here is trying to tell you that if you attempt to go to Turkey from here, there's a high probability that the Bulgarians will hang you. They now occupy North Macedonia, and the border is just a few kilometres from here. You would have to travel through that territory to get to Constantinople by land. The Germans have allowed the Bulgarians rights to this region in return for their military cooperation. Anyone who crosses into that area is sure to be arrested and tortured. The Bulgarians are worse than the Nazis. Several Greek families have already been slaughtered because they failed to leave the province. If you wish to go to Turkey, it's imperative that you proceed to a port and try to locate a cooperative boat owner to transport you by sea.'

'That's settled, then,' Patrick said with a hint of satisfaction. 'We go to Salonika.' Peter had no option but to agree.

Petros wished the pair safe travels and left with the local men. Peter slept fitfully, uncertain of what lay ahead. They rose well before dawn and made their way to the old woman's house to say farewell and thank her for her kindness. Her door was unlocked, but her rhythmic snoring told them she was still asleep. Not wanting to wake her, they left a note and some drachmas on the table along with a souvenir of their visit — a brass New Zealand Army badge depicting a wreath topped by a crown and inscribed with the word 'Onward'. Then they crept out, making sure they didn't disturb the sleeping woman.

After they were a safe distance from the village, Peter consulted the map and they discussed their next move.

'How long do you reckon it will take us to get to Salonika?' Patrick asked.

'Hard to say, Paddy. By the look of it, around two or three days if it's all plain sailing — more if we run into a Kraut patrol or have to hole up somewhere for a day or two. Anyway, Petros said we should head in this direction,' he said, poking his finger towards the road to the left.

'D'ya think it's safe to travel during the day?' Patrick wondered.

'Probably not, but it's Hobson's choice — we must push on. No point in hanging around here. At least our clothes don't look out of place, not like our army clobber. Besides, bugger-all Krauts speak Greek, so even if we do bump into Jerry, we're not likely to be questioned unless someone asks for our identity papers. If that happens, we're in real trouble.'

'We'll be in shitter's ditch then all right,' Patrick said.

The two men skirted around Miriofyton, heeding the teacher's warning, and made good headway until early evening, when they ran into a group of German soldiers lounging on the side of the road. 'Hey Greco,' one yelled. 'Zigaretten?' Peter shook his head and started to move off. To avoid trouble, Peter would have offered him a couple of fags if he'd had any. But he didn't.

'Not so fast, Greco. Stop! Now!'

Peter and Patrick kept walking, picking up their pace as they did, hoping that the soldier wouldn't pursue them. The clatter of boots on the hard road told them they weren't going to get away that easily.

'Do we run or do we stay?' Peter asked himself, then decided it was better to try to bluff their way out of their predicament than run and have a German patrol after them.

The soldier soon caught up, and shoved his gun into the small of Peter's back. It had a bayonet attached and Peter felt the sharp tip piercing his flesh.

'I said stop, Greco,' he said in German. 'Don't you peasants understand we make the rules around here and if I say stop, you'd better do as I say, or you'll have this rammed up your arse.' He jabbed the bayonet even harder into Peter's back to make the point. Thanks to his time in the POW camp Peter could make out some of the words, but he didn't need any knowledge of German to understand the soldier's intent. He tried telling him he didn't understand in the hope that he would leave them alone. 'Verstehe nicht,' Peter said in heavily accented German. The soldier pulled Peter around to face him and lifted the bayonet until it rested under his chin.

'Understand now, Greco?' He spat the words out with a venom that told Peter he wouldn't hesitate to use the rifle if they didn't obey. 'Now give me zigaretten or you'll get some of this!' he said, waving the bayonet dangerously close to Peter's face. Cigarettes were prized currency in wartime Greece. The occupiers could never get their hands on enough of the precious tobacco.

Peter rummaged through the small rucksack looped over his shoulder, pretending to search for cigarettes. Patrick looked on. The German turned and waved for the rest of his group to join him. Luckily, they seemed disinterested. Peter whispered into Patrick's ear, 'When I say run, we scarper as fast as we can.'

'Nein zigaretten,' Peter said, shaking his head, when the man turned to face him again. He opened the haversack to show that it was empty. He pulled out both trouser pockets to show that they were empty, too.

The soldier raised his rifle again and shouted something in German. The way he brandished his gun made it clear that if they wouldn't give him cigarettes, he would relish the opportunity to use violence. Suddenly, the German lifted his rifle stock and aimed it at Peter's head. Just as he slammed it down, Peter moved to the right, catching the wooden butt on his collarbone. He reeled back in pain. The soldier lifted his rifle again and swung it at Peter; he ducked, but the stock still grazed his scalp.

With no options left he charged at the German, striking the soldier's chin with his forehead and making the man stagger backwards towards Patrick, who grabbed him around the neck. But the soldier twisted free and elbowed Patrick in the stomach. He then threw a wild punch, hitting Peter with a glancing blow. With all the force he could muster, Peter head-butted the soldier. The German lost his balance; his rifle clattered to the ground.

'Now, Paddy — run!' he yelled at his companion. 'Go like the clappers.' Peter pushed the German hard in the chest as he struggled to his feet. The two men took off, racing along the road like two sprinters competing for Olympic gold. The soldier wouldn't be far behind.

The German fired two shots: one whistled past Peter and thwacked into a tree; the other was well wide of its intended mark and echoed harmlessly through the still evening air.

Peter and Patrick kept on running until they were sure no one was following, then pulled up off the side of the road, both doubled over and gasping for breath. The trunk of a large oak tree, about 100 metres in and concealed from the road, provided cover. They rested there to consider their next move.

'Jesus, Peter, that was a close shave. We might have been done for there.'

Peter just grunted, partly because he was still taking in air, but mostly because he was shaken by the skirmish with the aggressive soldier. His heart was pounding so hard that it felt like it would burst through his ribcage.

'If those cross-eyed bastards could shoot straight, it could have been curtains for us,' Patrick said, half-joking, to relieve the tension. 'I was shitting myself, I don't mind admitting it. We need to keep our distance from Jerry, or we'll be buggered. That was bloody lucky. Let's wait until it's dark before we push on to Salonika.'

Peter nodded, relieved to have come through the encounter largely unscathed.

Chapter
Four

'Iesous Christos! Patrikios!' Tasoula crossed herself. 'Christos, you — Patrikios. How happen?'

The knock on the door had startled Tasoula. She was cautious about night-time visitors and had almost decided not to answer. When she saw Patrick — and with another soldier — she was flummoxed, unable to believe that he had turned up on her doorstep again. To the best of her knowledge he was already safe in Turkey, or even back in England.

'Hello Mrs Tasoula,' Patrick beamed. 'It's nice to see you again.'

'Angliki no good, Patrikios. Thanasis get.' She put her finger to her lips, signalling for the two men to stop talking until her son arrived. Ushering the pair into a large sitting room, she directed them to a plush sofa pushed against the back wall.

'Thanasis, please come here,' Tasoula called out in Greek. A tall, lanky boy — about seventeen or eighteen — appeared in the doorway. A handsome lad with a chiselled, angular jaw reminiscent of Cary Grant, he had a thick crop of curly black hair slicked back over his prominent forehead and wore a traditional black Greek fisherman's cap perched at an odd angle on top of his head. What stood out for Peter, though, were his somewhat gangly arms — they seemed out of proportion to the rest of his body. Peter smiled at the boy.

'Mr Patrick! What . . . what happened?' The boy was clearly shocked by the reappearance of his mother's earlier guest. 'What you doing back in Greece? You supposed to be in . . .' — he halted, clearly realising that any further comment was redundant. Patrick was here in Thessaloniki, nowhere near Turkey.

Patrick wrapped both arms around the young boy and hugged him. 'It's great to see you again, too, Thanasis, although I wasn't expecting to. I'll explain everything soon, but first, an introduction. This is my good friend Peter Blunden. He's a New Zealand soldier. We're both on the run and hope that your mother can hide us here for a few days.'

'Of course. Of course. What am I thinking? Please comfortable make yourself.' Thanasis spoke very good English; apart from the occasional error in grammar and the odd missed verb, he was almost fluent.

'Now tell me everything,' Tasoula said, after Peter and Patrick had sat down.

Slowly, so that Thanasis could translate, Patrick explained how Madam Lapper's escape network had been compromised, infiltrated by the Gestapo. He described how he had been recaptured; how he and Peter had jumped the train on the way to a German POW camp; and how they had been helped by the Mouries villagers.

'You must warn Madam Lapper. She's in danger — the Germans are onto her. While they're still recapturing escaping soldiers they won't do anything, but once she has outlived her usefulness — or the Allied soldiers stop coming — they'll arrest her and everyone else in the escape chain will be at risk. You know what the Nazis are capable of. It would only be a matter of time before they forced her to reveal the names of others in the resistance.'

Listening closely, Tasoula nodded occasionally as Patrick emphasised the danger.

'As far as I'm aware, Mrs Tasoula, the Nazis have no idea who else is involved. They only intercept the POWs after they leave Madam Lapper's, so you're safe for the moment. But if she's arrested and tortured, she won't be able to hold out. She'll be beaten until she tells them everything.'

Tasoula was shocked, even though she already knew that what Patrick said was true.

'The Gestapo are masquerading as a British-backed escape organisation that helps to transfer escapees. They've convinced Madam Lapper that they'll arrange safe transport to Turkey, but the boat owner is on the Gestapo payroll. Soon after I boarded, they arrested me and sent me straight to Salonika, right back where I started.'

Tasoula turned to Thanasis. 'My God, I can't believe that Madam Lapper has been delivering dozens of British soldiers straight into the hands of the Germans. Terrible. Oh my God, she'll be devastated. Thanasis, please go and fetch Madam

Lapper. Tell her it's extremely urgent.'

'I'll come with you,' Patrick said. Thanasis looked to his mother for approval; instead, Tasoula raised a hand to say that Thanasis would go and Peter and Patrick would stay. Thanasis opened the door, glanced up and down the road, then headed down Adrianoupoleos towards Astipaleas Street.

Tasoula turned to her guests. 'Eat. Must eat,' she said matter-of-factly, as if they just returned home after a stroll in the park.

Patrick had fond memories of his brief stay with Tasoula and Thanasis, and while Tasoula was fossicking in the pantry for food, he explained to Peter how she helped many escaping British soldiers, risking her life every time she took someone in. 'She's a very courageous woman. The boy, too.'

'But we can't remain here, Paddy. We must leave — it's not safe for her if we stay. She's already done enough.'

Patrick laughed. 'You try telling her that, Peter. She'll take no notice, I can assure you. I insisted on leaving, too, but she flat-out refused. Told me she's determined to play her part in resisting the Germans. She knows the risks, but she's a proud Greek and figures that if she can help soldiers escape, the quicker they'll be back on the front lines fighting the enemy. Anyway, we'll only stay for a few days.'

Tasoula reappeared with two large plates of moussaka and fasolada, a traditional bean soup. The two men ate in silence while they waited for Madam Lapper.

Soon after the meal was finished, Thanasis arrived with Madam Lapper. She was agitated and distressed.

'What happened, Patrick? Thanasis has told me you were recaptured. I thought you made it safely to Turkey or all the way back to England.' Madam Lapper spoke near-perfect English, a language she had mastered long before the war; Thanasis translated for the benefit of his mother.

'Unfortunately not. After I left your place, I followed your directions to the port. Everything went well. The captain seemed friendly enough and said to go downstairs, where five others were waiting. "Make yourselves comfortable," he told us, "the boat will leave in an hour." I went into the cargo hold as instructed and waited. Another four escaped prisoners boarded, so there were ten of us in all. We sat around joking and laughing, all excited about the prospect of freedom and the opportunity to rejoin our units and have another crack at the enemy. But then, without warning, the door swung open and about eight Gestapo, all waving guns, confronted us. We didn't stand a chance, so had to surrender.'

Madam Lapper was incredulous. 'The Gestapo? Surely not the Gestapo.'

'Yes, the Gestapo. I could tell by the long black leather coats with swastika armbands. The boat's captain was with them, grinning. The senior officer handed him a wad of notes and the captain left, still grinning. The German officer told us we were fools; that the Gestapo were running the sham escape operation and had already recaptured dozens of others. He boasted that they knew all about the woman who was sending the soldiers, but while she was delivering prisoners straight into their hands they wouldn't arrest her.'

Madam Lapper shivered, visibly stunned by news she wasn't expecting. Her panicked eyes narrowed. 'So, they're aware it's me?' she asked, although the question was largely rhetorical.

'He didn't name names but, yes, I'm sure they know it's you. You're in great danger, Madam Lapper. The officer made it clear that they would deal with you when it suited them. And you know what *that* means. Fortunately I arrived at the boat alone, so none of my Greek friends were exposed. I'm not sure about the others, but I hope they came on their own, too. Madam Lapper, you must disband your escape group and leave Salonika as soon as you can.'

Madam Lapper squirmed in her chair, clasping and unclasping her hands. Her knees were locked tightly together. Peter could see the fear etched on her face. Although she did her best to hide it, straining to contain her emotions, the woman was petrified. She had every reason to be so — not only did the Nazis have her under surveillance, but they also had documented evidence of her treachery. Mercy would be out of the question. The best she could hope for would be the swiftness of a firing squad. But before that, she would have to endure brutal interrogation and torture.

Tasoula was thinking the same thing. The Nazis' torture techniques almost always yielded the names of other accomplices. And Tasoula's would be among them.

'Patrikios is right. You must leave Thessaloniki at once,' Tasoula said. 'There's no time to waste. Take what you're able to pack in a suitcase and get as far away from here as you can. I have a contact in Kolchiko. He'll look after you for a few days until you can make more permanent arrangements. You're a very brave woman and we're all grateful for everything you've done. We'll help you in any way we can.'

Eyes downcast, Madam Lapper nodded. 'You're right. I'll leave first thing tomorrow.' She hesitated. 'No, tonight. It's late but if I hurry, I'll make it to Kolchiko by morning. Thank you, Patrick, for risking your own life to warn me. You've saved mine. Eventually, the bastards would have come for me and . . .' She slid her forefinger across her throat to show that she understood what punishment awaited her.

'Paddy and I must leave, too,' Peter said. 'We can't put your lives in any more danger.'

'Nonsense,' Tasoula retorted. 'You'll stay here. No one knows about me, and we all have to play our part in fighting these Nazi devils. Providing refuge to you may not be a lot, but it's something I can do. Something I will continue to do.' Patrick looked at Peter with an I-told-you-so smirk.

'Thanasis, you go with Madam Lapper and help her pack while I make Petros and Patrikios comfortable.' Tasoula pulled her friend closer and embraced her. She handed her a piece of paper with an address in Kolchiko. 'Be safe,' were the only words of encouragement she could offer. Thanasis took Madam Lapper by the arm and led her out.

Peter could only watch and admire the courage of these patriotic Greeks who risked their lives — and might lose them — to help fugitives like Patrick and himself. As soldiers, their punishment, should they be recaptured, would be as lenient as a few weeks of solitary confinement — unless they were unlucky. But these two women had faced the death penalty from the moment they began welcoming Allied soldiers into their homes.

Peter was contrite. He had encouraged — in fact, pestered — Patrick to head straight for Turkey, and now he felt guilty about what would have happened to Madam Lapper if Patrick had followed his advice. He was relieved that his friend had prevailed. 'You made the right call, Paddy,' he said. 'It was an honourable thing to do and I'm truly sorry I tried to change your mind.'

Patrick just grunted, doubtless satisfied that his decision had been vindicated.

———————

After Thanasis returned, alone, Tasoula spoke to him for a few minutes before unlocking the door to a small room to the side of the front door.

'My mother says that this is where you'll stay,' Thanasis told the men. 'You must keep the door locked at all times. She has twelve dressmakers here during the day. None of them are aware we're hiding British soldiers, so you must be silent. And I mean silent. Not even a cough or a sneeze. Once they've gone for the day, you can come out.'

'Thanks, Thanasis. I know the drill. I've been here before, remember?' Patrick said. Thanasis smiled.

Peter looked around the small room that would be their home for as long as they stayed. Two single beds — about a metre apart — were pushed up against the side walls. A small, painted chest of drawers was squeezed into one corner; a wooden chair perched in the other. The walls were bare save for an oval, timber-framed mirror hanging from a chain above the chest of drawers, and a single window hidden behind a blind. Both beds were made up, each with a clean white pillow and a brightly coloured, hand-stitched patchwork quilt. Crafted from fabric remnants, Peter presumed. He wondered whether it might have been Thanasis's room before Tasoula started taking in Allied boarders.

'So, this is our home for the next few days, Peter. It's like staying at the Savoy compared with that shithole at Salonika.'

Tasoula returned a short time later and talked again to Thanasis. 'Mother says you must throw your clothes out. She'll get you new outfits.'

'We've come to the right place for that!' Patrick said, with a smile.

Tasoula produced a tape measure and, with her trained hand, ran it up their arms, around their chests and down their legs. Peter looked on in awe — this woman had just learned that her resistance network had been compromised, yet was carrying on as if she were simply measuring up a couple of clients for new suits.

Pointing to the bathroom, she gestured for them to leave their old clothes in a pile outside the door. She handed Peter a bottle of foul-smelling liquid, disinfectant for delousing. Peter was sure that anything that smelled *this* bad would kill any and all undesirables they might have picked up on their journey.

The two men took turns to scrub themselves in the small but pristine bathroom. Peter couldn't believe how much dirt had accumulated since they'd left Salonika. Neither of them had washed in over six days and Peter was repulsed by his own body odour. His grime-grey skin was peppered with red blotches from insect bites, scratches and parasite rashes. It took half an hour of intense scrubbing before he was sure he had rid himself of the filth and vermin. He now smelled like a hospital ward, but at least he was clean. It felt good.

Less than an hour later, Thanasis reappeared with a stack of pressed and folded shirts, jackets and trousers. 'Mother says that if she had more time, she would have tailored something. These belonged to my father. Mother has made some alterations, so they should fit.' Thanasis didn't express any emotion when he mentioned his father. Peter thought this a little strange, but didn't say anything.

With just a few more minor adjustments to the sleeves and trouser legs, which Tasoula did in minutes, the clothes fit well. She was an excellent judge of size.

All that night, Peter tossed and turned. The encounter with Madam Lapper had unnerved him. Up until then, he hadn't considered what the consequences might be for his hosts. He thought back to the Mouries villagers and what they had risked to protect him and Patrick while the Nazis searched the town. Patrick was also turning restlessly on his small single bed.

Chapter Five

Thalia arrived for work early on her first day, as she wanted to make a good impression on her new employer. She heard voices and scuffling inside after she rang the doorbell and waited for Tasoula to answer. An interior door slammed, and it took ages for her employer to appear.

'Thalia, you're early. I insist that my girls arrive on time, but not a minute before. Nine a.m. on the dot. Don't arrive early in future. Understand?'

Thalia trembled. She hadn't expected such a curt response to her early arrival; she'd just wanted to show that she was eager to start her new job. 'Of course, Mrs Tasoula. I didn't mean to upset you. It's my first day — I thought I should get here in plenty of time.'

Tasoula's tone softened. 'You weren't to know, dear, so welcome. Please come in.'

Tasoula waved Thalia into the parlour. Thalia had been far

too ill at ease to take much notice of Tasoula's house during her interview, but now she took it all in. She had never seen such a magnificent place. While waiting for Tasoula to answer the bell she had already been overawed by the huge arched entrance, which featured elaborately carved wooden doors with massive decorative black hinges bolted to the timber panels. A half-round wrought-iron panel sat like a crown above the doors and a hexagonal porch protruded from the roofline. It was a mansion, and it dominated the houses around Enou Place where tree-lined Adrianoupoleos Street intersected with Tifonos.

Inside, it was just as impressive. Compared with her parents' small two-bedroom apartment above the taverna they owned, it was a palace. It wasn't possible to see all the bedrooms — she thought there might have been four — but the living room was spacious, and the kitchen was big enough to cook for a football team. Off to one side was the dressmaking studio.

———————

Peter Blunden bore more than a passing resemblance to Jimmy Stewart, the famous actor: they had the same chiselled features, soulful eyes, heavy eyebrows and full mouth. Even their hairstyles were similar. Peter was more reserved than his celebrity look-alike, but his self-effacing exterior concealed a sharp wit and a born raconteur. He was no fashion icon — preferring traditional clothing styles — but the clothes he wore were smart and elegant.

Peter was everything Patrick wasn't. Patrick was short; Peter almost a head taller. Patrick had a quick temper; Peter was calm, diplomatic and dignified, although he did have a rebellious streak and didn't take kindly to being told what to do. Patrick swore a lot, Peter didn't; he abhorred foul language.

Patrick was outgoing, outspoken and gregarious; Peter quiet and unassuming, almost to the point of shyness. Patrick cared little about his appearance; Peter was meticulous about his. In fact, the only thing they had in common was hair parted on the right-hand side. And their friendship. Despite their very different personalities, they had become the closest of friends.

The two men soon settled into a daily routine: an early breakfast before the dressmakers arrived; a quick break for lunch when the girls left for theirs; cribbage and other card games for silent recreation; and — what they looked forward to most — some free time at the end of the workday when they were allowed to leave their tiny room. It was November 1941 and, with the nights closing in, they welcomed the opportunity to sit in the warmth of the potbelly stove, Patrick puffing on a cigarette and Peter sucking on his pipe. Both appreciated what Tasoula was doing for them. They understood the sacrifices she made and admired her bravery. Tasoula treated the two men like family: they always had food on the table and a warm place to sleep. Many Greeks had neither. But being cooped up in a small room in total silence for eight hours every day took an emotional toll. They couldn't communicate during the day unless they whispered; they couldn't even walk around the room. The boredom was mind-numbing. They even had to control their bodily functions to time their toilet breaks around the dressmakers' work hours.

They tried sleeping in the daytime and staying awake at

night, but the sound of customers coming and going, girls gossiping, and the monotonous clacking of sewing machines kept them awake. Besides, there was the genuine risk that their snoring might alert one of the girls to their presence, so they gave up on that idea.

Peter liked to read, and Thanasis lent him a few English-language books he had, including one with some fascinating stories about adventures in the south seas. Peter re-read them several times; it helped to while away the hours. To ward off the monotony and make their card games more interesting, they gambled with imaginary money. Patrick was the better player; if he ever cashed in the 'debt', Peter would have owed him thousands.

To pass the time, Peter also learned Greek. If they were to escape to freedom they would have to travel through Greece, and therefore one of them needed to master the language. He also wanted to become fluent enough to converse with Tasoula in her native tongue. Thanasis helped Peter at night. He was a patient but demanding teacher; Peter often became frustrated with his own lack of progress and poor pronunciation, which Thanasis corrected mercilessly. But it made him even more tenacious. He set himself a target of learning twenty words a day. With plenty of time on his hands, he exceeded that number by some margin.

But nothing staved off the boredom for long. Initially, the prospect of escaping to Turkey kept them motivated, but Tasoula insisted it would be too dangerous to leave; winter would make it impossible to traverse the treacherous terrain and a new escape network hadn't yet been set up. She was right: they would have to wait until a safe sea route to Turkey had been established — and that would be in spring at the earliest.

To make matters worse, following Madam Lapper's disappearance and the abandonment of her escape network, Nazi patrols had become more vigilant. Fugitives that they would have recaptured after they boarded the collaborator's boat now had to be hunted down. Peter and Patrick just had to bide their time and cope with being bored stiff.

Apart from evening conversations with their hosts, the two men's only contact with the outside world was through the small keyhole in the door. From time to time they caught glimpses of the young dressmakers as they passed by, along with customers who came for fittings or to pick up orders. It made a pleasant, if unsatisfying, change from the four walls of the locked room.

One dressmaker in particular was a more regular keyhole acquaintance than the others. Peter figured she must be an apprentice because Tasoula gave her all the lowly tasks: sweeping the floors, tidying up after her colleagues and cleaning the parlour adjoining their room. Although each sighting was fleeting, Peter noted that she was beautiful: long, flowing black hair cascading over slender shoulders; flawless olive skin; and penetrating brown eyes that exuded hope and optimism, in stark contrast to the despair and oppression that was enveloping Greece. He nicknamed her Cinderella because she was the beautiful girl given all the menial tasks. Not that she seemed to mind.

Peter could tell that the girl was curious about the locked room. She swept around the door for much longer than it would take to sweep away any dust. She twisted and rattled the handle every day, trying her best to open it. More than once, Peter knew she was peering through the gap at the bottom of the door because her head blocked some of the light that flowed through. Peter thought she would probably try to peek through the keyhole, too, so made sure he closed the swivelling keyhole cover on their side whenever she got too close. Once, they had left the door unlocked after returning from their daily lunch break and it took all of Peter's strength to hold the handle firm when the girl tried to open it. On another occasion Peter felt the urge to sneeze, but managed to suppress it. As far as he was aware, she didn't notice.

'She's onto us, Paddy,' Peter said one morning. 'I'm sure of it. She's curious and suspicious, so we need to be careful.'

Patrick agreed. 'I hope you're wrong, Peter, but somehow I doubt it.'

Each day, the inquisitive girl seemed to take longer to clean outside their room. Peter often heard her brushing up against the wall. She must have had her ear against it, listening for sounds inside. Any mistake — an inadvertent cough, shoes scuffing on the floorboards or some other involuntary sound — and she would discover their secret. They resolved to be even more careful whenever she approached. They were worried that she might be a collaborator — anyone reporting two Allied soldiers and a resistance fighter to the Germans would be offered a handsome reward. With food and money so scarce, and many Greeks struggling to survive, it would take only a small bribe to persuade some to betray two wanted fugitives.

Thalia's first weeks in her new job passed quickly. She had never been employed before and she wanted to please. She was a little worried about the prospect of another German raid on the property; the incident during her interview had unnerved her and she sensed that Tasoula had something to hide. But everything seemed normal in the workroom and Tasoula's calm manner put her at ease. There were no German soldiers in the immediate vicinity — not that Thalia noticed, anyway — and that further reassured her. Perhaps it had been a one-off. Although Tasoula *had* referred to previous searches. The buzz and excitement in the dressmaking studio quickly took her mind off that unfortunate encounter, however.

Tasoula was expert at guiding her clients to the right choice of fabrics, colours and styles to flatter their varying figures, and the orders flowed in; most from regular clientele, some from casual customers. Sometimes male customers would arrive, and Tasoula would produce a catalogue of all the latest fashions for men: double-breasted suits, overcoats, casual jackets, formal wear, waistcoats. The continuous clatter of sewing machines and the constant chatter of garrulous girls trying to be heard above them created an energetic workplace atmosphere. Bolts of fabric being unfurled on the long wooden table, as though they were red carpets for royalty, and the rhythmic swish of scissors working in unison to create the complex pattern outlines added to the hum of a busy studio.

At first, Thalia's duties comprised only the most basic work: sweeping floors, fetching fabrics, oiling the Pfaff machines, cutting pattern outlines (where the margin for error allowed for mistakes), and sorting through fabric remnants to find anything suitable for making into scarves, belts, ties and hats. From time to time, Tasoula entrusted her with measurements for minor alterations.

The other girls welcomed Thalia. She connected immediately with Fifi, one of the more experienced dressmakers, and with Pauline who, in an unguarded moment, confided that her family was Jewish and at risk of being persecuted by the Nazis. Thalia was a cheerful person with a great sense of humour and the three girls giggled and laughed their way through the days. Thalia was enjoying her new job — even though she was the lowly apprentice. She was a quick learner, though, and Tasoula soon offered her more responsibility: sewing lace and trim, attaching buttons and some simple machine-stitching. All in addition to her sweeping and cleaning duties.

The locked room near the front door intrigued Thalia. Why had Tasoula been so keen to check it when the Germans raided the house during her interview? Did she, as Thalia suspected, want to make sure that it was securely snibbed? Tasoula's actions that day were mystifying to Thalia; suspicious even. Thalia couldn't help herself: she tried the door every day. It was always locked.

Thalia instinctively knew that the room contained a secret. She had no idea what could be behind the locked door, but there was *something*. She tried to find out more: rattling the doorknob, peeking underneath the door, and sometimes putting her ear against the wall to listen to what might be going on inside. She tried spying through the keyhole but could see nothing because some object on the other side blocked her view. Thalia even knocked on the door as if she were a visitor expecting someone to open it. Once, she thought she picked up a muffled sound but wasn't sure.

She plucked up enough courage to ask her employer. 'Mrs Tasoula, I hope you don't mind me asking, but what's in the closed room?'

'Nothing Thalia. Really, there's nothing in there but a few treasured family heirlooms and a couple of quite valuable paintings. I keep it locked for safe-keeping. I don't want anyone poking around in there and taking my precious stuff. The Nazis in particular — they might raid the place at any time.'

Tasoula's explanation didn't convince Thalia, but she knew better than to keep questioning her employer. 'I understand, Mrs Tasoula. You can't be too careful these days. The Germans are everywhere, I realise that, but it must get very dusty in there and I'd be happy to clean it. It wouldn't be a problem. Under your supervision, of course,' she added.

'That won't be necessary, Thalia. There's no need for you to concern yourself with that room. No need at all!' Tasoula snapped. Taking a long breath, she forced herself to simmer down. 'Now, back to the workshop. You're making great progress. With a bit more work we'll make a decent seamstress out of you yet.'

Tasoula's response raised more questions for Thalia than it answered. 'Heirlooms and artworks indeed! Mrs Tasoula is hiding something in that room,' she thought. Her mind started working overtime. Was there a stash of guns for the partisans hidden there? Tasoula hated the Germans, but Thalia didn't think she had anything to do with the resistance. Or was it so untidy and full of junk that Mrs Tasoula was embarrassed to let anyone see it? Or did the room hold unpleasant memories? Perhaps someone had died in there and Mrs Tasoula couldn't face going into the room again. That might be one explanation, Thalia conceded. But she still wasn't satisfied.

Every day, Thalia spent more and more time sweeping and looking and knocking and listening. She *had* to find out what was behind that locked door.

———

'Jesus, Paddy,' Peter whispered, 'look who's here.' He shuddered. Patrick moved him to one side so that he could peer through the keyhole. The two men had just returned to their room, a few minutes before the girls came back from lunch.

'Christ, a bloody Kraut,' he whispered back. 'Better make sure we're deathly quiet.'

Patrick moved to the rear of the room, but Peter's eye remained glued to the keyhole. He had heard the sharp rap on the door and a German voice as Tasoula opened it, but didn't expect to see a Wehrmacht major in full regalia: green tunic and breeches, peaked cap with a silver-braid wreath. The embroidered eagle on the tunic gave Peter the shivers. He had seen the same symbol on the officer who had interrogated him after his capture. That major had been a brute. This was another very senior German officer.

Tasoula directed the man to a chair while she summoned Thalia, the only one of her girls who spoke German. Emerging from the workshop, Thalia broke into German when she saw the officer. 'How can we assist?' she asked.

'Good morning Fräulein,' he said with a smile. 'How are you on this fine day?'

'Good,' Thalia replied, although she was anything but. A German anywhere near her made her want to vomit. 'What can we do for you?'

'I'd like my uniform altered, if you don't mind.' He was almost apologetic. 'It doesn't fit well. Look here . . .' He tugged at one of the sleeves, which hung down to his fingertips. 'And here,' he said, pulling at the buttons on his tunic to show that it was baggy at the front. 'I've just been promoted, you see. To major.' Thalia could tell he was very pleased with himself. 'I want my dress uniform to fit perfectly. I need to set a good example, you understand. To the men.'

'Of course. We'd be happy to help any officer of the German army. It would be our privilege,' Thalia said, with a mock sincerity that seemed lost on the ingenuous officer.

'Thank you so much. But first, there's something I must do. I'm sorry, but my superiors have instructed me to do a quick inspection of every place I visit. Just to check for anything illegal — illicit radios, forbidden propaganda material, that sort of thing. We even discovered a hidden British soldier once.' The officer laughed. 'Not that I'm suggesting there's anything like that here. It's just a precaution, you understand. Standard practice. Do you mind if I have a look around?'

'You won't find anything here. There's just the owner and us dressmaking girls.'

'I know. I know. But it's my duty. Orders, you understand. It won't take long. Just a quick check. You don't mind, do you?' The officer didn't seem to be suspicious, but Tasoula appeared to be on edge. She was shaking slightly.

'Of course not. You can start with the studio where all the work's done.'

'What about that room over there?' he said, waving towards the locked room. 'That's the closest. I'll start there.'

Thalia translated for Tasoula, who stiffened. The request clearly unnerved her, and Thalia recalled her stern warning about no one being allowed in that room. Looking for direction, Thalia searched Tasoula's eyes. An almost imperceptible shake of the older woman's head told Thalia all she needed to know.

Peter had been watching the exchange through his spyhole. The man had pulled at his uniform and played with the buttons on his tunic. It had to be something to do with tailoring; otherwise, why would he be there? It wouldn't be a surprise raid — a lone officer would never conduct a full-scale search without support. Perhaps he wanted his uniform altered. Although Peter couldn't see much through the narrow slit, it was enough to tell that the outfit was far too big for such a slight fellow. That had to be it. A simple tailoring job. Peter relaxed.

Then things changed. Peter saw the German looking around the house, seeming more interested in his surroundings than whatever he had come for. He didn't seem to be agitated, though, which was a good sign. The girl, the suspicious one, jabbed her finger towards the dressmaking studio, but without warning the German swung on his heels and pointed at their room instead. Trouble was looming. The man moved towards their door.

'Hell's teeth, Paddy,' Peter breathed to his friend, 'I think we have a problem. Not sure what's going on, but it doesn't look good.'

Now the major was grasping the door handle of the locked room. Thalia hesitated, unsure exactly how to respond. Her throat had dried up.

'Of co . . . course you can go in there.' Thalia was stuttering, struggling to get the words out. Then, just as the major was about to twist the handle, she reacted instinctively. 'Of course,' she said, more confidently, 'that's fine. You're welcome to check all the rooms — but first, let me take your measurements. Then you can do your inspection after we've taken down all the details.'

Before the officer could turn the handle, Thalia took him by the arm and guided him to a small wooden tailoring platform. Anxious to distract the man, she grabbed a measuring tape and put it around his chest, making a point of rubbing her hands across his ribcage as she called out the measurements. Tasoula noted them down as if *she* were the apprentice, not Thalia.

'We can make this fit as well as any tailor-made suit,' she assured the officer, looking directly into his eyes as she spoke. 'Now let's have a look at the arms.' She unrolled the tape, stroking his muscles as she ran the measuring ribbon from shoulder to wrist. 'Hmm, very strong I see.' The German straightened his shoulders and puffed his chest out. Thalia thought she saw a self-satisfied smirk spread across his face at the compliment.

'Now, let's sort out these breeches,' she said, not giving the

German a chance to protest. She measured his waist, calling out the correct size as she did. Thalia then slid the tape between his legs and wrapped it around one thigh, as close to his crotch as she dared. She did the same to the other thigh, taking her time with each measurement.

'There, finished,' she said, looking at him again, engaging his eyes for long enough to suggest that she was interested in more than just his alterations. 'Now let's get these clothes off so that we can start work on the adjustments. You can change over there,' she said, directing him to a curtain that partitioned off a small fitting room by one of the sewing stations. Tasoula said nothing, but nodded her approval as the officer changed into a spare outfit he had brought with him. He reappeared in an ill-fitting captain's uniform and smiled at Thalia.

'I'll make it my personal business to do the alterations myself,' she said. 'Come back in three days and your uniform will fit you like a glove. Everywhere,' she added.

Any thoughts of searching the house had long passed. The officer tipped his peaked cap, gazed longingly at Thalia — and left.

'Pig!' Thalia said in Greek, as soon as she shut the door behind him. 'These animals have no place in our country.'

'You were wonderful, Thalia. I wouldn't have handled that situation any better. And I've had a lot more experience dealing with the Germans than you have.'

'It was revolting,' Thalia said. 'I have no idea what came over me. One minute, I was terrified. Couldn't speak. The next I was acting like a brazen hussy.'

'Sometimes we just do what we have to, Thalia. We react

instinctively. There's something else you should know. I'm in . . .'
She stopped mid-sentence. 'One day I'll tell you more, but for
now, all I can say is thank you.'

From the keyhole, Peter looked on in awe. He didn't quite
understand what had just happened, but it was clear that the
young Greek girl had saved them from recapture. And had
saved Tasoula from a much worse fate.

After the girls had left for the day, Tasoula explained
everything to Peter and Patrick. Reflecting on the encounter
later that night, the two men realised just what a close call it
had been. 'That was a near thing, Peter. We'd have been well
and truly buggered if that Kraut had rumbled us. God knows
what would have happened.'

'Too true. We've only got one person to thank for getting us
out of that scrape. How she steered that major away from our
door I'll never know. She's not only easy on the eye, Paddy —
she's also very brave.'

The officer came back three days later. As a precaution,
Tasoula had shifted Peter and Patrick to another safe house,
owned by a Mrs Koula Angelidou. The German major tried
on his uniform, expressed his satisfaction with the alterations,
flirted with Thalia, and left.

Chapter Six

The encounter with the German officer had shaken Thalia. At the time, she had reacted without considering the consequences; only later, as she reflected on the incident, did she realise that Tasoula had been terrified at the prospect of the house being searched again. She had seemed even more concerned about the locked room being inspected.

Thalia was becoming increasingly suspicious about the room and Tasoula's reluctance to explain why she wouldn't allow anyone in there. She also had her suspicions about Tasoula herself, having seen her deep in conversation with strangers who had no interest in dressmaking. Different men came and went, and Tasoula took care to make sure no one was listening when they talked. These secretive meetings heightened Thalia's interest in Tasoula's clandestine activities and the room that was never opened.

Once, she did overhear Tasoula talking to one of the men

— a thickset fellow with Popeye muscles and several missing teeth. While she wasn't close enough to pick up everything, she did catch snatches of their conversation. 'Nazi swine,' Tasoula said at one point; '. . . wary or be captured' was another phrase she used. On another occasion, she heard Tasoula instructing Thanasis to buy wine and tobacco 'for the men'.

'What men?' she wondered. No men lived in the house apart from Thanasis, and Thalia didn't think he qualified. And no one smoked.

'What's Mrs Tasoula up to?' she asked herself. Her reference to 'Nazi swine' didn't surprise Thalia, but the fact that she'd said it to a relative stranger did. Thalia felt the same way about the Nazis as Tasoula did, but loose talk — even to friends — about German oppression or derogatory comments about the occupiers was dangerous in wartime Greece.

Thalia found the answers to her many questions in the most unexpected way. One Friday in late November, she left at midday as usual but returned to work early because she had a tight deadline to meet. She had to hand-sew ornate lace and elaborate embroidery onto a dress — a laborious and painstaking task, made even more difficult by the tight timeframe. It was due to be picked up at 5 o'clock. Tasoula had never entrusted her with such intricate work before, and she was eager to please her employer.

When Thalia walked in ten minutes before her lunch break ended, she couldn't believe what she was seeing: two men sitting at the kitchen table, engrossed in conversation, while Mrs Tasoula cleared their lunch plates away.

'Oh my God . . .' she said, startled by the presence of

two men talking in a foreign language. For a split second she thought they might be Nazis about to conduct another search. But neither man wore a uniform, and they weren't speaking German. It suddenly dawned on her that these two men must be the occupants of the locked room. 'Oh my God . . .' she repeated. 'I knew it. I *knew* it. I knew there was something or someone in that room.'

'Let me explain,' Tasoula said, but Thalia interrupted: 'It's them, isn't it?' she said, pointing towards the men. 'They're the ones in the room, aren't they?'

Peter was just as shocked. He started to speak, but Tasoula held up her open palm to block any further comment. He turned instead to look at the girl who had sprung them. He knew who she was: the one who had coaxed the German officer into having his measurements taken instead of searching the house. The same girl who tried the door handle every day and peered under the door. He had watched her often enough through the keyhole, but hadn't expected to see her in person. She looked even more beautiful than his restricted keyhole view had allowed him to appreciate. Her dark brown eyes mesmerised Peter even though he was perturbed that he and Patrick had just been exposed.

Tasoula turned to Thalia. 'Enough,' she said, exerting her authority. 'I'll explain everything, but the other girls are due back in a few minutes, so we'll have to leave it until later. Can you stay after five tonight?'

Thalia was lost for words. She just nodded.

'Now back to work, Thalia. And not a word of this to anyone. Not *anyone*. Understand?'

Thalia nodded again and headed for the studio.

This was the moment of truth; Tasoula would now have to tell the girl everything. Her doubts about Thalia's trustworthiness came flooding back. This was what she had dreaded: relying on someone else to keep such a dangerous secret. If Thalia chose to report the information, the young girl would profit: a word to the authorities would be well rewarded. And even if she didn't report Tasoula, an overheard conversation between friends, a slip of the tongue at the wrong time, or a casual remark about a hidden British soldier would all mean immediate arrest. The stakes couldn't be higher: Tasoula would now have to rely — hopefully — on a seventeen-year-old girl's promise not to reveal the truth about her employer. Still, she had no option. The girl had seen the two men and immediately deduced that they were the ones hidden in the locked room.

Peter was just as concerned. 'Whadd'ya think, Paddy? Are we done for here?' he asked after they had retreated to their locked sanctuary.

'Nah. I'm sure we can trust her. I hope so, anyway.' But Patrick was the reckless one who never seemed to worry about anything, so his assurance did little to reassure Peter.

'I hope you're right, Paddy. There's nothing I can put my finger on, but there's something about her. I'm not sure why, but I doubt that she'll dob us in.'

Peter pictured the innocence, the vulnerability, that those brown eyes exuded.

'Yes, we can trust her,' he said confidently.

Thalia could hardly contain her excitement. Who were these men? Foreign spies? Guerrilla fighters here to help the resistance? Or just a couple of foreigners trapped in Greece since the outbreak of the war? Were they dangerous? Was Tasoula being forced to hide them? Did they possess secret documents? Were they English? Or American? Or Dutch? Or some other nationality she had never heard of?

The girl couldn't concentrate on her work. A myriad of theories raced through her adrenaline-fuelled brain until it became a jumbled mess of disconnected thoughts. Almost mechanically, she sewed the lace and embroidery panels onto the dress, hoping it would pass Tasoula's stringent inspection. 'If it's not perfect, it's not good enough,' the dressmaker would often say. This time, however, Tasoula didn't even check the work, telling Thalia to hang it on the timber collection rack, ready to be picked up.

Just before 5, the customer collected the garment, inspected the work, and expressed her approval. Tasoula ushered her out the door, dispensing with the convivial chat she liked to exchange with clients. She had other things on her mind. As soon as the other girls had left, she summoned Thalia into the parlour. The two men and Thanasis were already seated.

'There's a lot I have to tell you, Thalia. But first, some introductions.' She waved her hand towards Peter. 'This is Peter Blunden — Petros in Greek — a brave New Zealand soldier who fought to save Greece. Petros, this is Thalia.'

Thalia didn't know where New Zealand was, but didn't want to show her ignorance. Somewhere near England, maybe? She looked at the man with enquiring eyes. Peter extended his hand. Thalia took it tentatively, as if she were afraid he would crush her fingers.

'Thalia? Pleased to meet you. Thalia. That's a pretty name.'

Thalia didn't understand what he said, but as he was smiling, she took it as a compliment. Tasoula then pointed at Patrick. 'And this is Patrick Minogue — Patrikios — an Australian soldier who also fought for Greece.' Patrick also shook hands with Thalia.

'The Germans captured both men, but they escaped from a prisoner-of-war camp and found their way here.'

This revelation bewildered Thalia. She knew that Australia was many thousands of kilometres from Greece, and yet here were these men, from the other side of the world, sitting in the parlour of a Greek dressmaking studio. Why would they be fighting someone else's war?

Tasoula sensed her confusion. 'I'll explain it all, but first I need to know I can trust you. Thanasis and I are active members of the Greek resistance, and if you betray us, we'll likely be executed. At the very least, the Germans will imprison and torture us.'

'Y . . . y . . . yes. I understand,' Thalia stammered, unsettled by the news and uncertain how to respond. Still astounded, she gaped at Tasoula, then at the two men, before composing herself. 'I *hate* the Germans — just as you do — so, yes, you can trust me. I won't say a word about this to anyone. Not even my parents. I won't let you down.'

Thalia felt a surge of admiration for Tasoula and her son. And for the two men who had fought so valiantly for her beloved country. It had been clear that Tasoula had secrets she didn't share with Thalia or the other girls, but Thalia had never for a moment thought that she might be in the Greek resistance movement. And had no idea that she harboured escaped Allied soldiers.

Tasoula told Thalia everything — almost everything — while Thanasis translated for the benefit of Peter and Patrick. There was no point in holding back — Thalia already knew enough to have them arrested if she betrayed them. Tasoula explained how she had decided that she would do everything in her power to combat, disrupt and frustrate the occupiers. The only thing she didn't mention was the illicit radio and the stash of stolen German weapons hidden in the attic of the locked room. That information was best kept to herself unless someone *needed* to know.

'Thanasis is too young to join fighting units and I'm not cut out for armed warfare.' Instead, she had volunteered to help soldiers escape from Greece into Turkey, and to help the resistance in other ways. Tasoula had been among the first in the Charilaou district to sign up and had provided refuge for many soldiers on the run. Her role, she explained, was to house them until they could be safely escorted to Turkey. Peter and Patrick were the latest 'guests', as she called them, but others had stayed before — including Patrick when he escaped the first time. Thalia thought to herself that what Mrs Tasoula was doing was no less dangerous than guerrilla warfare; just different.

Tasoula described Madam Lapper's role in the escape chain and how the Gestapo had infiltrated the network. 'We must be cautious and vigilant,' she said. 'The Germans know about Madam Lapper and it might not take them long to figure out who else is involved. They may already have their suspicions about me, but can't prove anything. And then there are the collaborators who would betray me for a cup of olive oil and a favourable report from the German authorities. I'm not frightened for myself — my biggest concern is Thanasis. He's only a boy, and I must do everything to protect him.'

'Don't worry about me, Mamá,' Thanasis chimed in. 'I'm just as committed to ridding Greece of these devils as you are. Nazis have no place here.' Tasoula shook her head to admonish Thanasis, but Thalia could tell that she was proud of her son's patriotism.

'So, Thalia, that's our story. Now it's over to you. You can choose to turn us into the authorities — and be well paid for the information — but that's a risk we have to take.'

'You needn't worry, Mrs Tasoula. I would never betray you, no matter what. I despise the Germans, too, and if I can help you in some small way, I will. Your secret is safe with me.'

Tasoula had no doubts about Thaila's sincerity, but equally, had no illusions about what she would be forced to reveal if she were interrogated. 'Thanks, Thalia. That means a lot. I was sure I could rely on you.'

Thanasis was struggling to keep up with the translation, but Peter got the essence of the conversation. He turned to Thanasis. 'Tell Thalia that Patrick and I are very grateful, too. Mrs Tasoula has risked her life to help us and it's important for us to be sure that she can depend on Thalia's loyalty.'

Thanasis relayed Peter's message. Thalia smiled. It was the first time Peter had seen her smile. He looked at her again. Thalia turned her head slightly, and blushed.

Chapter
Seven

Tasoula had lived through adversity before. The Turks had forced her family from Anatolia when they defeated Greece in 1922; her parents had had to rely on help from the Refugee Rehabilitation Service in Thessaloniki to survive. That was bad enough. Then she had separated from her first husband — a drunkard and abuser — and was forced to start again with nothing, raising Thanasis on her own. That was even more difficult. And ever since the German occupation and her subsequent involvement with the resistance she had lived with the daily fear of discovery. *That* was terrifying.

But none of this compared to the misery and hardship that Greece now faced. Not only was the country in the oppressive grip of Hitler's brutal regime, but it was also suffering the worst famine in modern times. Thousands died of starvation every week; many more were barely alive, struggling to find food and unable to find work to get the money to buy it, but still desperately resisting the inevitability of death. The economy was deteriorating at an alarming rate, with unemployment soaring and inflation so rampant that prices rose every day. With cheese at 80,000 drachmas a kilo, butter much more at 120,000 and milk at 5000 drachmas a litre, only the wealthy could afford even the essentials. Life was grim.

To add to her woes, Thanasis and his friends had formed a loose-knit resistance unit, putting him in much more danger than the more covert work of helping Tasoula with the Allied soldiers. They called themselves the Sixth Phalanx. Young, headstrong and full of hope for the future of Greece, they roamed the streets on most nights looking for opportunities to thwart and disrupt the Germans. They harassed a group of known Greek collaborators, distributed resistance propaganda, painted patriotic slogans on bare walls — anything they could do to obstruct the occupiers. For the most part it was youthful bravado, but the Germans didn't discriminate between adult and juvenile saboteurs. If the Nazis caught him, she would never forgive herself for failing to protect him. The weight of the world seemed to be pressing down on her.

By now, seven months after the Germans had invaded Greece, the war was also taking its toll on Tasoula's business. Her once-thriving dressmaking studio was suddenly failing. And fast. In less than a month, orders had halved. Even those customers she once considered rich now struggled to pay. The others, who were able to afford tailored clothes only for special occasions, now relied on hand-me-downs or minor alterations to their existing wardrobes.

On top of her financial worries, Tasoula had every reason to be concerned about betrayal and discovery. The Germans were becoming more thorough, using more sophisticated methods to root out resistance fighters and those opposed to their regime. Tasoula trusted most of her girls, but had her doubts about some. Thalia, on the other hand, had quickly become Tasoula's must trustworthy confidante. As the only one of her girls who knew about the soldiers, Thalia had the ear of her employer and they shared confidences that Tasoula couldn't share with the others. 'Thalia, what do we do?' Tasoula asked, one evening after her workers had left for the day. 'Work has dried up, money is tight, and prices are out of control.' Thalia could see first-hand what was happening to her country. Many businesses had been forced to close down, and the Germans had taken over many of those that had been flourishing before the war. But she had no answers.

'Whatever you decide to do, Mrs Tasoula, I'll support you.'

'And there's Petros and Patrikios to think about. What do we do about them?'

'There's no easy solution, Mrs Tasoula. But we can't let these men down. They fought to save Greece and, at the very least, we owe it to them to ensure their safety. If we can't provide for them, we must find someone who can.'

Tasoula sighed; the weary sigh of a woman close to defeat. 'Oh Thalia, dear, we *must* protect these men — and we will — but what if we can't afford to feed them? What then?'

Thalia pulled up a chair and sat beside Tasoula. Eyes closed and deep in thought, she considered what she might do to help. She treasured her job with Tasoula, but if there was no longer enough work to support all twelve girls, she would make it easier for her.

'I'll resign, Mrs Tasoula. I'll hand in my notice. That's what I'll do. That's one less person to pay. One less girl to worry about. It's the least I can do.'

'Nonsense, Thalia. If I must let some girls go, *you* won't be one of them. You're a good worker and I trust you. Trust is important in these turbulent times. We should never forget that. There may come a time when I have to close the studio altogether, but until then, you'll stay. I won't have any more talk of you resigning. We can survive for now, but the situation is getting worse by the day. If it gets much worse, I'm not sure what I'll do.'

While Thalia was relieved that Tasoula wanted her to stay — and flattered that she valued her loyalty — she knew that what Tasoula said was true: the economic outlook was worsening daily.

The normally implacable Tasoula was struggling with the weight of her decision. She stroked her chin thoughtfully as she weighed up the options. She had to face up to reality: if she didn't act now, it wouldn't be long before she couldn't afford to pay all the wages. Reluctantly, she came to a decision.

'Here's what we'll do, Thalia. I've got no option; I'll have to let some girls go. There's not enough work for everyone — we both know that — and in these tough times, demand for dressmakers is likely to drop off even more. Besides, the other girls will find out about Petros and Patrikios eventually and, if I'm honest, I can't trust them all. I'll keep the six I think I can rely on and, sadly, I'll tell the others there's no more work for them. I'll be sorry to let them go, but I can't see any other way.'

'What about Petros and Patrikios?'

'That's more difficult. The fact is, I can't afford to house and feed them both. I have another resistance contact whom I'm sure will look after one, so that's what I'll do. Keep one at our house but make certain the other is in safe hands. Petros will remain with us, and I'll arrange for Patrikios to stay with my resistance friend.'

Thalia felt strangely relieved. In the short time she had known him, she had grown very fond of Peter.

———————

It was a sad day for Tasoula when the six girls left. She didn't want to let them go; circumstances had forced her hand. Tears in her eyes, she hugged each of the departing dressmakers and promised that if business picked up, she would take them on again. Everyone was upset, but they all understood. Those lucky enough to be staying realised that their turn might come at any time, and those leaving knew that Tasoula had no choice. The devastating impacts of the German occupation and the deadly famine had made it almost impossible for most Greeks — apart from the obscenely wealthy and the unscrupulous collaborators — to make ends meet.

Tasoula pressed a small envelope into the hands of each of the departing girls — the few extra drachmas she'd added to their final pay packets wasn't much, but it would help. After the six had bade farewell, promising to keep in touch, Tasoula summoned Thalia into the kitchen.

'Thalia,' she said, still wiping her tears away. 'What do we do now? Do we tell the others about Petros and Patrikios?'

'Mrs Tasoula, these are dangerous times — I understand that — but I'm sure we can trust the girls who are staying on. They hate the Germans like we do. And they'll find out about the men sooner or later. Just as I did.'

Tasoula hesitated for a moment. But there was only one sensible answer: she should tell them, on her terms, before they found out for themselves. 'You're right, Thalia. Best I tell them now.'

The following morning, Tasoula summoned the remaining dressmakers into the parlour. 'Please sit,' she said. 'I have something important to tell you, but first I must swear you to secrecy. What I'm about to say might have disastrous consequences for Thanasis and me if the Germans ever got to learn about it. Can I rely on you to tell no one? I mean *no one*. Not your parents. Not your neighbours. Not even your best friends.'

One by one, the girls nodded, clearly intrigued by the mystery surrounding their employer's impending revelation. Tasoula's eyes swept around the room, signalling her gratitude. Then, she told them about Peter and Patrick; about how Thalia had discovered the two soldiers; about her work with the resistance; and about the raids on her property by the Germans. She felt that if she wanted their trust, she had to tell them almost everything about her involvement with the resistance. However, she didn't mention the Nazi-infiltrated escape network or the other families who were hiding Allied soldiers. Such knowledge would compromise her underground colleagues if any of her employees revealed what they knew.

'And that's it,' she concluded. 'Now you know my secret.'

Thalia could tell that the other dressmakers were dumbstruck — wide, saucer-like eyes and slack jaws betrayed their astonishment. Who would believe that a humble dressmaker was a key resistance operative, hiding soldiers under their very noses? And under the noses of the Nazi occupiers? No one spoke a word until Fifi broke the silence.

'Thank you, Mrs Tasoula, for confiding in us. We won't let you down. I can speak for us all when I say that we despise the Germans as much as you do. Every one of us. We've talked about it often. I'm proud to be working for a true patriot. Very proud.'

'Me too,' Pauline said and, in unison, the rest echoed her sentiments. Being Jewish, Pauline had more reason than any of them to hate the Nazis — and to fear the repercussions if they ever learned of her nationality.

'Thank you all,' Tasoula said, buoyed by their support. 'Thank you so much. I felt sure I could trust you. Now let me introduce you to Petros and Patrikios.' Thalia opened the locked door and beckoned to the two men to come out. Peter was apprehensive; on the one hand, these young women had the power to decide his fate; on the other, this knowledge also put *them* at risk.

There was an air of anticipation as Tasoula introduced first Peter and then Patrick to each of the dressmakers. The buzz of excited chatter filled the room as the girls expressed their views about Hitler's occupation; they all had their own stories of Nazi atrocities to tell. The presence of the two men from the other side of the world intrigued them. Some had met foreigners before, but none had encountered anyone from as far away as New Zealand or Australia.

To restore order, Tasoula clapped her hands several times. 'Now, back to work everyone.' But for once, no one complied. They were far too exuberant to contemplate work. Tasoula shrugged, and relented. 'All right, today is an exception. You can have the rest of the day off — but it's business as usual tomorrow, mind. We still have orders to finish.'

A few days later, Tasoula had the difficult task of breaking the news to Patrick that he, too, would be leaving. Tasoula explained her predicament to the men: she wasn't earning enough to house and feed them both. Patrick would be moved to Mrs Koula Angelidou's place in Kato Toumba, which was close by, and Peter would stay. Patrick didn't seem to mind; Tasoula sensed that he had been expecting something like this. He had always been the more extroverted and carefree of the two soldiers, and would soon adapt to the new housing arrangement.

———————

Since he no longer had to hide from the girls, Peter welcomed the opportunity to sit in the workroom in front of the potbelly stove. He also ventured outdoors from time to time — most often in the neighbourhood, but occasionally further afield. Meanwhile, Patrick settled in well at Mrs Koula's and visited often. The girls sometimes stayed after work and there was music, singing and laughter. Life was as good as it could be under the circumstances. Even Peter's yearning for New Zealand waned.

Then an SS officer arrived.

A sharp knock on the door sent Peter scurrying into his room; Tasoula locked it behind him. Although Tasoula feared that it might be another raid, she opened to door to find just a single German officer. He entered the room with all the swagger of a schoolyard bully, his distinctive black uniform with the SS epaulettes and leather-holstered pistol sending shivers up Tasoula's spine. The SS man clicked his heels together like a tap dancer, stretched his arm above his head with a flourish and *Heil Hitler*-ed the assembled group, which by then included all the dressmakers.

No one said a word. Peter watched silently from the keyhole.

Again Thalia was called on to communicate with the German. 'How can we be of assistance, officer?' She asked. The back of her neck was prickling at the sight of the SS man.

'Lodging,' was the one-word reply. It was as if the German didn't think Thalia worthy of receiving any further explanation. Thalia pretended she didn't understand.

'I want a room!' the man snapped, looking around the spacious living area, admiring the decor. The magnificent entrance had doubtless impressed him, and he must have thought it a fitting residence for an SS officer.

'Sorry, there are no rooms to spare.'

Not for you. Not now. Not ever, she thought to herself, while still smiling at the officer.

'Well, you'd better find one — throw someone out if you have to. I want a room and I'll have a room. In fact, I'll look around myself and decide which room I want. And if I like it here, I'll bring some of my junior colleagues to stay as well.'

The tension in the exchange was palpable, and Peter watched with mounting apprehension.

Pushing Thalia to one side, the SS bully moved towards the locked door. Peter saw him coming closer, but suddenly Thalia was blocking his view. 'No!' she said with authority. 'You can't stay here. It wouldn't be proper for a man to be housed with six girls.'

'I wouldn't mind,' the officer said, with a lascivious smirk. 'I wouldn't mind at all'.

Thalis knew that the German High Command had instructed all officers to treat Greek women with respect — not that they always observed this instruction — and despite the man's bravado, she could sense some hesitancy.

Regathering himself, the officer squared his shoulders. 'Move aside, girl,' he said, elbowing his way past Thalia again. 'I'll inspect the rooms and the rest of the house. This place looks like it would suit our purposes well.'

Thalia froze, her mind blank. All of a sudden the normally garrulous, quick-witted girl — the life and soul of any party — could think of nothing to say. Tasoula, looking on, couldn't understand the words but was apprehensive about what was happening. But as the officer moved towards the sewing workshop and Tasoula's bedroom, both women breathed a sigh of relief. At least it was away from Peter's room.

'Mmm, nice place you've got here. This will be perfect. How many bedrooms?'

'I— I don't . . . don't know. I only work here.' Thalia's lips quivered and she looked at Tasoula for guidance. Tasoula widened her eyes and nodded fractionally to say that she trusted Thalia's judgement.

'No matter. I'll look for myself.' The bombastic officer strutted through the dressmaking studio, fingering half-finished tailored dresses with all the arrogance he clearly felt his position gave him. Moving into the living quarters, he opened cupboards and drawers, lifting ornaments as he went, and threw open the door to Tasoula's and Thanasis's bedrooms, leaving them ajar as he left.

Then he returned to the parlour. 'Now this one,' he said, jabbing his finger towards Peter's room. 'What's in there?'

'You can't . . . You can't go in there, it's not . . .'

'Why not?' the officer snarled. He stepped up to the door.

Through the keyhole, Peter saw the German approaching. The officer tried the door handle; when it wouldn't open, he twisted it again and pushed his weight against the door. Peter felt panicked. If the man got into the room, he would surely notice the attic hatch and the small ladder parked against the back wall. And if he searched the attic, he would find the radio, weapons and ammunition. Not to mention Peter himself.

Then, just as the German tried the handle again, Peter sneezed. He couldn't help it. Perhaps it was the dust circulating in the room; perhaps it was his anxiety. He didn't know. He sneezed again, this time louder.

'There's someone in there,' the German said, as if this wasn't obvious. 'Open the door. *Now!*' He bashed his shoulder against the door, which didn't budge. He put a jackboot to it, with the same result. Peter moved to one side of the door; if he was going to be arrested, it wouldn't be without a fight. He would tackle the man as he entered and attempt to overpower him. The officer kicked the door again, this time further up, and Peter saw it buckling.

Thalia saw that the door would give way before long. Somehow, it gave her courage. Without pausing to think, she addressed the German officer with a forcefulness she hadn't realised she was capable of.

'It's not . . . it's not safe in there. That's what I was trying to tell you. But if you want to go in, you're welcome. You're most welcome. There's no need to break the door down. What I wanted to tell you is that the boy who's in there — the one who sneezed, the owner's son — is very sick with diphtheria. It's highly infectious — that's why he's locked in. We can't afford to get ill, so it's best that he can't get out. But go in there if you want to. Please do.'

She took a key at random from a hook on the wall and held it out to the officer, terrified that he would take it. It was a dangerous ploy, but she was counting on the officer's awareness of infectious diseases. Before the war, the health authorities in Europe had issued widespread warnings about the risk of death from diphtheria and she was counting on the German knowing this.

The officer twitched and took a rapid step backwards, yanking a handkerchief from his pocket and covering his nose and mouth. He clicked his heels together again, swivelled around on the balls of his feet and, ignoring Thalia and Tasoula, marched out. Any thoughts of taking a room had clearly disappeared.

When he was certain the man had left, Peter rushed out and hugged Thalia. He could almost feel the emotion draining from her.

'You were wonderful. How can I ever thank you enough? Without your quick thinking, I'd have been dead meat.' Thalia didn't understand, of course, but the gratitude in his face said it all. She was proud of what she had done to protect Peter and Tasoula.

'It was nothing,' Thalia said, although her quivering hands and drawn face said otherwise.

———————

The close call with the SS officer made them even more cautious; it was the second incident that might have resulted in a disastrous outcome. Tasoula vowed to take more stringent precautions. It wasn't just Germans that concerned her, either — there were other unwelcome visitors she didn't trust, and Peter often had to scurry to his room at short notice. The situation came to a head soon afterwards; Peter had another narrow escape when a suspected collaborator called in unexpectedly to pick up some alterations. He felt sure she had glimpsed him as he slammed the door to his room. At the very least she would have heard it closing, and that alone might have been enough to arouse her suspicions.

Peter, Tasoula and Thalia discussed ways to set up some sort of early warning system. His Greek was getting quite good now, and Thanasis only occasionally had to step in to translate.

'Perhaps we should have a secret signal to give to trusted visitors,' Tasoula suggested. 'Say, three knocks in quick succession, followed by two long knocks. Or some other code.'

'Wouldn't work, I don't think, Mrs Tasoula,' Peter said. 'If anyone passed the signal on, it might get into the hands of the Germans. We'd still be on edge whenever anybody used the secret knock. We need a warning we can control from inside.'

'I've got an idea,' Thalia piped up. 'Why don't we rig up a bell? That will give Petros more time to hide. Whoever answers the door can check who's there and ring the bell if it's an unknown visitor or someone we can't trust.'

'Great idea,' Peter enthused. 'We can hang it by the door so it's easy to ring.'

'No. You don't understand. We must have the bell on a pulley so that it rings in here, in the dressmaking studio, where you can hear it clearly.'

'But it's simpler to install near the entrance, and it would be easier to ring.'

'No. No. That won't do. For a start, you might not hear it from so far away. And anyone at the door will definitely hear it and wonder why a bell is ringing. No, the pulley to the workroom is the best option. If someone does hear it, they'll think it's there to call Mrs Tasoula to the front door.'

Peter protested. But Thalia was a headstrong young woman; not one to be intimidated by some New Zealand soldier who didn't understand her logic. He was wrong, and that was that.

Peter tried one last time. 'But it will work just as well—'

Thalia cut him off. 'Can't you see you're wrong? My way is the best, and that's the way we're doing it.'

This time, Peter was defeated: beaten by a young girl who refused to give in. 'Okay,' he sighed, 'we'll do it your way.'

Thalia dashed off to get some string from the sewing room and a couple of pulley wheels lying on a shelf in the storeroom.

Peter installed the pulley wheels, tied one end of the string to the bell, threaded the other through the wheels and attached it to a hook he screwed into the door frame. Anyone answering the door just had to pull the string and the bell would ring in the workshop.

Peter had to admit that Thalia's solution was a good one. 'You were right. Thalia. Yours was the best option,' he said, admiring their handiwork. He turned to congratulate her. She was standing right behind him, and as he swivelled around, his lips brushed against her cheek. It was the briefest of touches, barely noticeable.

Thalia recoiled, surprised. Peter stepped back, and their eyes locked. Unmoving, Thalia returned his gaze. Peter was mesmerised.

It was over in just a few seconds, as Tasoula came into the room and clapped her hands. 'Well done, you two. It works well. Now, back to work, Thalia.' Peter didn't know if Tasoula had seen them gazing at each other, but her untimely entrance suggested that she had.

When Peter looked at Thalia again, she turned away. Peter thought she was either embarrassed or offended. But in fact, Thalia was confused. She couldn't explain why she had held Peter's gaze: a respectable Greek girl would have looked away, not wanting to encourage the attention of any man. But she hadn't.

Neither knew what that moment meant, but both knew it meant something.

Chapter
Eight

It was late. Tasoula glanced at her watch: 11:15. The loud hammering on the door had startled her. Her first thought was that it must be a German patrol. They used to be too lackadaisical to conduct late-night raids, but since they had stepped up their surveillance, snap searches at all hours had become more common.

The pounding continued, getting louder. Hard enough to rattle the hinges. Apprehensive, Tasoula approached the door, Thanasis watching keenly from the kitchen. 'Who's there?' she shouted through the thick timber, unwilling to open the door until she knew who was behind it.

A muffled voice answered. In Greek. She could just make out the words: 'I'm wounded. I need help.' The voice was urgent, desperate. Tasoula remained cautious: trust was a virtue best reserved only for her closest friends. 'How can I be sure what you say is true?'

'Please, I need help,' the voice pleaded. 'There's nowhere else I can go. Please let me in.'

The man sounded genuine, but an imposter might also sound just as desperate. Still unsure, Tasoula inched the door open, ready to slam it shut if she had any doubts about the visitor. A putrid stench greeted her before she could see the wounded man. His old Greek army tunic eased her fears somewhat. The man was in a terrible state: dirty, bloodstained bandages covered most of his head, and his mismatched uniform was in tatters. Both sleeves were missing, revealing a gash on his right arm. It hadn't healed properly and fresh blood had blended with dark red patches that had dried long ago. Tasoula wondered how someone with such serious injuries had the strength to bash so hard on the door.

'Come in. Be quick, though. No one must see you here.' The man stumbled into the house, trembling as he gripped the small hall table for support. Thanasis moved closer in case he fell.

'You look awful. What happened?' Tasoula asked as she pulled out a chair at the kitchen table. 'How did you come by these dreadful wounds?'

The man didn't answer right away. His lips quivered and he burst into tears. 'My family,' he said finally, sobbing. 'They're not there. Killed, all of them. My mother, father, and brothers. All dead.'

'Not where?' Tasoula asked. 'How do you know they're dead?'

'Not at our home,' he managed to get out. 'Shot dead.'

Tasoula tried to comfort the man, but nothing would pacify him. 'Best let him cry it out,' she thought. Since she was now satisfied that he was friend, not foe, she invited Peter into the kitchen. The New Zealander took one look at the man. 'Good God, the poor blighter. He's in a bad way. We must help him.'

When the soldier calmed down, Tasoula asked about his family and what had happened to them.

'Slaughtered. My whole family. All of them,' he said between sobs. 'Many other villagers, too. The Nazis razed the town to the ground. Bastards.' He explained that he was a resistance fighter, wounded in a skirmish with the Germans that had wiped out the rest of his unit. He had hidden in a ditch until the enemy left. A kind woman in a neighbouring village had patched him up as best she could. She had insisted that he stay with her while he recovered, but he was desperate to get back to his home, so left. His parents lived in a village near Thessaloniki, and the massacre had been retribution for another resistance attack that killed five German soldiers. The men in the village — the ones they found — were all lined up and shot.

'They targeted my family for more severe punishment because my father was a resistance leader. My best friend, our neighbour, told me everything. He escaped by hiding in his basement. My friend advised me to get away from the village — in my state, I'd be a sitting duck if the Germans returned. He was second in command to my father, so he's well connected and has resistance contacts all over this area. He gave me your address and said you might help.'

Tasoula couldn't imagine how arduous that journey to Thessaloniki must have been — in the depths of winter, with just a sleeveless, threadbare army jacket, thin trousers and a fisherman's hat for warmth. A makeshift crutch fashioned from a gnarled oak branch was all he had to support himself.

'I have a cousin in Saint Athanasios and I'll head there in the morning. If you would let me rest here tonight, I would be most grateful.' Peter looked at the man's lacerations. There was no way he would be in a fit state to leave in the morning.

'Of course, of course,' said Tasoula. 'But first you must eat. Then we'll look at your injuries. After that, you can clean yourself up.'

'Give the poor devil the soup and dried sausage we saved for tomorrow, Mrs Tasoula,' Peter said. 'It won't do me any harm to go without.'

The man wolfed the soup down, as though he were worried it would evaporate if he didn't eat it quickly enough. When there was no more to be extracted with the spoon, he lifted the bowl to his mouth and drained the dregs. He devoured the sausage with the same urgency.

After he had eaten, Tasoula told him to lie on the couch while she attended to his injuries. She peeled away the grimy head bandage. It had fused with a deep cut that ran all the way from his left ear down to his jawbone. As soon as she prised the gauze from his skin, lifting the crusty scab with it, it started bleeding. The gash on his arm was much deeper than she had thought, but worse was a wound to his stomach: blood was oozing through the torn strip of sheet he'd strapped around his midriff.

'Bullet,' he said in answer to Tasoula's unasked question. He was weak from blood loss and needed stitches. Lots of stitches. The bullet would have to be removed, too, if he were to survive.

There was little they could do at this late hour, save cleaning the wounds and making him as comfortable as possible. Peter looped one of his arms under the man's right shoulder and around his back for support. Thanasis did the same to his left. They half-dragged, half-carried him into Peter's bedroom, laying him on the bed, then removed the rest of his clothes and bathed him with a wet cloth.

'I smell bad,' he said, acknowledging the odour that permeated the room.

'That's the least of our concerns. Let's get you patched up and then we'll worry about hygiene.'

Peter motioned to Tasoula to come into the bedroom. 'What do we do, Mrs Tasoula?' he asked. 'He needs a doctor. And soon.'

'We'll let him rest tonight, and first thing in the morning we'll get help. There's a doctor in Filippou Street in the city who has stitched up wounded resistance fighters in the past. I'll get Thalia to bring him here to do what he can for this poor wretch.'

Tasoula and Peter did their best to tend to the man's injuries, disinfecting the wounds and applying fresh bandages. He was almost insensible, his eyes closed. Whether he had drifted off into a deep sleep or into unconsciousness was uncertain. Peter and Tasoula took turns to sit with him during the night. In the morning, Tasoula was relieved to find him still breathing. He even managed a brief smile.

Tasoula pulled Thalia aside as soon as she arrived for work. 'Thalia, I need your help. There's a wounded Greek resistance fighter in Peter's room. He's in bad shape and needs a doctor. He has a bullet wound in his stomach and multiple injuries that need stitching up.' She handed Thalia a piece of paper. 'There's a physician we can trust at this address. Please go there and bring him back. And please hurry.'

'Of course, Mrs Tasoula, I'll go straight away and be back as quick as I can.'

Having glanced at the soldier lying on the bed in Peter's room, Thalia could tell that this was an urgent mission. It would normally take almost an hour to walk to the doctor's, but she ran most of the way and made it in half that time. The house was a large, two-storey pink property with a pitched roof and white shutters. A marble statue of some dignitary Thalia didn't recognise sat opposite. She banged on the door as hard as she could. An elderly, bespectacled man in a dark suit answered.

'Doctor Soulis?' Thalia asked.

'Yes, that's me. What can I do for you?'

'Mrs Tasoula Paschilidou sent me. You must hurry, sir. There's a wounded man who needs urgent medical attention. Please come now.'

The doctor looked her up and down, suspicion etched on his face. 'Hold on, young lady. I don't know any Tasoula Paschilidou. Where does she live?'

Thalia realised that this was a proof of identity test; a sensible precaution under the circumstances. Thalia recited Tasoula's address.

'Ah, perhaps I do know her. Does this Mrs Paschilidou have any children?'

'Yes, sir, a son — Thanasis. Please, we must hurry.'

The doctor was silent for a few seconds, doubtless weighing up whether or not he should trust this girl. 'Wait a minute,' he finally said. 'Let me get my bag. What will I need to take?'

'I'm not sure, sir, but Mrs Tasoula said he needed stitches and mentioned something about a bullet in the stomach.'

The physician reappeared with a battered leather doctor's bag, and they set off for Enou Place. The doctor was old and slow, so the journey took much longer than Thalia liked. They had only walked a short way when a group of German soldiers setting up a checkpoint flagged them down. The checkpoint hadn't been there when Thalia had passed by earlier, but now they had no option but to wait in line while the Germans checked their papers.

When their turn came, the soldier took a cursory glance at their identity documents before handing them back. Thalia was relieved.

'And where are you off to today?' the young sentry asked as the pair pocketed their IDs. The doctor didn't speak German, so Thalia had to answer for both of them. 'This is Doctor Soulis and we're going to the Charilaou district. To attend to someone who has suffered terrible injuries.'

The Wehrmacht guard raised his eyebrows, pleasantry replaced by suspicion. 'Interesting,' he said. 'And why would you fetch a doctor from here to go all the way to Charilaou? It's several kilometres away and there are plenty of doctors much closer.'

Thalia immediately regretted her stupid mistake. Now she had to act fast. She could see that the guard was sceptical.

'I— I can . . . I can explain. It's because . . .' she said, pausing to give herself time to come up with a plausible explanation. 'It's because . . . I only shifted to Charilaou a few weeks ago. Until then I lived near here. This is our family doctor. I'm . . . I'm not familiar with any doctors where we are now, so I came to fetch him.' Thalia was shaking, her heart thumping. The doctor looked on, puzzled but clearly aware that something was awry.

'And this injured person. A close friend? A relative?'

Thalia wasn't sure what to say. If she said friend or relative, it would doubtless lead to more questions about the fictitious person's identity. A stranger was the best option. 'No, I've never seen him before. But he's in a bad way. There was blood splattered everywhere.'

'Mmm. So, this person's a complete stranger, yet you've come all this way?'

'Yes . . . I couldn't leave him lying there. He might die without help.'

Thalia's weak excuse didn't convince the soldier. He changed tack. 'You say you used to live around here. Whereabouts exactly?'

Thalia hesitated; she wasn't familiar with Thessaloniki city at all. But she had to say something.

'Just . . . just along the road from the doctor.'

'So, your parents are rich then?'

Thalia was flustered. She wasn't sure of the significance of the question. The quaver in her voice betrayed her trepidation.

'No . . . no . . . not at all. They get by, but they're not . . . not *rich* by any means.'

'Is that so? This is a very wealthy neighbourhood, so which of the mansions on Filippou Street did they own?'

Thalia faltered again, her heart thumping harder. This was not going well.

'The house belonged to a family friend. We lived with them.' This was a feeble answer, and Thalia realised how improbable it sounded.

'You look like a nice young girl, but something doesn't add up here.'

Another soldier joined the conversation. 'My colleague here might think you're an innocent young thing, but I don't. You tell us some ridiculous story about living in a family friend's luxury house in Filippou Street and that you're walking several kilometres with an old doctor to tend to some injured person you can't even identify. You expect us to believe that baloney? No one walks that distance to get a doctor to treat someone so far away. It must be an hour each way. No, this makes no sense — there's something wrong here. We should continue this discussion elsewhere.'

The soldiers exchanged glances; then one motioned towards a staff car, a black Mercedes, parked outside a taverna. Thalia and the doctor were guided into the back seat. It smelled of new leather. The men slid into the front seats and they drove off. No one spoke a word. The doctor sat still, hunched over and visibly shaken. He was trembling. If the Nazis discovered he had been treating resistance fighters, the consequences for him didn't bear thinking about.

The interrogation room was in a large mansion the Germans occupied on Olympiados Street. Judging by the pleated French drapes, Thalia guessed it had formerly been a bedroom. The men directed her and the doctor to a wooden table with four matching chairs, telling them to sit. Two men in black uniforms then entered the room. SS. The four men conferred for a few minutes, then the soldiers left.

'Now, let's have your ID cards,' one SS officer said. Thalia translated for the doctor and handed over both IDs. The officer studied hers for what seemed like minutes. He noted down the details in a large notepad.

'Christidou?' he drawled, stretching out each syllable. 'Thalia Christidou. I wonder what you're up to, dragging a doctor from the city to the Charilaou district?'

At first, the questions were innocuous. Why did you come all this way to fetch a doctor? Why would you go to so much trouble for a stranger? Why didn't you call the police to deal with the incident? But Thalia's evasive responses prompted a harder line.

'I've had enough of these lies,' the more senior officer said. 'No more. Understood? Now, tell us the truth — it'll be worse for you if you don't.'

Thalia bowed her head. She was cursing herself for making such a basic mistake. There were so many other things she might have said. Such as the doctor was her grandfather. Or they were visiting relatives in another district. She might have pretended that she didn't speak German. But it was too late for that now.

'I told your colleagues — I went to get a doctor to tend to someone who has serious injuries.'

'I don't believe you. No lies, I said. Now I'll ask you again: why were you and the doctor here walking almost five kilometres to see this so-called injured person?'

'I've already told the other soldiers: I don't know any other doctors.'

'Yes. So you say, but that's not true, is it? Where is this injured person?'

Thalia hesitated. She couldn't give Mrs Tasoula's address, and didn't want to give hers. 'Just opposite the Asteriadis pharmacy on Marasli Street,' she said, giving him the name of the first shop she thought of. 'He was lying in a pool of blood when I left him.'

'And you know this person?'

'No, I've already said I don't. I just came across him and he needed help. There were others there, but no one made a move to assist.'

He persisted with the same line of questioning. Thalia did her best to hold out, but her quaking body was at odds with her pretence of innocence.

A third SS officer — a fat, unsavoury-looking character — waddled into the room and dismissed the other two with a curt wave. They retreated to the back of the room. 'Christidou? That's your name, right?' he asked, glancing at the information on the notepad. Thalia nodded.

'Well, Thalia Christidou, I won't be as gentle with you as those two wimps,' he said, pointing towards the officers standing against the back wall. 'I'm here to find the truth and I'll do whatever it takes to get it.' Grabbing Thalia by the shoulders, he shook her violently. Her chair almost toppled over. Thalia felt the anger in his grip. He lifted her up and slammed her down on the chair again, then raised his fist, seemingly about to strike her. But suddenly, he stopped mid-air and seemed to calm down, smoothing his tunic with both hands while Thalia swallowed air in raspy breaths. The doctor looked on, aghast but unable to intervene.

'There's worse to come. Much worse. If you don't tell us the truth, you'll regret it.'

'I can only tell you what I told the others. I came to fetch my family doctor. I was just trying to help somebody who's injured and now here I am being questioned by someone accusing me of making it all up.'

'Bloody lies. All bloody lies. You know it and we know it!' He fixed Thalia with a ferocious stare, then struck her across the face three times with the back of his leather-gloved hand. The blows stung, but weren't hard enough to inflict any real pain.

'I've told you everything,' she stammered. 'There's nothing more. The doctor and I are simply trying to be good Samaritans.'

The three officers huddled in a corner, whispering. Then the fat one addressed Thalia. 'We don't believe a word you say. Not a word. Something's not right, that's certain. I have no idea why you're lying or what you're up to, but we intend to get the truth. Whatever it is, it's something illegal, I'm sure of that. You'll be spending the night in the cells. If you're deceiving us, we'll find out. And then . . .' His voice trailed off, but his meaning was clear.

The doctor, still not understanding a word, nevertheless

could recognise what was going on — and he had seen the violence. But he could do little else but just sit there, nonplussed.

'Before we lock you up, you'll take us to this so-called "injured" man. Then we'll see if you're telling the truth. Take us there — now.'

Thalia was taken aback. She hadn't expected this. She needed inspiration, and fast. If she tried to dissuade the SS officers, they would force her to lead them to the non-existent casualty anyway; and, of course, they would find no one lying there in a pool of blood. She decided to brazen it out. Quick thinking had saved her in the past; once again, she had to rely on her wits. An idea came to her.

'Of course, you're welcome to come but it's not a man, it's a boy. It was an unprovoked attack by two German soldiers on a young Greek boy. They beat him senseless. He may even be dead by now. In fact, I'd very much like you to come with us. Then you'll be able to file a report. Plenty of people saw the vicious assault, so you'll get lots of witness statements. Let's go,' she said, getting up and walking towards the door.

Thalia didn't know why she reacted the way she did under duress. She was independent and headstrong — opinionated, even — but that didn't explain why she could act with such confidence and lie with such conviction when she was put under pressure. She didn't consider what she would do if they insisted on taking her; that would be a problem for later, if it happened.

The overweight officer hesitated. The German obsession with reports and record-keeping would mean masses of paperwork and many time-consuming interviews. Thalia knew this, and she also knew that an allegation of a grievous assault on a young Greek civilian would mean even more documentation. Not to mention a military inquiry into the incident.

The two junior officers looked towards their superior for direction. He shook his head. 'Get out. Now!' he barked. 'Go and deal with your Greek friend, if he exists. We don't want to be involved with this shit. Next time, find a doctor who's closer. And — Christidou,' he said ominously, 'remember we'll be watching you. Make a wrong move, and we'll have you.'

A mixture of relief and fear enveloped Thalia: relief at being released; fear because somewhere among the myriad of German files there would now be one marked 'Christidou, Thalia'.

As they continued their interrupted journey to Tasoula's, the doctor asked Thalia what had happened. She brushed it off as if it had been a routine inspection. 'Just a random check. These Germans are brutes. They never leave us alone.'

Once at Tasoula's, the doctor removed the bullet and stitched up the resistance fighter. He left again as soon as he had inserted the last suture. Late the next day, the soldier hobbled out, determined to find his cousin in Saint Athanasios.

Chapter
Nine

Winter now had Greece fully in its icy grip, and Christmas was fast approaching. Peter's Greek was still improving by the day, and he took every opportunity to practise by conversing with Tasoula and the girls. On 15 December, Peter's birthday, Tasoula decided that even though Greeks didn't normally recognise birthdays — they celebrated Name Day, the day associated with a person's namesake saint — this birthday would be a good excuse to forget, briefly, the strife and poverty of wartime Greece.

How she did it, Peter would never know, but there in front of them stood a table laden with dried meat, spinach pies, cheese pies, stuffed eggplants, bougiourdi — baked feta cheese with tomatoes and peppers — and all manner of other local delicacies. The girls had strung ribbons made from fabric remnants from wall to wall; crisp white linen tablecloths covered the long wooden cutting table, repurposed as a dining table for the occasion; and white dinner plates with blue scalloped edges — Tasoula's best — were stacked high on a small side table. Patrick joined them for the celebration.

'*Xronia polla*, Petros,' Tasoula announced to cheers from all the girls. Thanasis had taught them the words to 'Happy Birthday', and they all sang it in English. The chorus of heavily accented voices touched Peter. Their attempt at 'For He's A Jolly Good Fellow' wasn't nearly as successful, but it didn't matter. Patrick tried a few popular wartime tunes on his mouth organ — 'The White Cliffs of Dover', 'We'll Meet Again' and others — but his hosts didn't recognise them, so he gave up and played the few Greek songs he did know. Before long, they were all singing and dancing. Thalia was in her element — she loved socialising and had a great sense of rhythm. Peter wanted to ask to her to dance, but was too shy. Besides, his dancing skills were limited to the 'back-country shuffle' and that would never do here. The Greeks danced the hand-to-shoulder *hasapiko* with enthusiasm, kicking their legs high and upping the tempo of each step until it was all a blur to the two soldiers.

Thalia glanced over at Peter as if she expected him to join in, but Tasoula interrupted the moment and sent Thalia to nearby Dagli's Taverna to get more wine. Towards the end of the very convivial evening, however, Thalia managed to approach Peter. 'I have something for you, Petros,' she said. The tremor in her voice betrayed her nervousness. 'It's a small gift I hope you will remember me by.'

Peter pulled at the string bow holding the package together to unravel it, then removed a square box from the brown paper wrapping. In it sat a pair of onyx cufflinks. Peter was on the verge of tears. 'Thalia, they're beautiful. You're so kind and thoughtful. Of course I'll remember you. And,' he joked, 'as soon as I get a shirt with two long sleeves, I'll wear them all the time.' They both laughed. Earlier Peter had ripped one of his shirtsleeves on a wire fence and now had one long sleeve and one short.

That night, his eyes welling up, Peter kept thinking about Thalia's present. It must have cost her almost half a week's pay. He felt guilty. With all the hardship the Greeks had suffered, it didn't seem right to accept such a precious gift. He promised himself he would cherish the cufflinks and wear them at every opportunity.

His thoughts drifted to his father and New Zealand. Birthdays had always been special occasions for the Blunden family, and he wondered what they might be doing on his. His mother had died in 1939, but he remembered how she had made such a fuss of him on his birthdays. Peter had no way of letting his father know he was alive and well; in fact, he was certain his family thought he had been killed. With no confirmation of his survival — just a note on his record to say he hadn't made it from Salonika to the Stalag 8B POW camp — they would think the worst.

Peter was also beginning to realise that his fondness for Thalia was about more than just friendship. He couldn't get the young Greek girl off his mind. In turn, Thalia was intrigued by Peter. So much mystery surrounded him, and he had an aura that was magnetic. Above all else, though, one thing puzzled her.

'Tell me something, Petros,' she said one day. 'There's something about you I don't understand.'

'What's that, Thalia?'

'Well, I don't understand why you and Patrikios would travel to the other side of the world to fight a war in Europe. What's this conflict got to do with New Zealand? Why would you come all this way and risk your life to fight another country's war?'

'I can see why you might be confused, Thalia. Greece is a long way from home, but the answer is quite simple. This is not just Europe's war — it's everyone's war. It's a war for democracy. It's a war against a tyrant who plans to rule the entire world, and every peace-loving country has a part to play.'

'Hitler is a demon, I get that, but it still doesn't explain why you're fighting for Greece. Did your government tell you to join the army? Were you forced to go to war?'

'Not at all. I . . .' Peter fumbled for the Greek word for 'volunteered', but couldn't grasp it. 'I . . . I enlisted of my own free will. No one told me to join up or to come to Europe to face the Germans.'

'So, you decided for yourself that you wanted to help defeat the Nazis? That's very brave, Petros.'

'Not brave — simply doing the right thing. If we don't stop Hitler now, God knows what the world will be like for our children and grandchildren. You can see what's happening in Greece already. And, this may surprise you, but now that Japan has joined Germany, New Zealand is in the firing line. Japan already has its eye on the South Pacific. Living under Japanese rule would be even worse than living under Hitler's regime.'

'Ahh, yes. The Japanese. I had forgotten about them.'

'Thalia, we're all fighting for the same cause, even though we're thousands of miles apart. If Germany and Japan win this war, the world will be a very grim, dark place. Just like it is now in Greece. So, yes, Thalia, this is *everyone's* war, and we must win it.'

Thalia felt a surge of respect for Peter: here was someone who had put her country ahead of his own safety. 'You're right, Petros. I hadn't thought of it that way. Now I get it.'

The more Thalia learned about this man from a faraway country, the more she admired him. They would have talked more, but Tasoula summoned Thalia back to the dressmaking studio.

———————

That Christmas of 1941 gave the household no cause to celebrate — apart from one memorable meal. In return for making a silk blouse, Tasoula was given pork for the traditional Christmas Eve dinner, and they all enjoyed gourounopoula, a roast pork dish with lemony roast potatoes. The new year also passed with little fanfare, and little hope for a better future. The situation in Greece was worsening and the winter nights were paralysingly cold. Peter had always thought that Greece enjoyed warm temperatures year-round — sweltering summers and mild winters — but the reality was quite different. The scorching summers morphed into freezing winters. And this was one of the coldest winters on record.

What distressed Peter most was not the cold itself, but the impact of winter on the most vulnerable. Each day he ventured out, he would encounter matchstick-like figures begging for food and warm clothing. Many were on the verge of starvation — some of those lying on the pavements had already succumbed — and all were suffering the effects of malnutrition. Two or three homeless people often huddled together for warmth. Having a strong social conscience, Peter did what he could: slipping a few drachmas into frostbitten hands or handing out a slice of bread and dried sausage. Once, Peter stripped off his sweater and gave it to one poor soul who was shivering so much that Peter feared he might die in front of him. It was a harsh reminder of the deplorable conditions that those living on the streets had to endure.

The Germans did little to help; they dismissed these unfortunates as being unworthy of alms or assistance. Tasoula told Peter that Himmler had made the Nazis' position clear: they didn't care how many Greeks starved to death so long as no German did. Where she got this information from, Peter didn't know, but he didn't doubt its veracity. The outlook for 1942 looked dire.

In January that year, Peter met Tasoula's brother-in-law, Giorgos. From their first meeting. Peter took to the ebullient Greek. He was exuberant, upbeat and high-spirited despite the wartime woes. Giorgos was a slight fellow with a round face, prominent nose and fast-receding hairline. Even in the grim conditions, he dressed nattily. Peter had never seen him out of a suit, seldom without a hat, and he lost count of the number of different pairs of shoes Giorgos wore. He and Giorgos soon formed a close friendship. The Greek might have been diminutive, but Giorgos feared nothing and no one.

Before the war, Giorgos had owned the Alatini bakery, but soon after the occupation the Germans seized it. The Nazis had also appropriated many other small enterprises, in particular those supplying food, essentials and strategic assets. Giorgos had gone from owner to lowly paid employee. That he had been given a job at all — demeaning though it was — was because the Germans had no idea how to run a bakery. Owners of companies that *didn't* require specialist skills had been tossed out onto the streets to fend for themselves. Sometimes the Nazis offered them a few occupation Reichsmarks, which were next to worthless, but most often they gave no compensation at all.

Those businesses that the Germans didn't take over, they plundered and robbed. Giorgos recounted the story of a friend who owned a leather-goods shop. Soldiers stole all his suitcases and leather bags in a daytime raid. Then they looted the shop next door, filling the stolen suitcases and bags with shirts, hats and other apparel. Many businesses suffered a similar fate. The Germans took what they wanted, leaving little or nothing for the locals. One thing, more than any other, incensed Giorgos: all his bread went to German soldiers, while his regular customers went without.

'I took this up with the officer who was pretending to run the bakery,' he said to Tasoula and Peter one night. 'I told that slimy bastard that we had to reserve some of our bread for our loyal customers. I knew I was asking for trouble, but I thought what the hell, they've taken everything I have and they can't run the place without me, so what do I have to lose?'

'That was either brave or stupid,' Peter said.

'Stupid, I think. The guy started acting like a maniac. A bit like Hitler, I suppose,' he joked. 'He slammed my head against an oven. Fortunately it had cooled down. Then he pushed his face right up against mine, called me an ignorant Greek peasant and told me that the bread would be kept for the soldiers, *not* the Greek riffraff. "Get that into your thick skull!" he said to me.'

'What happened next?' Peter asked.

'Well, the bastard calmed down a bit, and then he said something that chilled me to the bone. He said word had come from the top, Field-Marshal Keitel no less, that the Nazis have no interest in the welfare of Greeks: that to them a Greek life is worthless.' This didn't surprise Peter; he was already aware that the Nazi hierarchy placed no value on any human life other than a German one.

'It was all pointless, anyway. Within a month, the price of bread rose to an extortionate six thousand drachmas, so my regular customers can't afford it anyway. It's a terrible thing when ordinary people haven't got the money to buy a loaf of bread.'

Peter admired Giorgos's courage. But he had done a dangerous thing: challenging a German officer did nothing to improve one's life expectancy. Giorgos, however, was an irrepressible character who wouldn't be subdued. He took every setback in his stride. If he sniffed danger or had the odds stacked against him, he would invariably go on the offensive. And he was never short of impulsive ideas. Like most other necessities, wood was in short supply. When Tasoula ran out of logs for the potbelly stove, Giorgos came up with another of his audacious schemes.

'We'll steal some from the Germans. Well, not from the Germans themselves, but from property the Germans believe they own. We'll chop branches from the roadside trees. It will give us a chance to get our own back.'

Peter, who always thought things through and considered any pitfalls, didn't like this idea at all. 'Too risky, Giorgos. Far too risky.'

'Nonsense, Petros. We'll be up the tree in no time, cut down a few branches and be back here before you can say *gamíste ta nazistiká gouroúnia.*' This impolite invitation for the Nazis to leave Greece was accompanied by a bellowing laugh.

Giorgos's irrepressibility was matched by his powers of persuasion; before Peter could protest, Giorgos thrust a saw into his hand and dragged him out the door. Thanasis didn't seem to be keen on the idea either, but he followed dutifully. 'If we get caught, we can take a couple of Nazis with us,' he joked, brandishing an axe.

Sycamore trees lined Adrianopoulos Street. They each clambered up one and started hacking at branches. Before long, as Giorgos had promised, the trio had cut almost as much firewood as they could carry. Just as the last branch cracked and fell to the ground, a beam of torchlight blinded Peter. A second torch and then a third illuminated the other two culprits.

'Stop!' a voice yelled. 'Police! Get down, all of you. You're under arrest for damaging public property.'

Peter didn't know what to do. He had no identity card, and it would soon become obvious to the authorities that he was an illegal alien. The police generally sympathised with the Germans, so there would be little chance of leniency. 'What do I do?' he whispered to Giorgos as they assembled on the ground. Giorgos didn't seem to be concerned. 'Say nothing.

Just act dumb,' he said, as if this was nothing out of the ordinary. 'Leave it to me'.

They were marched into the police station, a nondescript building with a narrow entrance and plain, workaday furniture. A German flag adorned one wall, with gilt-framed photos of Hitler and his top henchmen — Himmler, Göring, Goebbels and Bormann — on another. Red, white and black swastika banners hung on either side of the door. It didn't bode well.

The police officer who had ordered them down from the trees — the one who seemed to be in charge — demanded to see their ID cards. Giorgos and Thanasis handed theirs over. 'What about him?' the policeman asked, poking his finger at Peter.

'Don't worry about him,' Giorgos said. 'He's deaf and dumb — can't hear or say anything. He's also a bit simple. He helps me out from time to time. I have no idea where he lives or what he does; he just turns up. The fool has probably left his identity card at home — if he has a home — or lost it. I doubt the idiot even knows what an identity card is.'

Peter looked straight ahead with a vacant stare. He was petrified, so it wasn't hard to act the part.

'You can call him anything you like. He can't hear what you're saying. Hey, stupid, I bet you're too dumb to count to ten. You retarded imbecile.' Peter said nothing, his only expression a blank look.

The police officer joined in the fun. 'You dumb shit.' They all laughed except Peter, whose glazed eyes confirmed Giorgos's description of him.

The policeman was clearly enjoying the joke at Peter's

expense. He called him a brainless moron, declared his mother a shameless whore, and invited him to bend over while he kicked his arse. Eventually he tired of the jibes, and Giorgos addressed him again. 'You can see he's a simpleton. You can't expect him to understand that he's got to carry an identity card everywhere.'

The policeman sighed, then turned serious. 'Okay, but what about chopping down the branches? That's a crime. I'll have to charge you with the wilful destruction of trees on public land. The Germans have insisted that we punish anyone who damages their property. You'll be spending the night in the cells.'

Now Giorgos flared up, fixing the policeman with a vicious stare. '*Their* property? *Their* bloody property! What about *our* property? What about Greek property? These intruders have no rights to *anything* on Greek soil!'

'Calm down, calm down. It will only be one night in jail. We'll process you all in the morning. You'll pay a small fine and you'll be free to go.' Peter was listening with mounting concern. 'Processing' would mean only one thing: a more careful scrutiny of their identities.

Giorgos continued eyeballing the policeman. He wasn't about to give in. 'But all we want is a bit of extra wood to keep us warm. You understand what it's like at this time of year. The branches would have fallen off anyway. We weren't doing anyone any harm.' A rapid-fire discussion ensued, too fast for Peter to keep up with. Giorgos became agitated. He was trying to convince the officer to let them go, but the man was adamant that they should spend the night in custody. It turned into a heated argument. Giorgos's propensity to live dangerously was plainly evident.

The furore culminated in a direct challenge from the exasperated Giorgos. He squared up to the officer, spittle spraying from his lips as he hissed at him: 'What are you? A true Greek or a Nazi puppet? Where are your loyalties? To them or to us?'

Peter could see that this would go one of two ways: either arrest for a more serious crime — perhaps sedition or subversion — or just a sharp rebuke and an order to go home if Giorgos's appeal to patriotism worked.

'Get out!' the policeman said. 'I'm no Nazi, but I am here to uphold law and order. Get out before I throw you in a cell.' Giorgos grabbed Peter and hauled him towards the door. Outside, they sprinted back to Tasoula's — stopping only to pick up the chopped branches and tools they had left behind.

———————

Firewood was one thing, but Tasoula's more pressing concern was food. With little demand for tailoring, even fewer alterations and just the odd repair job to patch up a worn dress on her books, she was struggling to pay the wages, never mind buy foodstuffs.

To make matters worse, food had become scarcer and even more expensive. Meat was a rarity — seldom available — and their staple diet comprised beans, lentils, goat's cheese, dandelion roots and other vegetables. Fish was sometimes on the menu, but rationed to make it last at least two meals.

Tasoula amazed Peter with what she could concoct from the most basic of ingredients. A marriage of beans and lentils with vegetable roots, weed leaves and flower stems produced dishes worthy of a Michelin-starred chef. Tasoula got milk coupons for the government-run milk station, each coupon buying one bottle, but that didn't go far. The only decent food was to be got on the black market, and exorbitant prices put that out of reach.

Thalia helped where she could. She fossicked for plants in the woods and helped cook the evening meals. She and Tasoula had become even closer, and she stayed for dinner most nights. On one of those nights, when they were lamenting the lack of provisions, the indomitable Giorgos came up with another of his wild ideas. 'I'll steal bread from the bakery,' he announced as they ate the last of the briam, a roasted vegetable dish Tasoula had served.

Giorgos's latest brainwave had come mere days after the tree-chopping escapade, and Peter hadn't yet recovered from that incident. Now he had more of Giorgos's impetuous ideas to contend with. Giorgos and Thanasis had hatched a plan. It was dangerous, but Giorgos waved away any concerns with a dramatic flourish. He had got Thanasis a job at the bakery, and together they worked out what they would do. Giorgos would steal the bread and Thanasis would conceal it.

'But how?' Tasoula asked. 'How are you going to pinch loaves from the bakery without the Germans finding out? You know what they'll do. You can't afford to take that risk. Anyway, I'll not have Thanasis getting involved with any of your hare-brained schemes. And that's final.'

'But Mamá . . .'

Giorgos tried to intervene, but his sister-in-law was just as strong-willed and obstinate as he was. Peter agreed with Tasoula. 'Thanasis, it's far too dangerous. You're risking your life. For what? A loaf of bread?' But the persuasive Giorgos had convinced Thanasis, and they were determined to go ahead. All pleas for reason fell on deaf ears.

'Sorry, Thanasis,' Tasoula said, shaking a finger at her son. 'I forbid it — and that's that. I appreciate what you're trying to do, and I can't deny that extra bread would be a big help, but I'll not have you putting yourself in danger.'

'Well, Mamá, I'm going to do it. I'll not stand by and let the Germans trample all over us. They've taken everything we have, so we'll take something from them. It may not be a lot, but it's one way I can fight back.'

Tasoula had already argued with Thanasis over his night-time sabotage missions, even though she respected his desire to combat the occupiers. She was torn between admiration for his fervent patriotism and despair at failing in her maternal duty to protect him. 'No, Thanasis. No,' she said, with as much authority as she could manage. But in her heart, she knew she was losing the argument.

Giorgos stayed silent. Thanasis sulked. Thalia was sitting quietly in her chair, deep in thought. Suddenly, her eyes brightened. 'Mrs Tasoula, what if we sewed a loop on the back of Thanasis's shirt collar and attached a string and a small pouch big enough to fit a round loaf of flatbread? If Giorgos can steal the bread without the Germans noticing, he could slip it into the pouch when they're about to leave for the day.

The bag would hang in the small of Thanasis's back and the Germans would never see it under his overcoat. It would be easy enough to sew a loop on the shirt.'

This wasn't enough to convince Tasoula, but Thalia could see she was thinking about it.

'I can steal the bread, no trouble,' Giorgos boasted. 'It's a great idea, and I know exactly where I can hide it until we're ready to leave. Thanasis will be safe. The round loaf will only be concealed on him for the few seconds it takes to walk away from the bakery. I'd do it myself, but the bastards hate me and often search me from top to toe. Once they insisted I drop my trousers to see if I had anything hidden in my underpants; I should have farted. But they've never once inspected Thanasis. He's a boy — they won't suspect him. Even if there is a search, they'll never think to check the back of his coat.'

'Mamá,' Thanasis implored. 'We need the food, and I'll be very careful.'

Tasoula stared at the ceiling, weighing up the risks. Finally, she spoke. 'It might work, Thalia, I'll grant you that. But Thanasis would have to be very careful. Stealing a loaf of bread would be enough to have him arrested. And who knows what would happen then? Thanasis, I'll think about it. In the meantime, let's see how Thalia's idea might work.'

Thanasis needed no encouragement. Within minutes, Thalia had sewn the loop on the yoke of his shirt, just below the collar, to take the extra weight. She then sewed a pouch from surplus fabric and attached the string. Peter found a small S-shaped metal hook, and tied one end to the shirt loop and the other to the pouch. Thanasis changed into the shirt, put a spare loaf of bread in the bag and put his overcoat on. It was impossible to tell that the loaf was there.

Tasoula conceded that the idea had merit and, even more reluctantly, agreed that Thanasis could trial it.

The following day, with a triumphant flourish, Thanasis produced a much-needed loaf of fresh bread and placed it on the table. Tasoula sliced it and they devoured it within minutes. The promise of more to come each day made a welcome addition to a depleted pantry. Giorgos boasted that he could steal half a dozen loaves, but Tasoula shut him up before he had a chance to elaborate on his new ploy. She had a quiet word with him later, making him promise that he wouldn't involve Thanasis in any more of his reckless ventures.

The extra loaves helped, but it still wasn't enough. Although Tasoula was much better off than most, with only a trickle of work coming in, her situation could only get worse. Also, the Germans had become more vigilant than ever, and that posed a much bigger threat.

Chapter
Ten

'Halt!' the soldier said. 'Halt! Ausweis bitte.' Papers, please. Peter sensed trouble. He kept walking.

'Now!' the soldier barked, as if he were giving the order to a firing squad. Peter glanced sideways. The soldier was young — very young — most likely on his first posting, and he seemed determined to make an impression. He was now pointing his rifle at Peter, his hands shaking so much that Peter feared it would go off.

The evening had started uneventfully. Thalia stayed for dinner and Tasoula shared her concern about the Germans stepping up their efforts to round up Greek dissidents and resistance families. The SS had already arrested two of her close contacts. The German authorities knew that patriotic Greeks were hiding soldiers, but not exactly where and who. They almost certainly had their suspicions — Tasoula herself might have been on the list — but suspicion wasn't leading to enough arrests. Random searches weren't producing enough results, either. The raids tended to be haphazard and the searches were seldom thorough. Most soldiers were lazy; more interested in looting and ransacking than catching militants or fugitives. Besides, some of the Allied soldiers would be tough customers — more than a match for their German counterparts. The High Command decided on another strategy. Tasoula heard about it through Mrs Koula, whose cousin was a police officer.

'We need to be extra vigilant,' Tasoula warned. 'Even more wary than before. The Germans' latest plan is to surround city blocks and search house to house. All the streets are to be blocked off, with armed soldiers on every corner, so there's no escape route. Senior officers will supervise, so the searches will be thorough. This is already happening, and the Germans have targeted at least two districts I'm aware of. I've no idea when our turn will come, but you can be sure it will be soon.'

Peter had many questions, but Tasoula had few answers. She only knew what Mrs Koula told her, and that wasn't much. Only that the Germans had co-opted local police to conduct searches under German supervision. 'Getting us to do their dirty work,' the cousin had complained.

The trio discussed contingency plans for evading the search parties. Peter would move out — stay away for a night if necessary — then come back when the Germans had left the area. They were still talking about where he might go when Thanasis, who had been out with his resistance friends, charged through the door, breathless.

'They're here,' he said, stopping to take in air. 'The

Germans are just up the road and they're going from house to house. They're everywhere and they'll be here before long.' All of them had been caught out. The plan for Peter to leave as soon as any patrols approached Enou Place required advance notice; he needed time to get out of the area. But that wouldn't work now; the search party was too close. Peter was pondering his next move when a soft hand gripped his. Thalia's. 'Come,' she said, pulling him towards the door. 'Come with me.' The next minute, he was out on a street packed with Wehrmacht soldiers and Greek police.

———————

Now they found themselves confronted by a trigger-happy juvenile with a rifle, yelling at them to stop.

Thalia gripped Peter's hand more tightly and pulled herself closer. 'We're young lovers, you and me,' she whispered. 'Just keep walking. Play your part and they'll leave us alone.'

Peter hesitated. Thalia took the initiative and wrapped her arm around his waist. Peter knew he must act, too. He put his hand over her shoulder, brushing her neck as he reached for her arm.

The soldier yelled out again. 'Halt! Now! Halt!'

Thalia said nothing. She freed herself from Peter's arm and swung around, now moving backwards to press her back against a brick wall. She grabbed Peter's arms and drew him towards her. The German shouted the order again, but Thalia ignored him. She pulled Peter even closer. She could feel the warmth of his breath; the contours of his body. She gripped him tightly, as if she were frightened to let go.

Peter now understood what he had to do. With one hand around her shoulders, he cradled her head with the other, and pressed his lips against her cheek. They didn't kiss — Peter was too chivalrous to take advantage of the situation — but to the soldier it would look like they were locked in a passionate embrace. Other soldiers nearby cheered the two lovers with lewd comments and suggestive gestures. The youthful soldier, probably too embarrassed to pursue the pair, lowered his rifle and joined in the boorish chants with his older colleagues. Soon they all lost interest and resumed their search, leaving Peter and Thalia propped against the wall. After waiting a short while, they walked out of the search zone unimpeded. Meanwhile, the patrol searched Tasoula's house and found nothing. For the third time, Peter had Thalia to thank for saving him from certain arrest.

As soon as the soldiers had left the area, Thalia and Peter hurried back to the house. The place was littered with upturned furniture, broken plates, discarded papers and smashed ornaments. The usual destructive mess.

'Thalia, Petros, you're back!' Tasoula said, relieved to see them unharmed. 'Thank God. I was so worried that those Nazi dogs would detain you. How did you do it? How did you get away?'

Thalia blushed. She was too self-conscious to tell Tasoula what she had done. Peter was, too. He avoided Tasoula's gaze, his cheeks flaring. 'It was all thanks to Thalia' was all he would say.

'No matter. You're both safe — that's the important thing. Now let's get this place cleared up.'

Peter had held Thalia close. So close that their bodies moulded together as naturally as petals to a rosebud. It felt good. Now Peter chastised himself for taking pleasure from the brief embrace. Thalia had acted solely out of a desire to protect him; he had no right to assume any emotional connection. He kept thanking her profusely. Over and over. But he wouldn't put his arms around her again. It didn't seem right. He was embarrassed. And he presumed that Thalia felt nothing.

Thalia wasn't sure what had made her clutch Peter the way she had. They could have just huddled together in the darkness, as far away from the soldiers as possible — that would have been enough to keep up the pretence of them being young lovers. Instead, she had held him with an urgency she couldn't explain. It had started as a spur-of-the-moment decision; an instinctive move to protect him. But somehow, it was more than that.

She believed that Peter's only interest had been self-preservation. That he had embraced her purely to avoid detection and recapture. She was proud that she had helped, but now was confused by what she felt. Whatever it was, it troubled her.

Chapter
Eleven

Peter cleared his throat, then addressed Tasoula, Thanasis and Thalia in near-perfect Greek.

'I'm leaving. I can't put you in any more danger. My presence here is putting everyone at risk, and I can't do that. I'll go by the end of the week.' The various encounters with Germans had made Peter realise just how close they had come to exposure. He would not compromise his hosts any longer.

'Nonsense,' Tasoula said, 'you're staying right where you are. We've pledged to fight the Nazis — if you leave, we'll just take someone else in. We know we can trust you, and would rather you stayed than some stranger. Anyway, our other resistance work puts us in more danger than having you around.'

Peter knew nothing about Tasoula's 'other resistance work' and knew better than to ask. She would often go out at night, not returning until late — sometimes early in the morning. She had once told him it was better that she said nothing about her comings and goings. 'You can't reveal what you don't know,' were her words to him.

'Besides, Petros, we don't have an organised escape route anymore. You can't wander around aimlessly looking for someone to take you to Turkey. You'd be lucky to make it out of Thessaloniki, never mind across the Aegean Sea. My resistance friends and I are working on a new network, but until we have something in place you must stay here. After what happened to Madam Lapper, we need to make sure we have a safe passage out of Greece.'

Thanasis and Thalia voiced their support. A mix of guilt and relief swept over Peter. He hated endangering the family, but he did like being at Tasoula's. And what she said was true: trying to leave now would be futile. Staying put until an escape route had been established was the most sensible option. However, that didn't alter the fact that he was putting the family in jeopardy. Although Tasoula had brushed aside his concerns, Peter's close calls had reminded him that he was a wanted fugitive. One wrong move would be disastrous for both him and his hosts. Had Thalia not acted so selflessly, and so cleverly, they might now be languishing in some dingy prison cell or — worse — being grilled by the Gestapo.

Now that he was staying, Peter vowed to help Tasoula as much as he could: chopping firewood, tending the garden, and in the season foraging for mushrooms in the hills, gathering nuts and harvesting olives from the three trees in the backyard — anything that would make life easier for her. He even tried his hand at making charcoal bricks. With her wood supply depleted — and no further plans to hack down roadside branches — the bricks would keep the fire going during the still-cold late-February nights. Peter tackled the task with enthusiasm. 'This can't be that hard,' he said to himself, as he set about it. All he had to do was gather the charcoal dust, mix it with asvestos (lime) and water, shape the paste into small balls and leave them out in the sun to dry. Peter had seen Thanasis making them — it seemed easy, so he was confident that he would knock up a few bricks in no time. He whistled as he worked with the black paste, but the job proved to be more difficult than he had imagined and soon he was struggling.

Thalia walked in while he was trying to mould the paste into round balls. 'That's not the way to do it, Petros,' she said, staring at the mess he was making. 'Here, let me show you how. There's a certain knack to it, but once you've done it a few times, it's easy.'

Thalia made her first brick in what seemed like a few seconds. She explained the process to Peter while she finished her second in an even faster time. 'There,' she said. 'That's the way you do it.' But Peter made an even bigger mess of his second attempt. Thalia shook her head in exasperation; as far as she was concerned, her instructions had been crystal clear.

Peter had carried on whistling as he tried to follow Thalia's directions, and she started humming along. Now she couldn't get the tune out of her head. 'Tell me, Petros, what's that song you're whistling?'

'It's an old army song. We sing it while we're marching. It's called "Pack Up Your Troubles in Your Old Kit-Bag",' said Peter, translating the title into Greek as best he could.

'That sounds like a strange song. What does it mean?'

'It's about leaving all your troubles behind you when you go into . . .' Peter couldn't think of the Greek word for battle. He improvised, having become adept at using different words and phrases when particular words were beyond his vocabulary. '. . . when you go to war.'

'I don't understand. You sing a song about packing your troubles into an old bag when you go to war?'

'Well, sort of. It means that if you forget about all your troubles, you'll have a clear head when you're fighting. It also reminds us soldiers that there's no point in worrying about things that might never happen.'

Thalia raised her eyebrows. 'You English. You have the weirdest customs. I'll never understand.'

'It's not as silly as it sounds, Thalia. Here, I'll translate the complete song for you if you like. Some words may not translate easily into Greek, but I'll try.'

'That would be nice, Petros. Maybe it will help me understand.'

Peter recited the words:

Pack up your troubles in your old kit-bag,
And smile, smile, smile,
While you've a lucifer to light your fag,
Smile, boys, that's the style.
What's the use of worrying? It never was worthwhile
so pack up your troubles in your old kit-bag,
And smile, smile, smile.

Thalia frowned, confusion showing in her eyes. 'I still don't get it, Petros. You get rid of all your problems by shoving them into some old bag and forgetting about them? And you smile while you're doing it? How do you put problems into a bag? That doesn't make sense. I still think you English have some strange habits.'

'All you have to remember, Thalia, is that most things we worry about will never happen. Sometimes it's better to stop worrying and concentrate on positive things. Things that make us happy. The words of this song remind us of that.'

'You're right, Petros. People do worry too much. *I* worry too much.'

Despite her worries, Thalia felt comfortable around Peter. His confidence and calmness put her at ease. 'Thanks, Petros. I'll call this my "troubles" song and whenever I'm stressed or worried, I'll hum it to calm me down.'

'That's the spirit, Thalia. You *do* understand.'

Thalia smiled. An intoxicating smile; Peter had never seen her smile like that before. 'Now, Petros, let me get on with making the charcoal bricks. You're hopeless — I'll have to finish the job myself.'

Thalia hummed the song while she made the rest of the bricks and laid them out in neat rows to dry in the sun.

———————

Most nights now, Thalia stayed after work and joined the family for dinner. The highlight of these evenings was listening to the BBC news. Peter or Thanasis would go up into the attic to fetch the illegal radio. The only wireless sets the Germans allowed were 'sealed' radios, with fixed tuning that would pick up only the Public Radio Station of Athens, the German propaganda outlet. Possessing a radio capable of tuning into the BBC was considered an act of treason, punishable by a long spell in a prison or concentration camp. Tasoula took great care to hide her receiver where it wouldn't be found.

It was an old Schaub set, housed in a chipped mahogany case with a circular speaker covered with frayed brown fabric. That it was a German brand irked Tasoula, but she had owned it long before Hitler's troops invaded Greece. Before turning it on, Tasoula closed all the curtains, turned off the lights and locked the doors. The valves took a while to warm up — hissing and squawking as they did — and then the set would splutter into life. They all huddled expectantly around the small receiver while Tasoula twiddled the Bakelite knobs, waiting for the familiar introduction: 'This is the BBC European Service. This is London calling . . .' Crackly static and a reverberating echo made listening difficult, but Tasoula was hungry for accurate news and only the BBC was broadcasting credible accounts of Allied victories — and losses. It was a vital link to the outside world.

Churchill's regular broadcasts, once or twice a month, were in English, so Peter's job was to translate and relay the news. Most reports contained the same message: Churchill would open up the second front as soon as possible, but Greece had to be patient. Peter began to wonder if it would ever happen. He kept his doubts to himself, though, and gave a more upbeat account to Tasoula, who circulated the information to her close friends. Churchill's voice alone was enough to inspire confidence.

Thalia felt privileged to be treated as part of the family and looked forward to these evenings, as much for the camaraderie as for the news. She liked Peter and found it easy to relax in his company, enjoying his sense of humour and the many amusing stories he told. Now that he was so fluent in Greek, she was drawn into conversation with him more and more. Thalia asked lots of questions; for his part, Peter also wanted to learn more about her background.

'What's New Zealand like, Petros?' Thalia asked one evening, after they had talked about how the Germans had captured him and his escape to Thessaloniki.

'Well, Thalia, there are two main islands — the North Island and the South Island — with regular ferries that connect the two. Just like the Greek islands. The total population of the entire country is only about 1.6 million, so there are lots of open spaces. The scenery is wonderful. How do I describe it? Well, there are spectacular glaciers, picturesque fiords, rugged mountains and miles of coastline with gorgeous sandy beaches. It's exquisite, Thalia. But unlike here, New Zealand doesn't have the history, culture and tradition of Greece. It's very different.'

'It sounds amazing, Petros . . . and what did you do before the war?'

'I was a farmer, in a place called Lees Valley — that's a pretty remote spot in the South Island. I was looking after a fifteen-thousand-acre farm. That's about three times the size of the whole of Salonika, so it was a massive run. I was a high-country . . .' Peter groped for the Greek word for musterer, but it eluded him. 'I was a sort of shepherd, but with thousands of sheep to manage. It was a very isolated existence, but I had my dogs for company, and I enjoyed it.'

'I don't think we have farms like that here. Do they have electricity and running water in New Zealand? Things like that?'

Peter laughed. Not everyone in Greece had such comforts. 'Of course, Thalia. New Zealand has one of the highest standards of living in the world. We have everything. We might be a long way away, but we have all the modern conveniences. Most households have a car, and many have telephones. This may surprise you, Thalia, but a lot of Greeks live in New Zealand. Quite a few own restaurants.'

'I had no idea, Petros. I thought New Zealand was a primitive country.'

'What about you, Thalia? Tell me a bit more about yourself.'

'Well, I was born in Kolindros, about fifty kilometres from here, but I don't remember anything about my time there. We shifted to Thessaloniki when I was very young, and my earliest recollections are from here. My mother and father were very strict, so I didn't have much free time in those days. I had to work when I got home after school and had little time to play or make friends. To be honest, I didn't get on with my parents, especially my mother.' Her face clouded over.

'That's sad, Thalia. I'm sorry. Why did they treat you so harshly?'

'I never understood why, so I can't explain. They always put me down and criticised everything I did. They still do. Let's just say I had a difficult childhood. I don't like to talk about it — it wasn't a happy time for me.'

'But you always seem so bright and cheerful, Thalia.'

'I love it here. It's like having a proper family. Mrs Tasoula is so good to me and appreciates what I do. So, yes, I am very happy now.'

Thalia paused. It suddenly dawned on her that being around Peter also made her happy. This man from the other side of the world had come to mean something to her. She dwelt on that thought for a second or two before continuing.

'It wasn't all bad, Petros. I did have some good times in my younger days. I remember riding on mule-back and swimming at Panormos Beach and fishing for crabs around the breakwater at Skopelos Port. And we picked lots of fruit: grapes, watermelons, figs. To some people that might seem like work, but I enjoyed it. And whenever I got the chance, I would walk in the countryside or explore ancient ruins. I love Greece and everything about it.'

'I love Greece, too, Thalia. It's a beautiful country, full of beautiful and brave people.'

'It is, yes, but Greece also has its problems. Life was difficult for us Greeks even before this war. I don't follow politics much, but my parents often talked about the prospect of civil war and the conflict between the royalists and the antiroyal Venizelists. And there have been several political assassinations.'

Peter didn't know much about Greek politics either, but the army had briefed them before they'd left for Crete: unemployment was rampant, inflation was out of control, the economy was imploding, poverty was endemic, and civil tensions simmered uneasily below a fragile surface. 'I know a little about these troubles, Thalia, so I can imagine how difficult things are. What about your schooldays?'

'I liked school. It gave me a chance to get away from problems at home. I studied classical Greek, history and German, among other subjects, and enjoyed skipping and playing hopscotch. Gymnastics was my favourite sport. What about New Zealand? What are the most popular sports there, Petros?'

'Rugby is the major sport, so lots of people play or watch. The All Blacks are the most famous rugby team in the world.'

'A team of black men?'

'No, no, not at all, Thalia. Most of the players are white.'

'Oh,' said Thalia, surprised.

'Rugby is played in winter. The main summer sport is cricket. Some games last for five days. It's hard to explain, but sometimes these games end in a draw. Neither team wins.'

'So, let me get this right, Petros: you have an all-black team but most of the players are white, and you play this cricket game for five days and neither team wins? I'll never understand you English.'

'Well, no, Thalia. There's more to it than that. The All Blacks are called that because . . .' Peter stopped mid-sentence. It was too difficult to explain.

Thalia looked forward to chatting with Peter. She was fond of him. Very fond, if she was honest with herself. She couldn't explain why she found him so fascinating, but she enjoyed talking to him and she was intrigued by a country that was so far away and had such strange customs. It was a lifestyle she could barely comprehend. Thalia found it all very exotic — her whole life had been lived within 50 kilometres of Thessaloniki. She had never even ventured as far as Athens.

Chapter
Twelve

Tasoula suspected that she was under surveillance. There was no firm evidence, nothing concrete to suggest that she was being investigated, but her instincts were seldom wrong.

The Nazis were closing in on the resistance network and had already arrested several of Tasoula's colleagues. The Papadakis, husband and wife, had been shipped to a German concentration camp for harbouring a British soldier; Mrs Galanis, another underground contact, had been interrogated briefly. Her quick release prompted speculation that she might have co-operated with her interrogators, and Tasoula was worried that she might have been betrayed. Mrs Galanis knew of Tasoula's involvement in the escape chain, although not about her other resistance work.

The Germans were getting smarter, too: some disguised themselves in civilian clothes and masqueraded as escaping English soldiers looking for somewhere to hide. The Germans immediately arrested those who agreed to help. Another ploy they adopted to dupe locals into betraying their fellow Greeks concerned Tasoula even more. Well-dressed men in smart suits came to towns and villages, telling the residents that they worked for the British and offering to provide food and money to Greeks who harboured Allied soldiers. They even produced a forged letter of introduction from King George II, the Greek king in exile in Cairo, to prove their legitimacy. And the new tactic of cordoning off streets to conduct house-to-house searches had resulted in several arrests. Tasoula had been lucky so far, but how long would that luck hold out?

Peter offered many times to leave to protect her and Thanasis, but she ignored his pleas. 'I won't be cowed by these Nazi devils,' she told Peter one day. 'I'd rather die doing what I can for my country than give in to those animals.'

'But what about Thanasis? If I leave now, the Germans can't prove that you have been harbouring Allied fugitives.'

'Thanasis is my only concern — but he, too, wants to fight back. He doesn't want to grow old wondering if he could have done more. Besides, I'm convinced that the Nazis already have me on a list of suspects. They're just waiting for the right excuse, then they'll arrest me whether you're here or not. I'm going to send Thanasis to stay with a cousin in Koufalia. He won't like it, but at least he'll be safe.'

Peter realised it was pointless arguing, but he'd had to offer.

But nothing happened. For months, nothing happened. The Germans showed no sign of wanting to arrest Tasoula. She relaxed. Thanasis stayed. Perhaps the Germans had forgotten about her, or maybe they had more important suspects to chase. Peter feared that they were just biding their time.

But as time went on, Peter relaxed too. He got bolder. Now fluent in Greek, he ventured out most days: sometimes trekking in the hills behind Thessaloniki; sometimes walking in the countryside; sometimes just wandering around the neighbourhood. He even bought ouzo from the Karousaki liquor store on Marasli a few times, and often enjoyed a coffee at the Tombulidis kafenion further up the road. But he was never reckless. He always considered the risks and was confident that he could pass for a Greek if he were challenged.

———————

Tasoula seemed to have cousins everywhere. Peter was never sure if they were genuine cousins, or friends of cousins. Or just friends. She always greeted each person as if they were her favourite. They exchanged bread for potatoes, milk in return for eggs, and bartered anything else they had for something they didn't. Food was scarce, but what little they did have was everyone's to share. So when Tasoula learned that one of her cousins near Sindos had begun harvesting a large crop of zucchini, she sent Peter to pick some. 'You can stay for a few days. I'm sure they won't mind,' she told Peter.

The farm was a solid four-hour walk away, but Peter was fit and set a brisk pace, arriving there within three. The reception he got wasn't what he'd expected, however. Despite what Tasoula had promised, the farmer made it clear that Peter wasn't welcome. First he said that Peter couldn't stay because he didn't trust the neighbours, then he changed his story: German patrols were scouring the area.

Peter left empty-handed. Tasoula would be disappointed, but it couldn't be helped; he wouldn't stay where he wasn't wanted. He was on his way back when he rounded a bend and spotted a checkpoint in the distance; it hadn't been there that morning. Peter of course had no papers, and no way of proving he had any legitimate business in the area. Even a cursory check would reveal that something was amiss. A more thorough inspection would mean immediate arrest. And then . . .

He turned back; he would stay the night somewhere — in a barn or an abandoned shack — and return the following day after the checkpoint had been moved. It was inconvenient, as he would rather get back to Thessaloniki that night, but it was the safest option. He was thinking about where he might doss down when he saw four German soldiers approaching from the opposite direction. Now trapped between the checkpoint and the approaching soldiers, he spotted a farmer nearby with a horse-drawn cart full of watermelons, presumably heading for a local market. On the spur of the moment he asked for a ride, hoping that the checkpoint guards would simply wave the farmer through.

'Jump on,' the jovial Greek said. 'I've got about six kilometres to go to the market, so I'll drop you off there.'

Peter put one foot on the running board and hoisted himself up on to the bench seat as the cart moved off. As soon as he'd sat down, he regretted his decision — he had put the elderly farmer in danger along with himself. But it was too late to do anything else now. They were already around the corner and in plain view of the checkpoint. And this time, there was no quick-thinking Giorgos to get him out of the scrape.

'Halt!' the sentry yelled. The farmer pulled on the reins and brought the cart to a halt.

'What do we have here?' the German asked, as if the watermelons stacked high on the back of the wagon didn't make it obvious.

'Just watermelons for the market,' the old man said.

'Okay. Papers, *bitte*, then you can go.' They both got off the cart and the farmer handed over his identity card. Peter fumbled in his pockets, then spread his palms out to show that he couldn't find his. He looked under the seat, then at the road below, then once again in his pockets. Meanwhile, the farmer looked at him quizzically. When the sentry turned away to summon his colleagues, Peter shook his head to signal to the farmer that he had no ID.

Doubtless sensing an opportunity to make an arrest, the sentry pushed the old man to one side and jammed the butt of his rifle into Peter's chest. 'No papers, eh? You know what we do to people with no papers. We arrest them, that's what. And we hold them until we have proof of identity. The only place you're going today is a prison cell. We'll lock you up until we get the proof we need.'

Peter felt the fear rising from his gut. 'But how can I get my papers if I'm locked up?'

'Not our problem,' the soldier said with a smirk. 'Over here,' he called, waving his rifle towards another two men in black uniforms on the side of the road.

The men pushed Peter towards a black Mercedes with a Nazi flag mounted on each mudguard. Alarmed, Peter clutched at the small bag he was carrying. In it he kept a New Zealand badge — a gift from his father that he always took with him for good luck. As soon as the Germans saw the badge, they would realise he was not who he was pretending to be. His mouth tightened; he was about to be exposed. The farmer was standing by his cart, watching. He could have moved off, but he hadn't. Just as they reached the car, he intervened. Throwing his hands in the air in a gesture of exasperation, he shook his head and ambled towards the soldier who now had his hand on Peter's head, about to force him into the back seat.

'He's my son, the scatter-brained fool. He's always losing or forgetting things. His papers. His wallet. His keys. He even forgot to bring sacks for the market today. He'd lose his very tiny brain if it wasn't permanently trapped inside his thick skull. I keep telling him to keep his identity card in a safe place, but the young fool ignores me. Young people today, they think they know everything.'

The soldier nodded, even though he was younger than Peter.

'We'll miss this week's market if we don't hurry. The watermelons won't last until next week. He's my youngest son. I can vouch for that. He's nothing but trouble, this one. If I didn't need him to help at the market, I'd encourage you to lock him up — just to teach him a lesson.'

He gave Peter a sharp clip across the ear. It hurt. Peter wasn't quite sure whether the hard slap was just for the sake of authenticity or a deliberate rebuke from an angry man.

'Let us through this once, and I'll make sure he brings his paperwork next time. And you can take some watermelons for your trouble.'

The soldier grunted and waved them through, but not before he and his two colleagues had each gathered an armful of fruit.

When they were out of sight, Peter clasped the farmer's hand and held it tight. 'I can't thank you enough. You saved my skin. I'm a New Zealand soldier — they would have arrested and beaten me as soon as they learned the truth. Thank you again. And I'm sorry I put you in this position. Truly sorry.'

'Ah, it was nothing. I hate these bastards. Anything I can do to deceive them, I will. Here, take some fruit from the cart for yourself.'

Peter refused, but the farmer insisted. The rest of the journey was uneventful, thankfully, and he arrived back with four large watermelons for Tasoula.

Chapter
Thirteen

During the seven months that Peter had been staying at Tasoula's, he saw Patrick as often as he could — the Angelidous house was nearby — and he also visited Nugget Carmichael, another New Zealand soldier living locally, harboured by the French consul.

He now saw Thalia almost every day. He liked her; a lot. And not just as a friend. The more Peter saw of Thalia, the stronger the attraction he felt, even though Thalia had neither said nor done anything to suggest that she had any interest in him. He couldn't help his feelings — even if she didn't reciprocate them — and wasn't sure what he should do. Peter had had little experience with women; none, if he were honest with himself. Before the war his life had revolved around the farm, hunting and having a few beers with his mates. He had never sought female company.

Peter wanted to confide in someone about his fondness for

Thalia, but didn't know how to bring the subject up. One day, he just blurted it all out to Patrick. He hadn't meant to burden his friend, but couldn't stop himself.

'Paddy,' he said nervously, 'I need some advice. I realise it's wrong, but I can't get Thalia Christidou off my mind. I think I'm falling for her, and I'm not sure what to do. I doubt she has any interest in me, but I can't stop thinking about her. Should I tell her? What should I do?' The normally calm, reserved Peter was embarrassed to be talking about his intimate feelings; and Patrick was clearly taken aback.

'Jesus, Peter — that came out of the blue. I had no idea. She's a looker, I'll give you that, but she's Greek. Her life is here among her own people. You'll have to leave sometime soon. What then? You'll be twelve thousand miles away at the arse-end of the world. She would never follow you there. Now if it was Australia,' his friend joked, 'she'd be on the first ship out, but New Zealand? Never!'

'It's no laughing matter, Paddy. I'm serious. I understand it's wrong in many ways, but I can't help how I feel.'

'Okay Peter, I know, I know. But you can't tell her, you realise that? For starters, there's a bloody good chance you're right: she probably doesn't feel the same way about you. And think it through, man. If you tell her, she might end up in big trouble. If the Krauts ever find out that she's not only helped hide some Kiwi footslogger but she's also got a thing going with him, God knows what they'll do to her. And what happens when you bugger off back to Kiwiland? What then? She can hardly up sticks and leave her family and mates and bugger off to the other side of the world. And if, by some bloody miracle, she does hold a torch for you, you'll be breaking her heart. And that's not fair. No, Peter, you can't tell her. You're a decent chap and there's only one decent thing to do: keep it to yourself. Forget her.'

'I can't forget her, Paddy.' Peter rubbed his forehead and ran his hands through his hair as he chewed over Patrick's advice. One minute he was deciding to confront Thalia; the next, not to. He took a deep breath and exhaled, then made up his mind.

'I guess you're right, Paddy. I can't tell her. It would be unfair. And ungentlemanly. I'll say nothing. Besides, I'm sure she thinks I'm a big pillock. Thanks for listening, Paddy. It's not what I wanted to hear, but what you say makes sense.'

———————

Thalia needed to talk to someone. Ever since she and Peter had held each other's gaze for those few seconds after installing the warning bell, he had been on her mind. Their brief embrace in front of the German soldiers had just strengthened her feelings, and their regular evening chats drew her even closer. Peter had given her no sign that he was attracted to her — in fact, there was every chance he had no interest in her at all — but she couldn't help what she felt. He would no doubt be very experienced with women — had probably had many girlfriends, perhaps even a fiancée waiting back home — whereas she had only ever had one boyfriend.

Unable to erase Peter from her mind, she had to talk to someone. Someone who understood. Someone who cared, someone with her best interests at heart. For most girls her age that would be their best friend, or their mother. Fifi was her best friend but, while she sympathised, she discouraged Thalia from taking things any further. Fifi's advice was well meant, but she thought Thalia's interest in Peter was just adolescent infatuation. To Thalia, it was more than that.

Naturally, Thalia couldn't confide in her mother. Their relationship was strained, broken even; and discussing her romantic feelings about any man, let alone a foreigner, would have been pointless. Nothing Thalia said or did was ever good enough for her mother. Narcissistic and self-centred, she would never approve of any relationship of Thalia's unless it improved her own social standing.

That left Tasoula; the only other person Thalia trusted to talk with about such delicate matters. In the short time she had known her, Thalia had grown closer to Tasoula than to her own parents. She plucked up the courage to approach the older woman.

'Mrs Tasoula, can I talk to you about something personal?' The quaver in her voice suggested to Tasoula that this might be an uncomfortable conversation.

'Of course, Thalia. You can talk to me about anything. I would never break any confidences. Whatever you tell me won't go any further. My life depends on keeping secrets, so I've had plenty of practice.' She smiled.

Thalia was nervous. She shuffled about in her seat and jiggled one leg. 'It's difficult, Mrs Tasoula. I'm not sure where to start. It's about Petros.'

'Petros?' Tasoula asked, although she had an inkling of what was coming. She had noticed the emotional chemistry between the two.

'Yes, Petros. I think . . .' She hesitated. 'I think I'm in love with him.'

Tasoula had dreaded this moment. Even if the mutual attraction wasn't obvious to them, it was to her. She had been hoping it might be just a passing fancy; something they would both forget in time.

'I see. Petros,' she said, stroking her chin as she considered how to respond.

'I've told no one about this apart from Fifi and she didn't help much. I need your advice. What do I do, Mrs Tasoula? Do I tell him?'

Tasoula chose her next words carefully. 'Does he feel the same way about you?'

'I'm not sure. I don't think so.'

'This is difficult, Thalia. Very difficult. Petros is a wonderful man. Kind. Generous. Caring. If I were much younger, I might fall for him myself. I can see why you're enamoured with him, but it's very complicated.'

'Complicated? How? I don't understand, Mrs Tasoula.'

'Thalia, you're a beautiful young girl, and nothing would make me happier than seeing you happy. But wartime romances are . . . well . . . just *complicated*.'

'I still don't understand.'

'Well, for a start, Petros will have to leave sometime soon — in the next few months, I'm guessing. As soon as we establish an alternative escape route. When he does, he'll flee to Turkey or Egypt, and when this damned war finally ends, he'll return to his homeland: New Zealand. It's on the other side of the world, Thalia. Different people, different customs, different food. Different everything. It's so far away. I don't want to hurt you, Thalia, but there's no future for you with him — even if Petros does feel the same way as you do. I'm sorry, Thalia, but you must forget him.'

Tasoula saw tears forming in the corners of Thalia's eyes. They inched down her cheeks. More tears followed. Tasoula wrapped her arms around her protégé and held her close. She understood Thalia's emotional dilemma, but she knew what she must do.

'I appreciate that you don't want to hear this, but wartime romances seldom lead to future happiness. These are unusual times. Two people are thrown together amid this terrible conflict and, for a short time, they find solace in each other's company. A soldier — sometimes a German soldier — might fall for a local girl. But then he has to leave, and they're separated, often by thousands of kilometres, and sadly, they never see each other again. All they're left with are pleasant memories of something special that happened during a very turbulent period.'

'But Mrs Tasoula . . .'

'Please let me finish, Thalia. Even worse than the risk of the relationship breaking down is the personal risk to you. You remember what happened to Arianna Makris — the girl who admitted to the German authorities that she was engaged to an English soldier?'

'Of course I do. They executed her. By firing squad. But I would never say anything to the Germans. Never.'

'Thalia, you say that now. But what if you're interrogated,

or beaten by these pigs? You don't know what you'll say until it happens, and if the Germans have even the faintest suspicion that you're involved with an Allied soldier, they'll arrest you. And then you're in real trouble. If Petros is still here, they'll force you to tell them where he is, and they'll arrest him too. You have no idea what the Nazis are capable of. You *must* forget Petros. I hate saying this to you, but if you don't, you'll either have your heart broken or your head blown off. I can't put it any more bluntly than that.'

The thin streaks trailing down Thalia's cheeks became a constant stream. She rubbed the tears away with her knuckles. She was still only seventeen and had never been in love before. Not truly in love. Was Fifi right: was it just a teenage crush? She had had a boyfriend — they were childhood sweethearts — but she didn't have the same yearning for him as she did for Peter. She levelled her eyes at Tasoula.

'You're only seventeen, Thalia,' Tasoula said, as though she had read the girl's mind. 'You have plenty of time. You'll find someone who will make you happy. Forget Petros. It's for the best. For you, and for him.'

'But, what if he *does* . . .' Thalia stopped, bowing her head. Tasoula was right: there was no future with Peter.

'I understand what you're saying, Mrs Tasoula. I'll have to forget Petros.'

She wouldn't ever forget him, but decided that pursuing any relationship with him — real or imagined — would be futile.

Chapter
Fourteen

It was now early in June, and Thalia was running yet another errand. Despite being Tasoula's most trusted confidante she was still the junior, so she was expected to do all the menial tasks. Still, to some degree she resented it — she would much rather be honing her dressmaking skills. This time Tasoula had sent her to collect buttons from a wholesaler on Voulgari Street. She walked quickly, anxious to collect the order before the wholesaler could sell the precious buttons to a competitor prepared to pay a higher price.

Taking a shortcut through Aris Park, she saw a line of German soldiers at the far end and altered her route slightly to avoid them. Everywhere she walked, it seemed, there were grim reminders of the deadly impact of the famine, which was killing thousands every week. Sometimes bodies lay in the streets for days before being collected by men in black, wearing tall caps with side-flaps and wheeling white handcarts. At one point on this trip, she crossed the road to avoid stepping over yet another corpse. The stench was sickening. Thalia mouthed a silent prayer for the poor souls struck down by starvation.

She stopped briefly to salute a Greek flag on a pole outside some municipal offices. It was some small consolation that the Greeks hadn't suffered the indignity of having their national flag banned, as it had been in every other country in Nazi-occupied Europe. The patriotic Thalia took every opportunity to acknowledge the one symbol of national pride that was allowed by the occupiers.

The wholesaler's was a smallish building tucked in between a pharmacy and a butcher with a sparse display of overpriced meat. It comprised a large showroom with double swing doors leading to a warehouse. Both of the neighbouring shops had Nazi banners strung across their front windows. Thalia wondered what it would be like to be sandwiched between two German-controlled businesses. Surrounded by the enemy.

Inside the showroom, a man in a khaki shop-coat smiled at Thalia. 'Good afternoon, Miss. What can I do for you today?' he said.

'The button order for Mrs Tasoula Paschilidou, thank you sir.'

'Ahh, yes, Mrs Tasoula. A good customer. She's lucky to get buttons at this time, but I've saved hers . . . put them aside in the storeroom. Buttons are scarce, you understand. Everything these days is in short supply.' His eyes darted left and right. 'For the Greeks . . . not the Germans.'

His eyes engaged Thalia's, clearly searching for her response. Thalia sensed that he regretted making a glib remark about ready access to goods and services for the Nazis, which could well have landed him in trouble. What he said was true, though: the Germans had run down production in every sector, and systematically curtailed agriculture, shut down factories, closed warehouses and restricted essential supply routes. No wonder there were shortages of almost everything. She wanted to tell him that she felt the same way, but was wary of making inflammatory comments in case he was a German stooge feigning opposition to the regime to snare unsuspecting Greek patriots.

She compromised. 'How very true. Everything is so hard to get. I don't know what it's like for the Germans, but we Greeks struggle to find anything — even if we have the money to buy it.'

The shop assistant sighed, shaking his head. 'Yes, Miss, the world is a very different place now. And I'm not sure that Greece will ever be the same again. I'll go out back and get your order.' As he pushed through the swing doors to the storeroom, Thalia could see row upon row of tall metal shelves; most were empty. She glanced around the showroom. Plywood display boards lined the walls. One wall for zips, studs and fasteners; others for laces, embroidery and other haberdashery supplies. For show; not for sale.

The man came out, carrying a small cardboard box. 'Here they are, Miss. Please pass on my kind wishes to Mrs Tasoula. She's been a customer here for years.'

'Thank you again for holding the buttons for us. Mrs Tasoula will be very grateful.'

'Anything for Mrs Tasoula. Greece needs more people like her. Tell her I've slipped a couple of extra buttons into her package.'

Thalia wondered if the man knew more about Tasoula than he was giving away. She thanked him again, and left. She needed to get back to Tasoula's in good time to finish the dress she was working on before closing time. On the way back, she took care to avoid areas where the Germans liked to set up checkpoints. This wasn't a foolproof strategy, though. Recently the Germans had been imposing even stricter controls on the Greek population: they conducted more spot-checks and regularly roamed the city with armed patrols.

More soldiers had gathered at Aris Park, along with a crowd of locals. The Germans were herding everyone who entered the grounds, including Thalia, at bayonet point towards the crowd. Three men came into view, all being pushed and shoved against an iron fence by the soldiers. The men were wearing civilian clothes. Suddenly, in a moment of absolute shock, Thalia saw ropes looped around the railing of an upstairs balcony and placards dangling from the men's necks, and she realised what was happening. These men were about to be hanged.

The sight sickened her. She had been thrust close enough to see the men's faces. One was wailing, pleading to be freed.

'I've done nothing,' he cried, 'nothing. Please. My children, *please*.' Tears were streaming from his red-rimmed eyes. He pleaded again, and a Nazi officer punched him in the stomach. The man doubled over in agony.

'Greek scum. You worthless piece of shit!' The officer spat the words out, and as his victim straightened he rammed the butt of his pistol against the man's head.

The needless act of violence filled Thalia with disgust. She had never seen such hatred — these were ordinary people living ordinary lives. Peaceful. Respectful. Good parents, good friends, good neighbours. She dreaded what would come next. Her stomach tightening, she felt the anger rising from her gut.

'Who would do such a thing?' she said out loud.

A voice whispered in her ear. 'Resistance. It's because of the resistance — I heard they blew up a bridge over the Vardar River. Killed a few Germans. Now the bastards are killing innocent people in retribution.'

Another man, who was squeezed in beside her, whispered in her other ear. 'Yes, and this is only the start. These pigs have pledged to kill a hundred poor Greeks for every one of their bastard soldiers killed by the partisans. I got this from a reliable source. A hundred Greeks for one worthless German!' Thalia couldn't fathom why anyone would make such scathing comments about the occupiers to a complete stranger. It was such a dangerous thing to do. But he didn't seem to care.

She looked towards the victims. Thalia couldn't make out the words on the handwritten signs hanging from their necks, but assumed they referred to some bogus crime the men had been accused of. She wanted to get away, but was hemmed in by the crowd. The Germans clearly wanted an audience to witness the punishment as a deterrent; to remind Greeks that active resistance would be met with violence.

If they were frightened, the other two placard-bearers didn't show it. They faced their executioners without a flicker of fear in their eyes. Upright and emotionless, they awaited the inevitable.

The German soldiers lowered the three nooses looped

around the upstairs balcony. One by one, they slipped them over the heads of the men. Three makeshift platforms — upturned wooden packing boxes — sat, ominously, below the ropes. Grabbing the men, the soldiers forced them to step on to the platforms. Other soldiers tied the ends of each rope to a wrought iron façade along the shop frontage below, making sure there was no slack in the nooses.

Still desperately pleading for his life, the wailing man slipped and fell forward. As the rope tightened around his neck, his cries were reduced to a gurgling sound as he struggled for breath. Two soldiers grabbed him and shoved him back on to the box, holding him in place until the senior officer could give the order to execute. A red mark was visible around his neck where the noose had almost strangled him.

Suddenly, a priest was pushing his way through the crowd. Two soldiers crossed their rifles in front of him to prevent him passing. He halted, but shouted at the commanding officer. 'Leave these men alone. They've done nothing wrong. Shame on you. You'll earn a place in Hell for what you're doing to these poor souls.' It was an act of defiance that would not end well. Thalia just prayed that the priest wouldn't meet the same fate as the three other men.

Still shouting, the priest forced his way past the soldiers and strode towards the makeshift gallows. The officer ignored him, but he was quickly surrounded by soldiers. One pushed a rifle into his chest; another swung his like a baseball bat and smashed the elderly cleric to the ground. Thalia could see blood. The priest attempted to get back to his feet, but they hit him again. On the ground once more, a soldier kicked him in the stomach as he lay on the grass.

But the violence meted out to the priest had changed the mood of the bystanders; Thalia could see that the officer was concerned about the attitude of the crowd, which was now aggressive. He briefly surveyed the hostile group, then turned away and shouted something to his men. Thalia couldn't hear what he said above the mutterings of the onlookers.

From behind her, a woman's voice screamed out — a cry of 'Nazi pigs' rose above the din. Perhaps it was the wife of one of the condemned. Another voice, this time a man's, yelled 'Leave us alone, you bastards!' A few others joined in to yell similar vitriolic abuse, hoping, no doubt, that anonymity would save them from punishment. The commotion increased as concerned spectators around them tried to hush the offenders for fear that the Nazis might identify them and force them to join those on the platforms.

The commander looked again towards the unruly crowd, then swung around, perhaps deciding that he'd best get it over with before things got out of hand. 'Now!' he ordered, and simultaneously the soldiers booted the boxes from under the feet of their victims. The nooses tightened. The men jerked violently, kicking, squirming and twisting before life was drained from them. Soon two dangled silently, still swaying, but lifeless. The third — the one who had pleaded for his life — continued kicking, still clinging to the last seconds of life until he, too, gave up, his face contorted with pain.

For no discernible reason, the wind suddenly died. A Greek flag that had been fluttering proudly in the breeze above the execution site suddenly drooped, dangling limply in the still air.

Just as suddenly, birds that were silently perching in the trees started squawking raucously, as if to join the chorus of dissent.

As the angry crowd dispersed, eager to get away from the murder scene, the Nazi soldiers left the three corpses hanging as a sadistic reminder of their savagery. The grim spectacle of the three dead men, chosen for the gallows for no other reason than expediency, repulsed Thalia. She had heard rumours about Nazi reprisals, but until then they had been just that: rumours. The reality was far worse than anything she could have imagined. She might have thought she understood how brutal the Nazis could be, but she had now seen the true extent of their inhumanity.

Thalia ran the rest of the way back to Tasoula's, managing not to break down until she was there. Through her tears she described what she had just witnessed. 'It was horrific, Mrs Tasoula,' she sobbed. 'How can one nation treat another with such hatred?'

Tasoula folded the young girl in her arms and hugged her. 'Oh Thalia. There's so much you don't understand. These fiends have no hearts, no compassion. They kill without conscience. They murder without regret. They're animals. *Worse* than animals. Animals kill to survive — some of these beasts seem to kill for pleasure. Many German soldiers are decent men, but the savage deeds of the few taint the decency of the many.'

'But Mrs Tasoula, how do we stop this bloodshed? Innocent Greeks are being slaughtered like rabid dogs.'

'Thalia, sweet Thalia, these pigs have no respect for any human life but their own. But the Germans don't have it all their own way. Our people are fighting back. Last week . . .' she stopped. She had been about to tell Thalia about a resistance coup: a small detachment of Greek partisans had derailed a munitions train on the Thessaloniki to Larissa line, near Aiginio, and stolen rifles, grenades and ammunition — enough to arm their unit for several weeks. But it was better that Thalia knew only what she needed to, in case the SS or Gestapo ever interrogated her. She had already put the girl in enough danger.

'Well, that story will have to wait for another day. You're upset, of course, so go home now and rest. Try to put this out of your mind because we must still carry on with our lives, despite the savagery that surrounds us.'

Thalia went home as Tasoula instructed, heavy-hearted. She had just lost her innocence; lost all faith in human decency.

———————

Weeks passed, but Thalia couldn't forget the vivid images of the hanged bodies with their necks twisted sideways. It was the most awful thing she had ever seen. Each night she prayed that she would never again be an unwilling spectator to Nazi retribution or callous cruelty. But of course, it did happen again — and this time much closer to home.

'They've got Pauline. The pigs have got Pauline!' Thalia said through breathless sobs as she burst into the house. 'I saw them taking her away. They've arrested Pauline.'

'Pauline? It can't be true,' Tasoula exclaimed, hoping that Thalia had made a mistake. The Nazis were targeting Jews, she knew, but Pauline had kept her religion and nationality secret. Only Tasoula, Thalia and Fifi knew.

'I'm sorry, Mrs Tasoula, but it's true. I can't believe it. The brutes dragged her and her parents out on to the street and put them in the back of a truck. There must have been sixty or more jammed in there. They treated the poor souls like cattle — worse than cattle. It was terrible, Mrs Tasoula. Just awful. The whole family had one small suitcase between them, and God knows where they'll take them. What will become of Pauline? She was such a good friend.' Thalia broke down in tears.

Pauline was one of Tasoula's best dressmakers and among her most trusted employees. She hated the Germans even more than Tasoula. 'It's just another example of Nazi inhumanity,' Tasoula said, wrapping her arms around Thalia. 'The Nazi swine hate the Jews. They've shut down synagogues, raided their libraries and ransacked their shops. The devils won't rest until they've wiped them out altogether. Poor beggars.'

Thalia had seen the 'Juden' posters plastered over shop windows and the anti-Semitic slogans crudely hand-painted on walls. The rounding up of Jewish people was deliberate and systematic. Most would never return home, the whispers said; the Nazi plan was to exterminate them. Subhuman, the Nazis called them — no better than animals. Tasoula was under no illusions as to the fate of Pauline and her family, but there was no way she could tell Thalia the truth.

Peter was also under no illusions about their fate, and was disconsolate. Pauline was one of the nicest of Tasoula's girls. Apart from Thalia, she was his favourite — always ready with a joke and sporting a genuine smile. Peter knew her parents, too — the family lived a few doors down the road. He had, in fact, just finished mending a clock for Pauline's father.

'*Bastards.*' Peter seldom swore, but the barbarity of the round-up and the persecution of thousands of innocent people justified the exception.

Many of Tasoula's friends were Jewish, as was most of Thessaloniki's population — it was commonly known as the Jerusalem of the Baltics. Their systematic persecution disgusted her, singled out as they were for no other reason than religion and ethnicity. But there was little she could do to help.

It had started on 11 July 1942, a Saturday. Black Sabbath, they called it, because the Nazis had timed their purge to coincide with the Jewish holy day. They'd forced thousands of men to gather in Eleftherias Square, in the heart of the city, in blazing heat. Dogs had attacked many in the crowd; the Germans had beaten others. Some had even been killed. One of Tasoula's friends, Abram Haïm, who had owned a hardware store before the war, was injured in the attacks. The Nazis had made their intentions clear: there was no place for Jews in Hitler's expanded Germany. This was the beginning of wholesale persecution of the Jewish people in Thessaloniki.

For weeks afterwards, the Nazis raided Jewish houses and businesses, and took their occupants away at gunpoint. Tasoula herself saw Jewish families evicted from their homes and packed into lorries — seventy to a truck — and taken away. To where, no one knew. Tasoula heard on the grapevine that the occupiers had sent them to forced labour camps, to break rocks, pave roads or undertake similar back-breaking work for the German military, or — worse — to the dreaded Pavlou Mela concentration camp in Thessaloniki itself.

Now Pauline and her family were among the victims.

Chapter
Fifteen

It was 30 August 1942 — summer was about to give way to autumn. Peter had realised that if he didn't go now, he was unlikely to escape successfully before winter set in. It would be difficult; Tasoula's colleagues had not yet established a new escape network. Peter had spent a lot of time looking for a partner to team up with, but most of the Allied soldiers in the area were either in custody, not interested in escaping or already on the run. Patrick might have been an option, but the Germans had already recaptured him after another of his spur-of-the-moment escape attempts. At first it had annoyed Peter that his friend hadn't invited him along, but in hindsight he was thankful he hadn't. Patrick's reckless streak had prompted him to make an unplanned getaway. Peter preferred to be more cautious and careful; better prepared and organised.

It wasn't that Peter had outlived his welcome at Tasoula's; he was now one of the family — the man about the house

— and he knew they enjoyed having him around. But he was now too well-known in the neighbourhood; it was becoming obvious that Tasoula had a foreign guest. Eventually, one of them would be betrayed. He also recognised the financial burden that Tasoula carried to keep him: she couldn't afford to do so for much longer. Her business had ground to a halt and she was looking for work in villages and towns around the region. The previous week, she'd been forced to let all the dressmakers go, even Thalia. One day she'd arrived at work as usual; the next she didn't turn up.

Tasoula told Peter it was because Thalia was ill. The truth was that the girl couldn't face saying a last goodbye to the New Zealander. Even though she had taken Tasoula's advice and accepted that there would be no future with him, seeing him and talking to him for the last time would have been too difficult. Soon afterwards, Tasoula informed Peter that Thalia was going to Giannitsa a few days later to seek work. Not being able to see her again disappointed Peter, but he was also strangely relieved. He had heeded Patrick's warning about the futility of pursuing a relationship; and at least now he didn't have to deal with the emotional turmoil of seeing her every day.

Peter's escape opportunity came when John Haycroft, an Australian soldier, approached him. They met in Enou Place, sitting together on a bench in the far corner of the park. After all the usual pleasantries, John got straight to the point. 'Peter, we don't know each other, but I'm planning to make a run for it, and I'd like you to join me. Nugget Carmichael tells me that you're a good bloke and speak fluent Greek.' Nugget, by now a close friend of Peter's, was the New Zealand soldier being sheltered by Jan Frère, the French consul.

Peter reacted with caution. He wasn't one to rush into important decisions. 'Yes . . . yes, my Greek is pretty good.'

'If I'm to make it out of Greece, I'll need to partner with someone who speaks the lingo. From what I've heard, you would fit the bill nicely.'

Peter eyeballed John, trying to get the measure of him. 'Thanks, John. I appreciate the offer. It's an interesting proposition, but I'll need more information. I don't want to make a rash call I'll regret. For one thing, the place is now crawling with Krauts — so how do you propose we get away from here without being caught?'

'It won't be a doddle, but you'd easily pass for a Greek, especially since you're fluent in the language. I reckon we can make it okay if we team up. And, bugger it, we can't just sit on our arses hoping that Hitler gets a dose of syphilis and croaks. We've gotta get ourselves back into this bloody war and on to the front lines again.'

'I'll second that. What about Nugget? Is he going to tag along?'

'Nah. Says he's comfortable where he is. Wants to sit out the war in Greece.'

Peter shook his head in disbelief. The odds of evading capture were diminishing with each German search patrol and resistance-family arrest. He feared that Nugget would be tracked down if he stayed.

'But, John, there's still no established escape network operating out of Salonika. We can't just bowl up to the port and ask some random captain if he wants to take a couple of British soldiers on a joyride to Turkey.'

'Well, the thing is, Peter, I have an English mate holed up in Saint Paraskevi with a local resistance leader. If we make our way there, to the Kassandra Peninsula, it's a short trip across the Aegean to Smyrna. The resistance chap will have contacts in the region who can help us get away.'

Saint Paraskevi was over a hundred kilometres from Salonika — a hike of several days through Nazi-infested territory — but Peter was warming to this affable Australian. He liked the man.

'Besides,' John added, 'I've come up with a plan.' The Australian explained how he would steal one of the launches used for transporting resin gathered from the pine trees on the Kassandra Peninsula and head for Turkey. Peter wasn't impressed. It sounded like the sort of madcap scheme Patrick would dream up. In fact, John was much like Patrick in many ways: brash, extroverted and outspoken. Still, he seemed like a decent fellow and Peter would have to make a move soon if he wanted to escape before winter. Besides, the resistance leader in Saint Paraskevi would be familiar with both the area and the best escape routes, and should have contacts who would help them get to Turkey. Liaising with a resistance group outside Thessaloniki was also what Tasoula had suggested. Peter would need to rely on his powers of persuasion to convince John to abandon his plan while they were on the run, but this was still his best chance to make it out of Greece and lessen the risks for Tasoula.

'I'm in,' he said to his new friend.

John then informed him they would leave the following day; under normal circumstances this would have been too rushed for Peter. But the opportunity had presented itself: he must either take it or delay his escape for who knew how long. It didn't give him much opportunity for farewells, but perhaps that was a good thing. Haste had its advantages: little time for second thoughts and less time for sadness.

Tasoula was staying in a nearby village, looking for work, and he felt really guilty about not being able to say a proper goodbye to her. Telling Thanasis was one of the most difficult things he had ever had to do; almost as difficult as saying farewell to his family when he'd boarded the ship from New Zealand bound for the Maadi training camp in Egypt.

Peter sat Thanasis down in the parlour and explained that he must leave, and why. Thanasis struggled to contain his tears. 'But Petros, you can stay here as long as you like. Please stay. We want you to stay. It won't be the same without you.'

'Thanasis, I'm very sad to be leaving, too. But I *must* go. If I stay, I'll put you in even greater danger. If I leave now, you'll be safe. No one will know I ever lived here. The Nazis will find nothing if they search the place. It's for the best, Thanasis. I must leave sometime and it's best that I go now.'

'But Petros . . .' Thanasis's voice trailed off. Peter understood the boy's reluctance to accept his decision, but sensed that he had.

'I'll miss you, my friend,' Thanasis said. 'I'll miss all the fun we had — even in these difficult times. I'll miss our Greek lessons, the adventures . . . and most of all, I'll miss *you*.'

'I'll miss everything, too, Thanasis. You and Mrs Tasoula

and the girls. I'll miss every one of you. And I'll never forget all you've done for me.'

'Promise me you won't. Promise me you'll visit us again when this bloody war is over.'

Peter nodded. He would never forget — he knew that for sure — but as for visiting again, that was a completely different matter. Looking straight at Thanasis, he hoped that the conviction in his eyes would convey his sincerity; but in his heart, he realised that it was unlikely he would ever see Tasoula, Thanasis or the girls again.

It had been ten months since he and Patrick had arrived on their doorstep. After all their shared experiences, he felt just as connected to Tasoula's family as he did to his own. Clearing out his room proved to be a heart-breaking task. There were just so many memories. Several times he stopped to dry tears with his handkerchief. He kept telling himself he was doing the right thing, even though it seemed wrong. 'I'm sorry I can't say goodbye, Mrs Tasoula,' he said to himself as he wiped the wetness away from his cheeks. 'Thank you for everything. You're a remarkable woman.' Briefly he thought about leaving her a note, but if the Germans discovered it, it would sign her death warrant. The best he could do was convey his feelings through Thanasis.

When he was certain there was no trace of him having been in the house, he sat down with Thanasis. They talked for hours: about Peter's gratitude for their kindness and the sacrifices they had made for him; about his love for Greece; their many escapades; his fondness for the girls and Uncle Giorgos; about everything they had been through in the past ten months. It was well after midnight when their conversation was exhausted.

'Where will you go, Petros?' Thanasis asked as they retired to their respective bedrooms.

'We'll head towards . . .' Peter hesitated. That knowledge was best kept to himself; if the Nazis arrested Thanasis and interrogated him, they would force him to reveal everything he knew. The Germans used brutality to very good effect. It would be better for them both if he misled his friend. He hated doing it, but he was protecting Thanasis — and himself — by lying about his plans.

'We'll head towards Ouranoupoli first thing in the morning and get a boat from there to Turkey. We should make Vasiloudi by nightfall.' Of course, Peter and John were actually planning to make their way to Saint Paraskevi. Ouranoupoli was in a different direction altogether from the town where Ted, the Englishman, was holed up in the safe house.

Unable to sleep, in part because he was sad to be leaving and in part because he was excited and apprehensive at what lay ahead, Peter rose early. He didn't want an emotional farewell — it would be too upsetting — so he simply woke Thanasis, put his arm around his good friend and, as was customary in Greece, kissed him on both cheeks. With a thumbs-up sign and a salutation of 'go well, my friend', he left.

Peter met John Haycroft at 6 a.m. at the agreed rendezvous on the far corner of Enou Place. 'There's just one thing I need to do before we go,' he told John. 'Wait here. I'll be back in a few minutes.'

Then Peter made his way to Thalia's house, hoping to catch

a glimpse of her before he left. The lights were on, but he saw no sign of Thalia. He waited for as long as he dared, then turned and walked away, disappointed. He hadn't gone far when he paused to look back one last time. 'I'll miss you, sweet Thalia,' he said out loud. 'We'll never meet again, but I'll miss you very much.'

With that, he turned away and strode back to Enou Place with a sense of purpose that belied his true feelings.

———————

The pair travelled all day, along back roads and seldom-used, overgrown tracks to avoid checkpoints and roving patrols. Boxes of apples found on the back of a horse-drawn cart provided some sustenance. While the circuitous route meant slower progress than they would have liked, they had almost reached Galarinos, just under a quarter of the way there, by sunset. They dossed down under some trees well away from the road.

The following morning, Peter left on his own to find food in the small village. Fair-haired, fair-skinned John looked too much like a German in disguise, but Peter was confident that his Greek would reassure the locals if they challenged him. The generous villagers gave all they could spare, and Peter returned with enough food to last a couple of days.

The mountainous terrain ahead would make the going much more difficult, but at least there was less likelihood of encountering Germans there, so they wouldn't have to move so slowly. It took a further two days to reach the top of the

Kassandra Peninsula, where John planned to steal a boat. 'We can take one from here,' he said, surveying the flotilla of small craft moored along the coastline.

'We could, but it would be easier to mix with that group down there,' Peter said, pointing to a cluster of Greeks waiting on a small pier outside a dilapidated shack that he presumed served as some sort of terminal.

John expressed surprise. 'But how will that help us steal a boat?'

'No need. The passenger ferry will take us across this canal, and we'll make our way to Saint Paraskevi from there. Leave it to me. I'll buy the tickets; you say nothing.'

Peter thought John looked overly conspicuous among the dark-haired Greeks, but nobody seemed to take any notice. Even so, they took seats away from the other passengers. The trip across the ancient Nea Potidea canal took only a few minutes. Just as they were getting ready to get off, however, a uniformed man blocked their way. He was at least six feet tall, with a thatch of unruly black hair, piercing eyes and a shadow of stubble covering his pitted face.

'Angliká!' he said in a voice that sounded as menacing as the look in his eyes. 'You Angliká.'

Peter didn't answer. If he said nothing the Greek might leave them alone; if he questioned them further, Peter would respond in Greek.

Peter leaned towards John. 'We may have to make a run for it,' he whispered. 'Push him aside and go for it if I give the word.'

The uniformed Greek wouldn't give up. He stabbed his

finger in their direction: 'Angliká. I know you Angliká.' John's fair complexion had doubtless given them away. Peter worried that this man would hold them until he could summon his German friends.

'No shit-bull me. You *Angliká*,' he said again.

Peter was about to give the word to scarper when the man broke into a broad smile that revealed a mouthful of nicotine-stained teeth. He extended an outstretched palm. 'I captain. You Angliká.'

Peter took the captain's hand and shook it vigorously, immensely relieved. In Greek, he explained that they were indeed English and on the run from the Germans.

'Ahh, Nazis. Bladdy Nazis. *Swine.*' The captain spat the words out with a venom that confirmed his deep-seated hatred of the invaders. He told them that the Nazis had executed one of his friends and he loathed them. He then pressed a wad of money into Peter's palm and produced a small pouch of tobacco. Rolling a cigarette, he told the men that they should avoid the first two villages — he didn't trust their inhabitants — but the villagers in the third one would provide them with food and shelter.

Peter tried to return the money, but the captain closed the New Zealander's fist around it. He wished them luck, then returned to the wheelhouse ready to ferry the next passengers across the narrow canal.

The escaping men avoided the villages the captain had warned them about and found a friendly welcome at the third, as he had promised. After a decent night's rest, they made their way to Saint Paraskevi, arriving just after dusk.

Chapter
Sixteen

'Where's the Christidou girl?' demanded the Wehrmacht officer, gripping Tasoula by the throat as she sat on the chair she'd been forced onto. He spoke passable Greek, though with a strong accent. 'She's on the list, so she must be here. *Where is she?* I'll tear the place apart if you hold back. Tell us now before we force it out of you.'

Tasoula tried to stall. 'Cressida? Cressida? I don't know any Cressida. What's her surname?' She just *had* to divert the officer's attention — if the soldiers searched the place again, they would find the illegal radio and the stash of weapons in the attic, and if that happened, she would be in even more trouble. She also needed to protect Thanasis. He had already seen more abuse, brutality, oppression and hardship than any eighteen-year-old should be subjected to.

'Bullshit! You know exactly who I'm talking about.' The German slapped Tasoula with the back of his hand and turned to Thanasis. 'Perhaps the kid will be more helpful.'

'Where is Christidou?' he said to Thanasis, emphasising the 't' and the 'ou'.

Thanasis looked at his mother for direction, but she was shielded from his sight by a soldier. His lips trembled. 'I don't . . . don't know any Christidou,' he said, chewing his bottom lip to disguise his fear. 'There's no one here by that name.' Tasoula felt a surge of pride in her son for refusing to back down.

'Liar! Bloody liar.' The Nazi grabbed Thanasis around the neck. 'Liar! She works here. She's worked here for months. The bitch is just as guilty as the rest of you. She's a traitor — and you understand what we do to traitors.' He sliced his forefinger across his throat to emphasise the point.

Tasoula knew that Thalia had left for Giannitsa the previous day. At least she would be safe. For now, at least.

The German turned his attention back to Tasoula. He lifted her from the chair and pushed her hard against the wall, his fingers pressed against her neck. She felt her gut clench with panic.

'Dumb bitch. Do you think we're stupid? We've been watching you for weeks. We know what goes on in here. We know about the soldiers. About your resistance work. And all about the Christidou girl's involvement in your treachery. We know *everything*.' The left side of his lips curled upwards in a caustic smile. Tasoula could tell that he was taking pleasure from the encounter. 'No more of your bullshit. Don't think you can fool us.'

Tasoula allowed herself a secret smile. She had been fooling the Germans for months — and she was certain they had now realised it. She said nothing.

'Stay silent if you like. It won't make any difference — we've got all the evidence we need against you and the boy. And we'll deal with the Christidou girl later. It's only a matter of time before we arrest her, too.'

His tone changed abruptly. 'Take them away.'

———————

It was 2 September 1942. A Wednesday. Two days after Peter had left.

One officer and three Wehrmacht soldiers had burst into the house and arrested both Tasoula and Thanasis. It wasn't unexpected. Despite Tasoula's best efforts to keep it secret, too many people were aware of the hidden Allied soldiers — and the Nazis relied on loose tongues to gather information they didn't have themselves. They carried out the raid with typical German efficiency: soldiers entered the property, informed the pair that they were under arrest, and sat them down with rifles pointed at their chests. No histrionics. No desperate scuffle. And no chance to escape.

The search of their home revealed nothing. The soldiers didn't discover the attic and there was no evidence of anyone having occupied Peter's room. Having been handcuffed, Tasoula and Thanasis were taken outside and bundled into the rear seat of a shiny Mercedes with blacked-out windows. The officer sat in front and one of the soldiers sat between Tasoula and Thanasis in the back. The other two remained behind.

No one spoke during the twenty-minute journey. Tasoula

wasn't sure where they were being taken, but she had a pretty good idea: Heptapyrgion prison was where the Nazis imprisoned resistance members. Tasoula steeled herself for what lay ahead. She prayed that Thanasis would withstand the punishment.

Soldiers dragged Tasoula and Thanasis from the car and pushed them towards the imposing wooden entrance gates. Tasoula fell as they manhandled her, grazing her knee on the cobblestoned road. A soldier pulled her to her feet. As she had predicted, they were outside Heptapyrgion.

Now they were frogmarched into two separate interrogation rooms. Tasoula was taken to a large room containing a solitary metal table, green paint peeling away from its edges. The walls were plastered in a depressing grey colour. Three matching chairs were positioned around the table: two on one side with cushions — for the interrogators, she presumed — and one with no padding. Tasoula could see torture equipment lining one wall: clubs and whips for beatings; nooses and ropes for hanging victims by their arms or upside down, by their feet; and a variety of hammers with odd-shaped heads. Several sets of pliers had been laid out according to size on a small trolley. For extracting fingernails, she thought. In almost any other location, these devices might have been standard workshop tools or farmyard accessories, but in this setting Tasoula had no illusions about what they would be used for.

A large floodlight had been placed behind the two cushioned chairs. The soldiers forced Tasoula onto the unpadded seat and shackled her to its tubular metal supports. The Wehrmacht officer who had brought her here entered the room, accompanied by a stranger in a Gestapo uniform: a corpulent man with florid cheeks, a bulbous blue-veined drinker's nose and close-cropped hair. He looked like a brute; Tasoula thought he would probably have been a bully at school. Things were not looking good for her.

At first, the questioning was civil. Why are you working with the resistance? Who do you report to? Who are your underground contacts? What about the English soldiers you were hiding? Where is the Christidou girl?

When Tasoula refused to answer, the mood hardened. The brutish Gestapo officer cracked her across one side of her jaw with the back of his pudgy hand, then did the same on the other. The blows stung, but she dared not show any sign of pain. The man leaned forward, so close that the sour smell of his stale whisky breath made her gag. He grabbed her by the hair and forced her head back until her nose was just centimetres away from his foul-smelling breath.

'Listen, bitch,' he said, the threat in his voice needing no interpretation. 'You'll give us names, you'll give us addresses — and more. We'll break you, break every bone in your treacherous body if we must. Scum like you deserve the worst we can dish out. You'll give us the information we want. Whatever it takes.'

He smashed Tasoula's head forward, ramming it against the edge of the metal table. 'That's just the start,' he said.

Blood dripped from Tasoula's nose, splattering onto her floral dress. The other officer turned the floodlight on, which blinded Tasoula with its fierce light. Even squeezing her eyes tightly shut wouldn't block out the piercing beam. Her head was throbbing.

'There's no point in denying anything. We know all about your soldiers — even who you hid.' He pushed his face closer to hers. 'As a matter of fact, Peter Blunden sends his regards. We captured him, of course, and he told us everything, the coward. It only took a bit of gentle persuasion, and he broke. He told us all about you and all the other resistance swine. Everything. Squealed like a pig. He wouldn't stop talking.'

Something in his eyes told Tasoula the man was lying. Peter wasn't the sort of person who would reveal anything unless they beat him to a pulp. Somehow she knew they were lying about capturing him, too. He was very resourceful — if anyone could outwit the Germans and make a clean getaway, it was Peter.

'Peter who?' Tasoula asked, feigning ignorance. 'Peter Bladen? I'm not familiar with any Peter Bladen.'

'Blund—' The officer stopped short, then changed his approach. 'Your half-witted cousin told us everything. We fooled her, the dumb peasant. All it cost us was a bottle of ouzo and a couple of loaves of bread. Stupid woman.'

Tasoula wasn't sure what cousin the Nazi was referring to, but she suspected a distant relative from Chalastra, who had seen Peter once when she visited. Her naïve cousin must have fallen for the German ploy of masquerading as British associates offering food and money to Greeks hiding Allied soldiers. She would have been trying to help, not have Tasoula arrested.

'No more of your bloody lies. Tell us everything. *Everything*, understand! We've already proved you're a traitor — an enemy of the Reich — so don't deny it.'

Tasoula remained silent.

Her recollection of the next few hours was hazy. She remembered being beaten with a rubber club, then being strung up by her hands with her feet off the ground. The pain was excruciating, and she could tell that the punishment had dislocated her shoulders. The questions kept coming, and the violence continued. Between bouts of torture, Tasoula lapsed into unconsciousness. Each time, the Gestapo officer plunged her head into a tub of ice-cold water to revive her.

When torture produced no results, the men tried the conciliatory approach. After she recovered consciousness once more, the Gestapo brute unshackled her and offered her water. The Wehrmacht officer took over the questioning.

'Tasoula,' he said, with mock sincerity, 'make it easy on yourself. There's no need to go through all this pain. We don't want to hurt you, but you're making us do it because you won't co-operate. All this will be over if you just answer our questions. We'll even put in a good word with the prison commandant, so you'll be treated well.'

Tasoula looked at the officer with contempt and spat at him, an act of defiance that only brought more punishment. The fat officer bashed his fist into her jaw and resumed his 'questioning'. But still they couldn't break her. After three or four hours — maybe five — they gave up for the day and left her alone, chained to the chair. The floodlight glared all night, pushing out its unrelenting light. Sleep was impossible, as intended, and Tasoula's exhausted brain was a scrambled mess. She alternated between hallucinating — vivid images of idyllic days in the sun, doubtless induced by the floodlight —

and plunging into the depths of despair, certain that her life was about to come to a tragic end. The only thing that kept her going was the thought of Thanasis, whose image came to her only intermittently.

Sometime in the middle of the night — she couldn't recall when — she wet herself. Urine dripped from the seat and down the metal chair-legs to form a puddle on the floor. In her confused state, she fretted over this personal indiscretion almost as much as she anguished over the prospect of further torturous punishment. Tasoula, who was meticulous about hygiene, was mortified.

Early the following morning — around 5:30, she thought, judging from a glimpse at the luminous dial on the guard's watch — she was unchained for a few minutes and served a bowl of diarrhoea-coloured gruel. A lone vegetable floated on top, its origin uncertain. Whatever it was, she ate it. It was her first meal in twenty-four hours and she needed to keep her strength up for the ordeal that lay ahead.

As soon as she had spooned the last of the slop from the chipped enamel bowl, a soldier cuffed her to the chair and the same two officers started the interrogation routine again. Who do you report to? Who else is hiding British soldiers? Who are the resistance leaders? Who publishes the resistance propaganda? Where are the illegal printing presses? They used the same torture tactics, with the same result: Tasoula said nothing. But dimly, through the haze of her jumbled brain, she realised that she wouldn't be able to hold out much longer.

She was at the point of giving in when another officer in a short-sleeved shirt and a blood-spattered white apron entered the room. He whispered something to the overweight Gestapo officer, then left. The interrogation and torment stopped. No one said a word as Tasoula was unshackled and the floodlight was turned off.

A few minutes later the aproned officer returned, half-dragging a battered and bloodied Thanasis. The sight of the boy horrified Tasoula. Blood was streaming from one nostril and more dripped from a cut across his cheek. One eye had closed up completely: a balloon of black, swollen flesh shrouded his eye socket. Tasoula realised that she must look just as bad, but seeing Thanasis in this state was more painful than any of the physical abuse they had inflicted on her.

Thanasis was crying. 'I'm sorry, Mamá. So sorry. I had to tell them about Petros. They threatened to shoot you if I didn't — force me to watch you die. I had to give them what they wanted. I had to do it, Mamá. I'm sorry, but I had to.'

Tasoula wanted to reassure Thanasis, but no sound would come from her swollen lips.

'I told them all about Petros and where he was going. I had no choice, Mamá. I couldn't let you die. Not ever. Petros is my friend, and I let him down. Poor Petros.' Tears dripped from his bloated eyes. Tasoula's heart sank. Perhaps they had captured Peter after all. But somehow she doubted it. Something was still convincing her he had made his getaway.

'The little prick wouldn't say anything for a start. It took a while, but I got him in the end,' the aproned officer said with a self-congratulatory smirk. Tasoula slumped forward in the chair then collapsed to the floor. Thanasis went to comfort his mother, but the aproned officer grabbed him by his collar and pulled him back.

There was now no point in denying that she had provided refuge to Allied soldiers. If the Germans hadn't captured Peter, then by now he would be far away. If they had, then admitting it wouldn't make any difference. They had already recaptured Patrick, so any information about *him* would be irrelevant. All she could do now was protect those whose identities weren't known to the Nazis, along with those like Thalia who were, but couldn't be located. She prayed that Thanasis had revealed nothing about anyone other than Peter.

'Okay. I'll tell you everything. But first you must promise you won't hurt my son anymore. Promise me that, and I'll give you what you want.'

'We don't make promises to traitors. The little brat deserved all he got. Here's what we'll do: if you don't give us what we want, we'll pulverise the kid in front of you. You won't be able to do anything but watch. And this time, we won't be as gentle.'

Tasoula looked over at Thanasis. He was now slumped in one corner of the room, head hunched forward, chin against his chest. She couldn't bear the thought of him suffering another beating, but she wouldn't betray the other brave Greeks fighting for their country. She made a decision: she would give up information already known to the Nazis. Nothing more.

'All right. All right. I'll talk. I'll tell you the truth,' she said, doing her best to sound like a defeated woman. 'I've only ever hidden two soldiers — Petros Blunden and Patrikios Minogue. That's the extent of my involvement. Thanasis has done nothing. He was aware of the two men, of course, but that's all.' She stopped and wiped some blood away with the back of her hand. She began to cry, not because of any emotional need but because she needed time to think.

'Petros . . . Peter . . . has been captured, so you already have him in custody. And he's talked, so there's nothing more I can tell you about him. As for Patrikios, I have no idea where he is. He left my place months ago and I haven't heard from him since. I presume he tried to escape from Greece. That's all I can tell you.'

'What about the other soldiers? We've arrested the French consul — he was hiding a New Zealander — and we have evidence of others. You must be able to tell us where they are.'

'The French consul? I didn't realise there *was* a French consul in Thessaloniki! I know nothing about any other soldiers. Only Petros and Patrikios.'

Of course Tasoula knew all about the French consul and where other soldiers were hidden. Either the Germans also did, in which case they would have already captured them; or they didn't, in which case Tasoula had no intention of telling them.

'You're lying again, you Greek whore. Give us the names of the scum who dare to hide enemy soldiers, and tell us who your resistance contacts are. *Who are they?*'

'All I did was look after the soldiers. I did nothing else for the resistance . . . I don't have any other information.'

The Gestapo officer punched her in the stomach. She doubled over, her gut burning.

'*Liar*. We've been watching you, Paschilidou. You're in the resistance all right. In as deep as the hole you're digging for yourself right now. There's no point in denying it. So save yourself from further punishment and tell us who your contacts are.' He struck her again, this time on the jaw. Her head snapped back, twisting her neck.

'Okay. Okay. The person who asked me to take the soldiers in went by a code name — Stavros — and we only ever met a few times. Always in a busy square or at a café with lots of people around. He never revealed his real identity, nor where he lives. They all go by code names . . . there's nothing more I can tell you.'

'Bullshit. Give us names, or we'll beat the boy again.'

The thought of Thanasis being pummelled again was too much for Tasoula to bear. She would have to give them *something*. She prevaricated, feigning reluctance to name anyone. After pausing for long enough to convince them of her reticence to divulge incriminating information, she bit her lip and answered.

'The only name I can give you is Sofia Petrou. She lives at Larisis 66.'

Sofia was a well-known collaborator who had been responsible for several resistance arrests and, according to Tasoula's underground contacts, at least one execution. Tasoula hated compromising any Greeks, even Nazi sympathisers, but this one deserved everything that was coming to her.

'If you only go by code names, how come you have this woman's name?' the suspicious German asked. Tasoula had to think fast. Again she wiped her tears away. 'She goes by the code name Lysandra. The only reason I can give you her real name is that I recognised her when we met. We used to work together before the war. That's how I know her name and where she lives.'

The officer seemed to be satisfied with her explanation, and made some notes. Eventually the Germans would realise she had duped them, but until then, life would be miserable for the duplicitous Mrs Petrou.

'And what about Madam Lapper?'

'Madam who?'

'Lapper. Madam Lapper. She organised the escape route out of Thessaloniki. You must be aware of her if you were hiding soldiers intending to escape.'

'I've never heard of her. Where does she live?'

'Not important. She has disappeared, and we want to find her.'

Tasoula looked up at the ceiling as if she were trying to recall the name. 'Leper? Madam Leper? No, sorry. I don't remember anyone by that name. Perhaps Petros can give you the information? This Madam Leper might have helped him escape. Ask *him*.' Tasoula sincerely hoped that Madam Lapper had evaded the Nazis and was now safe with friends in another village.

The three officers conferred. They made a half-hearted attempt to glean more information, but when none was forthcoming, they gave up.

'Take them back to their cells,' the Gestapo officer said. 'We're done here.'

Chapter
Seventeen

Yarnee Mavrodos was a short, wiry fellow with a dragon tattoo on one arm and a double-headed eagle on the other. Sinewy muscles stretched the sleeves of his plain white T-shirt and a neat, close-cropped beard flowed from a full head of hair. His expression was mostly grim — not surprising in wartime Greece — but when he did smile, it was a wide smile accentuated by unblemished white teeth. He was the resistance contact in Saint Paraskevi and greeted Peter and John as if they were old friends. John introduced Peter to the Englishman, Ted Anderson, then Yarnee informed the trio that they would stay for a few days until he could arrange for them to be transported to Turkey.

John outlined his plan to commandeer a launch to get them there.

'An interesting idea,' Yarnee said. 'It might even work. But it won't be necessary.' He already had an established escape route to Turkey, using a trusted trading-boat owner who made regular freight trips across the Aegean Sea. 'I'll talk to him, and with a bit of luck I'll be able to arrange a passage before the end of the week.'

Peter was relieved. He had no faith in John's plan, and now he didn't have to talk the Australian out of it.

Peter, John and Ted got on well, swapping stories about their pre-capture exploits. Ted had been with an English tank regiment in northern Greece; John had been in the Australian artillery. Neither had experienced the horrors of Crete. According to Ted, Yarnee was a key figure in the local resistance and well connected with underground leaders in other regions.

After enough ouzo to render discussion unintelligible, they retired for the night, in the hayloft of a barn. Peter couldn't sleep, reflecting on the past few days as he lay awake. He felt guilty about not saying goodbye to Tasoula and even guiltier for deceiving Thanasis, but was also relieved that they were no longer in danger because of his presence. He thought about Thalia, disappointed he hadn't seen her before leaving Thessaloniki. 'You have to forget her,' he said to himself. 'Face up to it, you'll never see her again.'

The next day, the men exchanged ideas about what they might do once they reached Turkey. The lure of freedom was seductive: they planned exotic excursions, nights out, fancy dinners — even a night at a luxury hotel if their back-pay stretched that far. Dreams were cheap; the reality was much more likely to be all-day training, a few beers in the evening if they were lucky, plain meals in the mess and an uncomfortable camp bed with a lumpy mattress in a crowded army barracks.

The following morning, Yarnee burst into the kitchen where the men were having a breakfast of pastries and strong coffee. 'Petros, something awful has happened. It's terrible news, I'm afraid — the Nazis have arrested Mrs Paschilidou and her son. They seized several others on the same day, all resistance members. Another New Zealand soldier — Nugget or something? — and the family he was staying with were also arrested. My contact told me it was the French consul and his family.'

A hollow feeling rose up from the pit of Peter's stomach; he felt sick inside. His face turned grey. 'Mrs Tasoula and Thanasis? No, no. There's no way it can be true. It's a mistake. It must be a mistake. It might have been someone else. How can you be sure it was Mrs Tasoula and Thanasis?'

'I'm sorry, Petros, there's no mistake. I understand your grief, but it's true. I have resistance contacts all over the region and my man in Thessaloniki has positively confirmed that Tasoula and Thanasis were among those arrested. Apparently, several suspected resistance members have been under surveillance for some time and the Nazis swooped last week. It must have been a couple of days after you left. I know no more than that. None of my associates have any idea where those Nazi arseholes have taken them, nor what they've done to them.'

Devastated by the news, Peter again protested that it must be a terrible mistake, but then stopped short. It *was* true; somehow the Germans had gathered the evidence they needed — or made it up. Although he was positive there would have been no trace of him having been there, he still felt he was to blame.

He, and he alone, had brought this horrible punishment on his friends.

John and Ted tried to console him, but Peter's guilt overwhelmed him. Yarnee put his arm around Peter's shoulders, trying to reassure him. 'Petros, Tasoula has been very active in the resistance, and not only by harbouring fugitives like you. She undertook many other perilous missions. The Nazis would have been watching her whether or not you stayed. She understood the risks — we all do — and accepted the consequences.'

Peter knew this to be true, but it didn't make him feel any better. Deep in despair, the sense of hopelessness worsened when he thought of Thalia. Had she also been caught up in the Nazi purge?

'What about Tasoula's girls? The dressmakers. Did they arrest any of them?

'I know nothing about any girls, but my informant says that they took no one else from Tasoula's place. The other captives came from known resistance families.'

Peter just grunted, the shock making him unwilling to believe this.

'Petros, I understand that this is hard for you to take in. We're all devastated whenever the Nazis arrest one of our own. But — that's the world we live in. It's sad, but it's true. I'm sorry, and I understand that you're upset, but there's another pressing matter we need to discuss. Did you tell anyone about the route you took? That you were coming here to Saint Pereskevi? It's very important — if you did, the Nazis will have wrung the information out of Tasoula or Thanasis and we'll all be in trouble.'

Peter raised his head, a glimmer of relief in his eyes. 'No, Yarnee. I told no one. In fact, I lied to Thanasis. I told him we intended to head towards Ouranoupoli, the wrong direction. I didn't like deceiving him, but thought it would be for the best.'

'Thank God for that. At least we're safe for now.'

Peter couldn't shake away the images of Tasoula and Thanasis being interrogated — most likely tortured. But as Yarnee had pointed out, the partisans understood and accepted the inevitability of retribution and death. Life had to go on. As much as he grieved for Tasoula and Thanasis, he also had to focus on his own survival. Dead men can't fight wars.

―――――――

When it came time to leave, Yarnee gave them just an hour's notice. Bursting into the room where they sat, he announced that everything had been arranged. They would leave at 11 p.m. to meet the boat at midnight. None of them had much to pack, and they were ready to go with time to spare.

The three of them, guided by Yarnee, arrived at Loutra Beach a few minutes before 12. Right on time a boat appeared through the mist, with only its dim cabin lights to announce its arrival. After hugging the three men and wishing them safe travels, Yarnee melted away into the darkness while a small rowboat ferried the escaping soldiers to their transport.

It was no luxury launch; the hull was rusting so badly that Peter wondered how many more voyages it had left before it succumbed to corrosion. The timber panelling looked like it hadn't seen varnish in decades. The wheelhouse was littered with empty ouzo bottles, which did little to inspire confidence in the captain, and old petrol cans that had been stacked against each side of the small, shanty-like cabin. An upturned wooden box that had once held bottles of olive oil served as the captain's perch. A tall, swarthy character, he could have passed for the brother of the Nea Potidea ferry captain.

The crewman showed the men to a cabin that stank of unwashed bodies and stale cigarette smoke. Despite the state of the boat, Peter was thrilled to be on his way to freedom. Exhausted but elated, he hauled himself up on to the tiny top bunk, wrapped himself in the grimy blanket and fell asleep almost instantly.

In the morning, Peter did his best to spruce himself up. He couldn't find any washing facilities — he doubted that washrooms were a top priority anyway — but he smoothed his hair with water from the galley tap and brushed down his shirt and jacket with the palms of both hands. Breakfast, served by the captain, was a buckled tin plate heaped with a greasy pile of what looked like scrambled eggs, flecked with black flakes from a dirty frying pan. John and Ted turned up soon afterwards, and he served them the same fare.

Just as Peter was chewing his way through the last of his morning meal, the crewman shouted a warning: he'd spotted a German patrol boat edging towards the rusting hull. A few minutes later, a loud foghorn and a megaphone-amplified German voice announced its arrival. Grabbing Peter by the arm, the captain pulled him towards a tall metal cabinet. Inside was a mini-arsenal: a Tommy gun, Allied grenades and ammunition. 'Here, take these. Hide behind the corn sacks on the deck until these bastards have gone. If they find you, open fire and lob the grenades on to their boat. Now, quick — behind the sacks. They're about to board.'

John and Ted dived behind the bags, Peter following with the cache of weapons. He could hear plenty of commotion further along the deck. The shouts and screams didn't sound like this was a routine inspection. Someone was speaking Greek in a foreign accent, so at least one of the Germans understood the local language.

Peering around the edge of the sacks, Peter saw the German patrol-boat commander push the captain to one side, banging his arm hard against an iron railing. Three other German sailors appeared — they were about to search the vessel. His heart sank. This unexpected intrusion could thwart all their plans; this was not how their story was meant to end.

The commander kicked some empty bottles lying on the deck; one smashed against a metal winch. He opened the wheelhouse door, pinching his nostrils as a waft of foul-smelling air assaulted him. Peter checked the Tommy gun and pushed the box of grenades towards John and Ted. 'Take these,' he whispered. 'If we get rumbled, I'll open fire and you throw the grenades at the German boat. I haven't come this far to be captured again, so let's give it to them if we have to.'

All four Germans were now moving around the vessel, coming closer to where they were hiding. The commander lifted the tatty lifeboat cover and peered inside. The corn sacks were right behind the lifeboat — he was inches away from their hiding place. Peter dared not make the slightest noise for fear of giving his position away. He gripped his Tommy gun and levelled it, ready to fire. John and Ted had a grenade in each hand.

Now the Germans were standing in front of the sacks. Peter saw the bags teetering as they pushed against them. A German sailor prodded one of the sacks at the top of the pile with his rifle butt. It toppled, catching Peter's right shoulder as it slid to the ground. He let out an involuntary cry. Quickly turning towards the source of the noise, the commander signalled his men to check. Peter caught his breath; any inspection, even a cursory one, would reveal not only the other two fugitives but also the small collection of Allied weapons. He couldn't let that happen.

Passing the Tommy gun to John, Peter jumped to his feet and emerged from his hiding place, rubbing his shoulder and feigning pain. He moved across to block the officer's path. 'Bloody hell, that hurt,' he said, hoping the German commander was the one who spoke Greek. 'I'd just started re-stacking the cargo when that damn corn sack came crashing down. Caught me right here,' he said, massaging his shoulder.

The officer was unmoved. 'Who are you? What are you doing here?' he said in Greek; Peter's hunch had been correct. He pushed Peter hard against the pile of sacks, which swayed. Peter prayed that the entire stack wouldn't tumble over and crush his friends.

'Just crew. Just doing my job. Checking on the cargo to make sure it's secure.'

'I don't care who the hell you are or what you're doing — just get out of my way while we search the vessel.' He stepped to his left to skirt around Peter, but Peter moved to block him. He had to think fast. If they discovered the others, all hell would break loose. He had to divert the commander's attention.

'Captain, there's nothing here. You can see it's just a pile of corn sacks. But if you'd like me to take you below decks to search the rest of the boat, I'll show you everything.'

'Move! Step aside now!'

'The skipper over there — he won't help you,' Peter said, pointing towards the Greek boat-owner and lowering his voice. 'He's a pig. Treats us no better than animals. Works us day and night and pays us next to nothing. If there's anything to find down there, I'll find it. It would give me great pleasure to see that rogue arrested and taken away.'

Peter sensed that the German relished the idea of finding something illegal on board. They were always on the lookout for contraband being smuggled from Greece into Turkey, or vice versa. He felt a slight sense of relief as the commander took the bait, although they were a long way from being safe.

'Okay, we'll search here later. Take us below decks first and we'll see what there is down there. Come,' he said, motioning to two sailors and Peter to follow.

Assisted by Peter, the Germans checked the engine room, the small recreation space, the captain's quarters and the two crew cabins. Nothing. But Peter had a plan. Earlier he had spotted several cartons of cigarettes stashed behind a wooden flour box in one of the galley cupboards. No contraband was prized more than cigarettes; revealing them could be a way to satisfy the Germans. It was a risk, but a risk he had to take.

He led them into the galley. It stank of old fat, fried garlic and spoiled fish. Unwashed tin plates had been piled high in the small sink. Peter looked first in the open shelves stacked with tinned foods, some so old they were rusting. He shook his head. Moving to the drawers under the sink he did likewise, then searched a pile of boxes filled with ouzo, beer and retsina. Finally, he opened the cigarette cupboard and, with a flourish, produced a carton of cigarettes. The coveted Pall Mall brand. Peter tossed it to the patrol-boat commander, who caught the carton and juggled it from one hand to the other.

'There are seven more of these,' Peter said, pulling the cartons out one by one. The commander's eyes widened. 'Pity,' he said to the sailors. 'On the last trip, we had dozens of these. I'm sure that bastard of a captain sells them on the black market in Turkey.'

'Here, take them,' Peter said, passing over another carton. 'At least you'll get something for your troubles.'

The currency of choice in wartime Europe, the cigarettes were too valuable to be ignored. The Germans glanced around the small room and then at each other. The commander lifted his head slightly and raised his eyebrows; a sign that the cigarettes now belonged to them. Peter handed the rest over.

Now that they had accepted the contraband, the Germans seemed eager to get back to their own boat. They went up on deck, and with a nod to Peter, a scowl aimed at the Greek captain and the obligatory *Heil Hitler*, the commander swung around on his heels and left with his men, presumably satisfied with their haul.

Once the patrol boat had disappeared into the distance, Peter explained to the others what had happened. The captain muttered something about there being no cigarettes for the rest of the journey, but then flashed Peter a broad grin.

'Jesus, Pete, that was ballsy,' said Ted. 'We might have gone for a Burton there. Thanks, mate. We owe you.' Peter didn't altogether understand the 'Burton' expression, but presumed it was English slang for being killed.

The rest of the three-day journey was uneventful. After passing between the islands of Lesbos and Chios, they arrived at a deserted inlet on the Turkish coast, close to Smyrna. They were free at last.

———————

After being welcomed by the British consul, followed by a hot shower — their first in days — and a nourishing meal, the three men were debriefed by an officer. He opened the conversation by telling them a cable would be sent to their families informing them that they were safe and well. Then it was their turn to tell him what they knew.

Peter passed on all the information he could about the German occupation of Greece, stressing the need for more support for the underground fighters. He made special mention of Tasoula, Thanasis and his other resistance friends. The officer made copious notes and promised to forward the request for additional resources for the partisans to his superiors.

The debriefing lasted until the early evening. Although jubilant, the men were exhausted after all they'd been through. 'Let's hit the grog, boys,' John said. It was their first night of freedom in over a year, so none of them needed any further encouragement. Naturally, they suffered the consequences the following morning.

Several weeks later, the British Consulate gave them new passports; passage had been arranged through Syria to Egypt. During the journey, a couple of unpleasant nights in a Turkish prison provided the only excitement. Ted had left the train during what he thought would be an extended stop at one station, to have a meal at a local restaurant. Unfortunately, he missed the train's departure, and even more unfortunately, he was carrying all the passports. With no passports and therefore no means of identifying themselves, Peter and John were jailed at the next stop while they waited for Ted to arrive on the next scheduled rail service. But it was really only a minor inconvenience.

Having arrived at Haifa, they were housed at the Allied reception camp while awaiting travel arrangements for a transfer to Cairo. With no money, Peter requested that they be given part of their back-pay to buy cigarettes, beer and other 'essentials', but the paymaster refused. This annoyed Peter. He thought about the generous Greeks who had very little themselves but shared everything. During the ten months he had been there he had never gone without, and even strangers had offered him food and money when they'd learned he was an English soldier. In contrast, the British Army did what felt like nothing. 'Not authorised' or 'against the rules' were the official excuses. It was a reminder that, despite the war, bureaucracy was still flourishing.

When they finally arrived at Maadi Camp in Cairo, British intelligence officers carried out another debrief. Peter disliked having to tell the story again. It troubled him to talk about Tasoula and Thanasis; he couldn't shake off the images of them languishing in a grim prison cell.

Chapter Eighteen

The letter arrived with several others. Thalia could tell by the handwriting that it was from Fifi.

My dear friend Thalia, Fifi wrote. *The most terrible thing happened the other day. The Germans arrested Mrs Tasoula and Thanasis. I was sitting in Enou Place minding my business when a German staff car pulled up outside Mrs Tasoula's. An officer got out and joined three soldiers who had been loitering nearby. The officer pointed towards Mrs Tasoula's and they started banging on the door. They made a dreadful racket. When Mrs Tasoula opened the door, they said something to her and went inside. Almost half an hour later, they marched Mrs Tasoula and Thanasis out of the house and bundled them into the car. It was awful, Thalia. Poor Mrs Tasoula. Young Thanasis looked terrified. Two men drove off with Mrs Tasoula and Thanasis and I've no idea what happened after that, but I fear the worst. I've asked around, but no one can tell me anything.*

After the car left, the soldiers who'd stayed behind came out of Mrs Tasoula's house laden with stuff they had looted. Bolts of cloth, half-finished dresses — whatever they could carry. They went back in and carried out a sewing machine — it was still bolted to the dressmaking table, so they took the lot. God knows what German soldiers would want with a sewing machine! They ransacked the place. I couldn't bear to watch any longer, so I left. I hate to think what they'll do to Mrs Tasoula and Thanasis.

Thalia, I thought you would want to be told, so I wrote straight away. I'm afraid I have no more information about this terrible event.

Please write back and tell me how you are.

Your loving friend, Fifi

PS: Apparently, Petros left a few days ago. Thank God he wasn't there, or Mrs Tasoula might have been in even more trouble.

Thalia read the letter twice, straining to hold it steady in her quivering hands. At first she couldn't take it all in; couldn't be sure that she truly grasped Fifi's message. Then she was horrified: Tasoula and Thanasis were being held somewhere. Panic set in. What if the Germans were looking for her, too? She was an accomplice, after all. She had helped shelter two Allied soldiers and duped two German officers. Thalia thought back to the checkpoint incident and the SS officer who now had a file on her.

Worse, she had assisted Tasoula with other resistance work. Nothing as dangerous as sabotage or distributing underground propaganda, but she had delivered packages to partisan contacts and twice passed on messages from Tasoula to a man she suspected was also part of the resistance movement. If they had arrested Tasoula, they would surely be aware that Thalia worked for the dressmaker. If the Germans had been watching Tasoula, they would have been watching her, too.

Worse still, too many people were aware that she was very close to Tasoula; if a friend or relative had betrayed Tasoula, they might also have betrayed Thalia. And if it was one of the other dressmakers, the Germans would now know everything.

She had to find out. Had someone denounced Tasoula? Where were she and Thanasis being held? What would happen to them? And she also had to decide what to do about her own situation. Were the Nazis looking for her? If they were, what could she do to protect herself? There were so many things to consider.

First, though, she had to warn her parents. Nikolaos and Desdemona Christidou owned a taverna close to Tasoula's house. So, she would go back to Thessaloniki. Most of the answers would be there anyway.

Thalia's relationship with her parents was strained, particularly that with her mother. Her father looked upon her more as a workhorse than a daughter, but he did provide for her and she had caught occasional glimpses of affection. Not so with her mother.

The following day, she set off from Giannitsa to Thessaloniki. That night, over dinner, she told her father: 'Dada, there's something I must tell you. Something very important. Something about me I haven't told you.'

'What is it, Thalia?'

'I think I'm in trouble. I've been working a bit with the resistance, and it's likely the Germans are looking for me. Mrs

Tasoula is a staunch partisan, and I've been helping her out from time to time. Nothing dangerous, mostly just passing on messages and that sort of thing.' She decided not to mention the Allied soldiers. 'The Nazis have arrested both Mrs Tasoula and Thanasis — there's no doubt the brutes will torture them and force them to confess everything. If the Germans don't know about me now, they soon will. Dada, what should I do?'

His cheeks flaming and his eyes glowering, Nikolaos exploded. 'You *stupid* fool. Why did you get involved with these people? Nothing good will come of it. You've put us all at risk. Now they'll be looking for us, too. Why? Why did you do such a foolish thing?' Desdemona just sat there, shaking her head with the same disapproving look she always had. She offered no comment on Nikolaos's tirade, just as she had never spoken out against him before. Now that she was older, Thalia realised he was controlling and a misogynist.

'You must go, Thalia. Go back to Giannitsa, where no one knows any of this. Stay there and don't contact us again until this is all over. We must learn to live with these Germans, not fight them. *Stupid* girl.'

His spineless outburst angered Thalia. She hadn't expected sympathy from her parents, but she did expect some understanding. But she never got that. It was one reason why she clashed with them so often.

'It is *you* who is the fool, Dada,' she said angrily, an instant later regretting the rebuke. But it was too late to stop now. 'These Germans won't rest until they have subdued all of Greece. We'll be second-class citizens in our own country. Can't you see what they're doing: executing innocent people, enforcing oppressive rules, using torture to get information, arresting anyone who dares to retaliate? And what about the poor Jews? Look at how they're treating them. It's people like you who make it easy for the Nazis to take over our country. I'm proud of the small part I've played in fighting back. My only regret is that I didn't do more. I'm going now, but you need to be aware that they may come looking for me. I trust I can rely on you not to tell them where I am.'

'You don't understand, Thalia — that's your problem. You can't see that these Germans are here to stay. They've conquered Greece and they'll conquer the rest of Europe. We've got to get along with them and accept their rules. Soon, having German masters will be normal. You'll see.'

A further rush of rage overwhelmed Thalia. 'You *can't* believe that. *Surely* not. You're *pathetic*, that's what you are. A weak coward. People like you — people who stand by and refuse to stand up for what they believe in — will allow these brutes to take away our national identity and cultural dignity. I'll not give in. *Never.*'

Nikolaos slammed his fist on the table. 'You know nothing, young girl. *Nothing.* What you did was foolish. I've got a good mind to turn you over to the authorities myself. I won't, but I should. Now *go.* Get out of Thessaloniki. Go back to Giannitsa. We won't tell anyone what you've done if that's what you're worried about, but go now before I change my mind and report you.'

'Perhaps it's best you say you haven't seen me in months. That you no longer have anything to do with me.'

Nikolaos just grunted as she walked out the door.

Thalia couldn't understand her father's attitude, his subservience to the occupiers. He even welcomed German soldiers into his taverna, and as a result his previously loyal local customers had deserted him. Thalia regretted some of the things she had said, but not her reasons for saying them.

———————

After some thought, Thalia decided to stay with Fifi for a few days. Surely her best friend would advise her what to do. But while Fifi welcomed her, as she always did, she didn't offer any concrete suggestions on how to find out where Tasoula and Thanasis were being held. 'The best you can do,' she said, 'is talk to her friends and relatives.'

So, Thalia set about finding out for herself. First she visited Mrs Koula's house, but it was empty, and the neighbour told her that soldiers had also arrested Mrs Koula and her husband on the same day. None of her other contacts could tell her anything other than that the Germans had taken Tasoula and Thanasis. Eventually, it was Giorgos who confirmed the worst. The authorities had officially informed Giorgos's wife, Katina — Tasoula's sister — of her arrest and imprisonment.

'They're being held at Heptapyrgion. It's a terrible place.'

Thalia shuddered. She had never been there, but she had heard the stories of callous cruelty, extreme violence and subhuman living conditions. An abandoned Byzantine fortress located in the north-eastern corner of the acropolis of Thessaloniki, its ten towers dominating the hill overlooking the city, it had been converted into a notorious jail.

Giorgos shook his head forlornly. 'She and Thanasis will go on trial soon. The outcome is a foregone conclusion, of course. Tasoula will get the death sentence; that's inevitable. Thanasis's age and the lack of firm evidence tying him to the resistance might mean a lighter penalty for him. But it will still be many years of hard labour.'

Thalia's jaw dropped. Until now she hadn't thought for a minute that Tasoula would pay the ultimate price for her so-called crime. 'The death sentence? Oh, surely not. Oh my God, that's terrible. Poor Mrs Tasoula and Thanasis.'

'Sadly, it's a certainty. Death is the only sentence given to resistance members who hide Allied soldiers. A few visitors are allowed while they're waiting to be tried, so I've been to visit Tasoula. She's as good as can be expected. After the trial, they'll ship her off to some forced labour or concentration camp to await her execution. That's if she's not executed straight away. God knows where the bastards will send her . . . or what will become of her. It's very sad, Thalia. I know you're very close to them both; so am I. In these desperate times, tragedy lurks around every corner. I'm lucky to be free myself, praise God. It's only a matter of time before they catch up with me, but we all understand the risks we're taking.'

'These beasts deserve to burn in hell. One day Greece will be rid of them, but in the meantime we must do what we can. Look, if I wanted to visit Mrs Tasoula before the trial, how would I go about it?'

'It's far too dangerous, Thalia. If the Germans have any inkling at all that you're implicated, they'll arrest you as soon as you set foot inside the prison. They might let you in, but they won't let you out. Don't go, Thalia, I beg you.'

'No. Of course not. I won't go,' she reassured him.

But the headstrong Thalia was not to be put off that easily. She had already decided to go and was forming a plan. If Fifi would agree, there might be a way to get into Heptapyrgion prison to visit Tasoula.

She told Fifi all about her conversation with Giorgos and about Tasoula's incarceration. 'Fifi,' she said after they had finished their evening meal in a little estiatorio off Plateon Street. 'I have a favour to ask. It's a lot to ask, I realise that, but I'd like to borrow your identity papers. Just for a few hours, that's all.'

Fifi looked puzzled.

'I'm desperate to visit Mrs Tasoula and if I use my own name, they might arrest me. I think they know about me and the help I've given Mrs Tasoula. If I borrow your ID, I should get past any prison checks.'

Thalia and Fifi were often mistaken for sisters. They were both the same height, had the same flowing black hair and similar facial features. Even their eyes were the same colour. Thalia could pass for Fifi without arousing suspicion.

'I'm not sure, Thalia. Normally I would be happy to give you my papers, but what if I'm also on a Nazi watchlist? What happens then? They'll arrest you instead of me, and I can't let that happen.'

Fifi was right, but Thalia just had to see Tasoula. 'I understand Fifi, I do. But I'll take that chance. If they apprehend me in place of you, at least I'll have kept you safe. If I don't return, you'll know it's not safe for you here and you can leave town.

Please Fifi, I must visit Mrs Tasoula. She was so good to me and if what I hear is true, I may never see her again. *Please*, Fifi.'

Fifi exhaled slowly, then nodded. Thalia sensed it was against her better judgement, but her plea seemed to have convinced Fifi. 'Okay, Thalia, I'll do it. I don't really want to, but I can see how important it is to you. You make an appointment to visit Mrs Tasoula and I'll give you my papers.'

———————

Three days later, Thalia took the bus past the graveyard and up the long, winding cobblestone road to the prison. The guard took only a cursory look at her papers — she could probably have used her own without being detected — before ushering her into a long, concrete-walled waiting room, bare except for wooden benches lining both sides. Ten others sat on the hard bench seats, waiting. Thalia waited with them.

Tasoula had been told to expect a visitor, but the prison official gave her no name. In the courtyard outside her small cell was an observation post, a square, yellow, concrete guard tower up a steep, narrow staircase. It was manned by a Greek lifer she had nicknamed Sapios, meaning rotten, on account of his foul, decaying teeth. His obsequious subservience to the Germans had gained him certain privileges. It was Sapios's job to announce the names of both those who were to receive visitors and those who were to be executed. No one knew which until he directed them to the left to the visitors' room. Or to the right.

'Paschilidou, Anastassia,' he shouted, using Tasoula's formal name. Usually Tasoula dreaded the harsh sound of his voice, uncertain whether he would send her left or right. But today she knew she was expecting a visitor. A prison warder led her into the visiting hall, a long, austere, cavernous chamber with metal tables bolted to the floor on either side of a wire-netting partition separating the prisoners from their visitors. Guards were posted at regular intervals on both sides. Visiting time was fifteen minutes, strictly enforced.

Thalia was already seated when Tasoula entered. The older woman's eyes widened when she recognised her visitor. 'Thal—' she began, but Thalia held up Fifi's identity card, hidden from the guard's sight in the palm of her hand, and Tasoula caught on straight away. She corrected herself. 'Fifi. How wonderful to see you, girl. And how nice of you to visit me.'

Tasoula's appearance shocked Thalia. Although she had only been in the prison for a short time, already she was thin and gaunt. The dark rings around her eyes, which Thalia had noticed the first time they met, during that initial interview, were now pitch-black, and pouches of wrinkled flesh below them were ageing her even more. She looked like a sickly old lady.

'How are you, Mrs Tasoula?' Thalia asked, trying not to show her surprise. 'We've all been worried about you.'

'Fifi, don't worry about me. I'm holding up all right. It's tough in here, but I make the best of it. They haven't given me a trial date yet. Not that it matters — any sort of mercy is out of the question,' she said with a sigh. 'I'm more concerned about Thanasis.'

Tasoula glanced both ways to make sure there were no guards within earshot. Even then, she whispered. Stooges were everywhere; Tasoula trusted no one. The elderly lady next to them was just as likely to be a spy as a prisoner.

'Thalia, you must be careful, dear. Very careful. I was betrayed and your name is also on the list. I can tell you this for sure because they questioned me about you when we were arrested. They made it clear they intended to arrest you, too. Remember Zenaida Pavlides, that distant cousin of mine from Chalastra? The one who used to visit us from time to time? It was she who alerted the Germans, but it wasn't her fault: the Germans tricked her. They hoodwinked her into telling them everything — about me, Thanasis, you, Mrs Koula, Father Andreas, the French consul. Maybe others. She visited often enough, so she was familiar with quite a few people in our circle. I'm sorry I've put you in this predicament. Stay away from Thessaloniki, Thalia. It's not safe for you here anymore.'

Panic clawed at Thalia's gut. Now she knew for certain that the Nazis wanted her. 'Thanks for the warning, Mrs Tasoula. I'll be careful.'

A guard edged closer. Tasoula raised her voice. 'Fifi, they treat me well in here, considering. Two meals a day and an hour for exercise,' she said, loud enough for the jailer to hear. She sighed, the weary sigh of a woman who had almost lost the will to fight. 'It will all be over soon enough.'

This remark unsettled Thalia. What would all be over soon enough? The war? Her trial? Or was Tasoula hinting at the unthinkable?

A beefy warder stationed herself right beside their metal table, so the rest of their allotted time passed with no further opportunity to talk in private.

'Fifi,' Tasoula said as the hefty female hauled her away. 'Remember me and think of me sometimes.'

Thalia saw the tears glistening on her cheeks. 'I think of you all the time Mrs Tasoula,' she said over her shoulder. 'I'll visit you again soon.' This was a lie: it was unlikely that she would ever see Tasoula again.

Thalia couldn't help weeping on the way back to Fifi's, but she had to be strong; this was no time for tears. With her name on an arrest list, she had to keep a clear head. After handing Fifi's identity papers back to her, she wrapped her arms around her friend and hugged her tightly before setting off to Giannitsa. She was frightened, but at least she now knew the truth: the Germans did have her in their sights.

Chapter
Nineteen

Tasoula was taken back to her cell, a small, dark room with water seeping down the bare concrete walls. There was no light, and no window to let any in. A small, half-round metal cover near the top of the bolted door provided the only connection to the outside world. The guards opened the door just three times a day — twice for stale bread and insipid soup; once for daily exercise. The rest of the time, Tasoula lay in complete darkness, day and night. She could pace out three metres from front to back and less than that from side to side. The prisoners referred to the cells as tombs for the living. The wooden slatted bench that served as a bed was pushed into one corner of this tiny space, with a rolled-up grey blanket sitting on the end to use as either a cover or a pillow. She opted for the comfort of a pillow.

Tasoula spent much of her time fretting about Thanasis. He had been imprisoned in the men's section and she in the women's, so they had no way of communicating with each other.

A trial would be several months away. She knew that, just as she knew what the outcome would be. The only question was how they would administer her sentence — the gallows or a firing squad. But anything that delayed the inevitable had to be worth pursuing, so she started preparing her defence, even though she realised it would make no difference to the judge's decision. Her Nazi-appointed lawyer showed little interest in helping her.

In the end, Tasoula's day in court came sooner than she'd expected. On 10 December 1942, a Thursday, they transferred her to the German military court on Vasilissis Sofias Street. Just over three months after her arrest, she was standing in front of the judge. The courtroom was a large timber-panelled room with tall marble columns and carved capitals. The judge sat behind a long wooden bench perched on a platform. Behind him, in between two draped Nazi banners, hung a huge framed portrait of Hitler, presumably presiding over proceedings to ensure that Nazi justice would be dispensed.

The judge delivered verdicts swiftly. Always the same judgement: guilty. The only difference was the severity of the punishment: a lenient sentence was several years' hard labour; a harsh one, the death penalty. Five defendants were sentenced before Tasoula. The judge handed down two sentences of death and three of hard labour, ranging from five to twelve years.

Tasoula's trial lasted just over an hour. Detailed prosecution evidence took up the first fifty-five minutes — the Nazis were nothing if not thorough — before Tasoula's lawyer stood up. No defence witnesses were called; none were allowed. The judge sat reading from a folder of documents, taking no interest in the proceedings as Tasoula's lawyer offered his 'defence', which amounted to a spurious claim of mistaken identity.

'Is that all?' the judge asked, without looking up from his papers. The lawyer confirmed that he had finished, and sat down. 'Defendant, have you anything to say for yourself?'

Tasoula stayed silent. Nothing she could say would make any difference.

'Nothing? No remorse for your treachery? No admission of guilt?'

Fixing her eyes on the royal coat of arms inlaid into the back wall, the one symbol of Greek nationalism that the Germans hadn't removed, Tasoula refused to answer.

The judge slammed his gavel down on its wooden block. 'Okay. Guilty as charged. Death. Next,' he said, as he continued poring over his documents. It was as if he were handing down a trivial fine for a minor offence.

Tasoula's Nazi lawyer promised to appeal, but she knew that was either an outright lie or, at best, he would go through the motions. The outcome would be the same, regardless. She felt nothing; she had expected this verdict. She was in the resistance: death was the only sentence given to so-called traitors to the Third Reich. At least she hadn't offered up any information that the Germans didn't already know.

Thanasis got five years of hard labour.

———————

Straight after the trial, Tasoula was transferred to another hellhole. A canopied truck waited outside Heptapyrgion to take her to Pavlou Mela concentration camp in the Stavroupoli district. Seven others were already on board; Thanasis wasn't among them.

As the vehicle turned towards the camp entrance, it slowed until it came almost to a halt. The youthful guard seated beside Tasoula pointed his pistol in the direction of a group of men and women lined up along a prominent rise opposite the camp. Tasoula knew it as Toumba Mound, the Nazis' favoured execution site. There must have been thirty or more people standing there; perhaps forty. All with their hands bound.

'There,' he said to Tasoula, 'take notice, you dirty traitor.'

Tasoula could see the gathering, but feigned ignorance. 'Where?' she asked.

Grabbing Tasoula by the hair, the guard twisted her head towards the mound. 'There,' he said again, poking his gun at the group. 'There! That's what we do to people like you. Traitors deserve to die. Resistance dogs, and loose-tongued gossips who spread false rumours about German soldiers, and Greek whores who tell lies about being raped. All of them are about to be shot. And make no mistake — your time will come soon enough.'

Tasoula refused to respond.

'Well, what have you got to say for yourself, woman?'

Tasoula still said nothing. She wasn't about to be baited by some pock-marked German kid just out of school. She fixed him with a withering stare that would have frightened off most boys his age, but this one had a gun and a uniform. Bravado comes easily when shackled prisoners have no way of retaliating.

'That lot,' he said, jerking his head towards the group standing on the mound, 'are about to be shot because your bloody resistance friends murdered one of our brave German generals at Naousa. Cowardly bastards. This is what happens when you defy the Reich.' As the truck moved out through the camp entrance, an orchestrated clatter of machine-gun fire shattered the silence. Tasoula's initiation into the horrors of Pavlou Mela had started before she had even entered its gates.

Situated in Thessaloniki's north-west, Pavlou Mela was the first of the Nazis' concentration camps in Greece and Tasoula had heard rumours that it was the worst. A former Greek army barracks, the long, austere, two-storied nineteenth-century building also housed the German administration head-quarters. It was a grim place, dank and dark with ten-foot-high walls, and two lengthy cellblocks with iron railings over the windows. The Nazis had converted it into an internment camp for convicted resistance insurgents, criminals, fraudsters and political enemies of the Reich.

A guard marched Tasoula past a cement trough with a row of taps for ablutions, and shoved her into a small windowless cell with a metal bed covered with a straw sack and a single thin sheet for 'warmth'. Making her strip, the guard deloused her with a foul-smelling chemical and gave her a set of unwashed prison clothing. She refused to think about why the previous wearer no longer needed it.

Conditions at Pavlou Mela were shocking. Breakfast comprised lukewarm tea or barley coffee with a slice of rock-hard black bread. Tasoula could only eat the bread by breaking off small chunks and dunking them in the tepid liquid. Dinner consisted of a bowl of insipid soup — often swede or cabbage and occasionally containing a skerrick of meat — and Kriegsbrot (war bread), made from sawdust and potato starch. Every once in a while, a sliver of poor-quality sausage or a small piece of cheese was served. Dysentery was rife.

The meals, if they could be called that, often amounted to only a few hundred calories a day, not nearly enough for the back-breaking labour demanded of most inmates. Some men were harnessed to heavy rollers and made to tow them for nine hours a day without a break; Tasoula saw others pulling loaded coal wagons. Those who collapsed, or were too weak to work, were often shot, the dead being loaded onto trucks bound for mass burial pits. A fellow inmate who spoke some German told Tasoula she'd heard one guard boasting that 'the more we shoot, the fewer we have to feed'. Tasoula was 'luckier' than most: as a condemned prisoner, she wasn't required to work.

Tasoula dreaded the daily roll call, or *Appel*. Woken before dawn, inmates were forced to stand outside in all weathers — sometimes for hours — while the SS guards counted and re-counted the prisoners to confirm that all were present. She was sure that in extreme temperatures, they deliberately extended *Appel* to inflict the maximum hardship. Inmates who collapsed from exhaustion, malnourishment or severe frostbite — or sunstroke in summer, she presumed — were dragged from the lines and flogged. Even bad posture attracted a beating.

Two months passed in this dreadful place. Tasoula had heard nothing about her appeal, and nothing of Thanasis. She resigned herself to an extended stay at Pavlou Mela. She settled into a depressing routine. Every morning she prayed that Thanasis was safe, that his youth would earn him better treatment, and thanked God she was still alive. With only rats and bugs for company in her small cell, the rest of the day was spent trying to stay sane. The only highlight was the hour they allowed her in the exercise yard. It provided not only an opportunity for some physical activity, but also gave her a chance to communicate with other prisoners.

Violence and brutality were an everyday occurrence at the camp. It was common knowledge that Pavlou Mela was the favoured source of victims for Nazi reprisals, picked at random from the inmates. They had no way of escaping, and as far as the Germans were concerned, these were convicted criminals who had no rights. Whenever the partisans notched up a victory against the occupiers, the Nazis despatched a truck to Pavlou Mela to select doomed convicts for execution on Toumba Mound, alongside suspected associates and even people taken at random from the streets. One hundred Greeks for every Nazi killed. Any elation over a resistance win was soon subdued by the sight of the unfortunate victims being led away. Most went defiantly, knowing that at least the Nazis had suffered losses, too.

So when Tasoula saw a large truck pulled up alongside the fence during her exercise break, she realised what was happening. Soldiers were herding prisoners into the stationary vehicle. At least twenty were already sitting waiting on the bench seats on both sides of the open-deck truck.

'What is it this time?' Tasoula asked one guard with whom she sometimes conversed. The guard, most likely unfit for active service or being punished for cowardice, was Austrian, not German, and had sometimes confided his pacifist views to Tasoula.

The Austrian scanned the yard to make sure no one was within earshot. 'It's always the same: the partisans attack a German unit or blow up a train; our side exacts revenge. Word is that this time it's in retaliation for a resistance strike near Langadas. At least twenty of our soldiers were killed and all their guns and ammunition were stolen. Those poor bastards,' he said, pointing at the now-loaded truck, 'they won't be back.'

Unable to show her sympathy to the guard, one of only a few who ever showed any compassion, Tasoula watched the truck drive off. 'When will this bloodshed and violence end?' she asked herself. But she already knew the answer. It would end when the Nazis left Greek soil forever, and not a moment sooner.

Tasoula had been imprisoned in the condemned block, the section reserved for those awaiting execution. Her cellmates were mostly Greek resistance fighters, along with some blameless citizens seized during Nazi raids or accused of political dissidence; the Germans didn't discriminate between the innocent and the guilty. Those of other nationalities — Yugoslav, Albanian, Polish, Russian and British — were housed in the main compound of the prison.

In Tasoula's block, communication with other inmates was restricted to cross-cell conversations — shouts to those in the cells farthest away; quiet discussions with those closest. Tasoula made friends with three inmates from Alexandroupolis crammed into the cell next door. Like her, the Nazi judiciary had convicted them and sentenced them to death; in their case, for forging fake IDs for the resistance and Allied refugees. She admired the trio, who seemed unfazed by the prospect of imminent death.

One evening, one of them announced the tragic news that nobody wanted to hear. 'It's our time tomorrow. We're praying for the firing squad — at least it will be quick. Apparently there have been a few botched hangings in recent months; that would be the worst way to die.'

Tasoula imagined herself swinging from a rope, still conscious while the noose slowly strangled the life from her. She shuddered. 'Aren't you frightened?' she asked, all too aware that her time would come soon enough.

'Of course we are. We're terrified. But nothing we do will change our fate; all we're praying for is a fast and painless end. We've made our peace with God and come to terms with death.'

Tasoula wasn't at all sure that she would be so courageous.

That night, the cellblock resembled a Mardi Gras party. The three next door burst into song and invited the rest to join in. They sang popular Greek songs into the early hours of the morning, until they were hoarse.

Three times the guards stepped in to halt the festivities, but there was little they could do — as soon as they left, the chorus started up again. The trio goaded the jailers, inviting them to shoot them on the spot. A single bullet then would be preferable to a dozen when the soldiers had them lined up against a wall.

Just after dawn, they were marched at rifle point down the cellblock, but stopped at each cell to say goodbye to their fellow inmates. The warders tried to push them along, but nothing they did worked. Of course the guards could have fired on them, but that would have suited the doomed prisoners. As they neared the doorway, Tasoula began to sing 'Hymn to Liberty', the Greek national anthem.

I know you from the blade
Of the sword, the terrifying blade . . .

Hesitantly at first, the others joined in and soon the full force of the inmates' choir was reverberating through the block as soldiers led the three out. Shortly afterwards, twelve gunshots told Tasoula that the prisoners' wish had been granted.

———————

Tasoula's lawyer did eventually lodge the promised 'appeal', though it was merely a symbolic gesture that had no chance of success. But at least it bought her a little more time. The court permitted her three petitions to successively higher authorities, and she intended to use them all. The longer she stayed alive, the more she could hope to live.

Her stay at Pavlou Mela ended without warning, however. One day, with no explanation, a guard dragged her from her cell and into a truck. This took her to a railway siding, where she was shoved into a crowded train — bound for where, she had no idea. Wherever it might be, she was certain that it couldn't be worse than Pavlou Mela. Her death sentence went with her.

The timber-sided livestock wagon, still littered with straw and dried animal droppings, was enclosed on all sides, with a brakeman's cabin attached to the rear. A faded sign on the outside of the boxcar showed that it had been designed to carry eight horses, but the Nazis had crammed in over a hundred humans, like penned sheep destined for the abattoir. Inside, a single latrine bucket was perched in one corner. With only one small, barred window for ventilation and no food or water, it resembled a death chamber rather than a carriage.

Despite the conditions, joy overwhelmed Tasoula when she saw Thanasis being pushed into another wagon. He looked gaunt and emaciated, but he was alive. That was all that mattered.

The train travelled at a snail's pace, pulling in at sidings every few hours to allow troop trains to pass. Scuffles broke out as the human cargo struggled to get to the sole source of air or fought their way to the latrine bucket. Most didn't make it. The stench was overpowering. Those who died along the way — at least three in Tasoula's carriage alone — were left where they lay. Sometimes the dead remained upright, propped up by the mass of bodies, until the survivors found space for them on the floor or the guards dumped them at the next stop. From time to time, the prisoners were allowed off the train; men and women shoved and jostled to be among the first to be able to snatch an extra few seconds of fresh air. At most stops, though, the soldiers kept the inmates locked inside, suffocating and sweltering. Armed guards with dogs stationed themselves between each wagon to control the crowd and prevent escapes; not that any of the prisoners had the strength to make a run for it.

During one of the irregular breaks, Tasoula spotted Thanasis. The mother-and-son reunion was brief and bittersweet; Tasoula wrapped her arms around him for a momentary embrace before being pulled off by a soldier and taken away.

'I love you, Thanasis,' she said over her shoulder as they pushed her into line. Thanasis cupped his hands around his mouth to project his voice, and shouted, 'I love you too, Mamá. May God protect you.' Then his voice trailed off, lost in the din of shouting guards, barking dogs and bustling prisoners.

The nightmare journey lasted three days. Stinking and barely alive, the feeble passengers, weak from malnutrition, were finally ordered from the train at a small station. The sign on the platform said 'Krems an der Donau'. Tasoula had no idea where the place was, but it had to be well over a thousand kilometres from her home.

Chapter
Twenty

Peter could tell there was bad news coming. The sombre face and the brisk, parade-ground-precision footsteps of the man in the sergeant's uniform told him that this was not a social visit for a friendly chat.

'What is it, Sarge? What's happened?'

'Bad news I'm afraid, Peter,' the man said, confirming Peter's suspicions. 'I'm not sure how to tell you this. You'd better sit down.'

'Spit it out, Sarge. You might as well let me have it.'

'It's your brother, Neil. There's no other way to put this, Peter: he's dead. Killed in action. Copped it from a Jerry fighter plane during an air-raid over the North Sea. Poor bastard. He almost made it out, but just as the chaps had been ordered back to base, a lone Messerschmitt tailgated his plane and blew it to smithereens.'

Peter was stunned. He had expected bad news, but not

about his brother. His shoulders slumped and his stomach heaved. 'What, Neil? It *can't* be. No, no. Not Neil. Please tell me it's not true,' he stammered, unable to believe what he had just been told.

''Fraid so, Peter. I wish I could give you better news, but sadly I can't. Neil is gone.'

It was too much for Peter to process. His dear brother, his best friend — dead. Never again to go hunting deer in the hills, watch a rugby game or share a beer in the local pub. To the air force, Neil was just another statistic; to Peter, he was irreplaceable flesh and blood.

'I know it's a lot to take in, Peter, so I'll leave you in peace to come to terms with your terrible loss. If you need someone to talk to, I'll be in my tent. And, of course, there's the chaplain. By the way, the desk-wallahs in Wellington have already informed your father.'

Peter felt tears welling up. He knew he should let his emotions flow, but he tried his best to suppress them; at least until he was alone. 'Thanks, Sarge,' he said, thinking how odd it was that he should thank the sergeant for delivering such a devastating blow. Peter understood that war meant death. But this was his *brother*. Brothers weren't meant to die.

Once the sergeant had left, Peter let his grief take hold. Normally a stoic individual, not one to let his feelings show, this time he cried until there were no tears left. He cursed Hitler, Himmler, Churchill, Freyberg and all the others responsible for this bloody conflict. He cursed the war itself. He cursed the German pilot who had downed his brother. He even cursed God for taking his brother at such a young age.

Later he sought out the chaplain, who gave him some words of encouragement and the usual reassurance that Neil was now in God's safe hands. It helped a little, but nothing anyone said or did really took away the pain. He tried whisky, but that just made him more morose. And talking to others made it worse — it kept reminding him how much he missed his sibling.

Peter moped for days, unable to sleep or eat. He couldn't muster up enthusiasm for anything. But deep down, he knew he must carry on. For Neil, if not for himself. They had both known the risks when they volunteered. He now made up his mind that he would do his best to avenge his brother's death.

———————

Peter had been excited about getting back to Cairo, but Neil's death dealt him a crushing blow. Everything he had looked forward to with such anticipation now seemed totally meaningless — pointless — without his brother. He had also found it difficult to adjust to the discipline of army life again, with its rigid protocols and hierarchical structure. It was too boring and rule-bound for Peter, who had become used to the relative freedom of Greece and of making his own decisions. He had always had a rebellious streak and didn't respond well to others, officers included, telling him what to do. And he had to admit that he missed the excitement of his Greek escapades.

Even three months' leave in New Zealand, granted before he returned to front-line duty, did little to lift his spirits. Peter was delighted to be reunited with his father and his siblings still at home, of course — and other relatives and friends — but that was the extent of his elation. No one seemed interested in soldiers on leave; many seemed to think that they should be back at the front lines. This attitude incensed Peter: he had volunteered at a time when plenty at home were sitting in comfortable leather chairs behind impressive desks or working on farms and building sites. Not all dodged the war — lots of young men attempted to join up but were refused for medical reasons — but some were nothing more than lead-swingers, malingerers.

Peter couldn't even get his ration of cigarettes. He had a weekly allocation of fifty, but no shopkeepers would supply him; they were more interested in conserving their stocks for regular civilian customers who would still be around when the soldiers left again for active duty. It didn't seem right.

By the time Peter's leave ended, he was looking forward to returning to his regiment. The voyage back to Egypt wasn't all plain sailing: a violent four-day storm tossed the ship around like a cork and Peter was thrown down a flight of stairs, breaking his arm. A stint in Helivan hospital followed emergency treatment on board, and then he was transferred to Cairo to recuperate.

His recovery period at Maadi was uneventful. Mostly.

'Arnold, what the hell are you doing here?' Peter yelled when he saw the distinctive figure of his older brother hobbling across the parade ground, supported by a wooden crutch. Arnold was just as shocked as Peter. 'Peter. My God, Peter. I might ask you the same question. How did you end up here?' The two men embraced, both surprised by the impromptu meeting and thrilled to see each other. There was sadness, too. Neil's death had devastated Arnold just as much as it had Peter.

Arnold explained how he had broken his leg and had to wait for transport back to New Zealand. Peter told his brother that he would be posted to Italy once his fractured arm healed and he passed his medical.

'I heard from Dad that you had escaped from Greece. I have to tell you we all thought you were a goner. God, it's good to see you.' Arnold took a step back, gripping Peter's shoulders as he took a better look at the brother he'd thought he'd lost.

'It's a long story, Arnold, so it will have to wait. I've got an appointment with the doc in five minutes, and you know how much of a stickler for time he is.'

'What are you doing tonight, Peter? I'll see if I can wangle you an invitation to the Warrant Officers' mess. The guvnor's a decent bloke. No promises, but I'll try my best.'

'That would be wonderful, Arnold. But if you can't get me into the mess, let's catch up for a few beers, anyway. There's a lot to talk about. Say five thirty?'

'Done. Let's meet at the Lowry Hut courtyard. If the mess is a no-go, we can have a few bevvies there.'

'Wouldn't miss it for quids,' Peter called out over his shoulder as he rushed off to his appointment.

———

When Arnold arrived, Peter was already sitting in the shade by the swimming pool with a bottle of Stella, the local Egyptian beer. Brewed from onions, so the rumour went.

'Throw this on, Peter,' Arnold said, tossing him a staff sergeant's tunic. 'The sergeant major told me to give you one of my spares and we'll be fine and dandy.'

The evening started quietly. Peter and Arnold talked about old times and caught up on all the wartime gossip. As the mess filled up, the mood became more boisterous. Men sidled over to join Arnold and the newcomer, and before long a school of regular drinkers had grouped themselves around the pair. Pints of beer flowed, and wisps of cigarette smoke hung hazily in the increasingly airless room.

Peter, a natural raconteur, regaled the men with stories of his escapades in Thessaloniki: his close calls and hair-raising encounters with German soldiers; the bravery of Mrs Tasoula and her resistance colleagues; German oppression and brutality; the escape from Greece to Turkey; the hazards of being a soldier on the run. Then the officers started telling their own tales — sometimes tall — of daring on the front lines. The wits among them lightened the mood with an array of rib-tickling jokes. Jokes about Hitler; jokes about Churchill. One-liners, limericks and double-entendres. Then the singing began. A rousing rendition of 'God Save the King' was followed by 'It's a Long Way to Tipperary' and 'Bless 'Em All', sung with more enthusiasm than harmony. There was laughter. Lots of laughter.

Much later, after too much booze had dulled their exuberance, the laughter turned to melancholic maundering: reminiscing about life at home; pining for absent friends and loved ones; mourning fallen comrades. Watery eyes glistened and more than one lip trembled. Peter choked up himself when his thoughts turned to Neil, Tasoula and Thanasis. And Thalia.

The following morning, he woke up with a humdinger of a hangover, able to remember only fragments of the night before. A continuous pounding in his head threatened to split it apart, and his stomach was heaving. He was dangerously close to throwing up. Moving, even standing, made things worse. Even after his brain-fog lifted, there were huge gaps in his recollection. He did have a fuzzy memory of one officer falling off his bar stool and knocking over several tables and countless pints. As best he could recall, it had almost started a brawl. But he wasn't even sure it had actually happened.

'Never again,' he swore to himself, still feeling terrible.

It seemed to take forever for the day to pass, but by late afternoon a revival of sorts was under way. Just as Peter was thinking that life might be worth living again, Arnold poked his head into his bell tent. He was holding the same tunic, now beer-stained and stinking of cigarette smoke.

'You're invited back to the mess tonight, Peter. You made quite an impression last night. Here, put this on again,' Arnold said as he handed Peter the grimy jacket.

Peter groaned. But he had to admit that he had enjoyed the night. It had been an opportunity to let off a bit of steam with his older brother. 'I suppose,' he said. 'I guess a couple of cold beers wouldn't hurt.'

The brothers found a quiet table away from the crowd and talked about family and friends. Peter even told Arnold about Thalia. Arnold gave him the same advice as Paddy: there's no future in it.

After a few pints, Peter perked up again and they joined

the others in the mess. It was another entertaining night, with more war stories and tall tales. But around 10 p.m. Peter left, the other men all still swilling and singing and telling bawdy jokes. He woke the next morning with a much clearer head. And no memory lapses.

Chapter
Twenty One

After her visit to Heptapyrgion, Thalia couldn't erase from her mind the image of the weary Tasoula in her prison garb. Night after night she had nightmares about it. The thought of the woman she cared for being pronounced guilty and then being led to the gallows or facing a firing squad was almost too much to bear. She feared that the Germans had already executed Tasoula — several months had passed, and she had heard nothing more about her. On one of her trips to Thessaloniki, she asked Giorgos; he knew nothing either. No one could tell her anything. It was as if Tasoula didn't exist anymore.

Thalia was heartbroken; Tasoula had been more of a mother to her than her own. The girl had always felt there was something missing in her relationship with her parents. She was constantly at loggerheads with them, and nothing she said or did was ever good enough for Nikolaos and Desdemona.

Tasoula, on the other hand, valued and trusted Thalia and had been kind and compassionate.

Unable to sleep or focus on her work, Thalia couldn't even enjoy the company of friends. She needed to talk to someone. Fifi had been understanding — she, too, was troubled by Tasoula's imprisonment — but Thalia needed the wise counsel of somebody older, someone with more life experience. She thought of her Aunt Metis, the dressmaker who had taught her so much about her profession. This was the aunt she had confided in about personal matters that she could never discuss with her parents.

They met at a small café on Egnatia Street. Metis didn't come to Thessaloniki often, so it was best to meet somewhere central, conveniently close to the train station.

'Aunt, I have to talk to someone. Mrs Tasoula — the dressmaker, the lady who employed me — has been sentenced to death. I'm devastated. She's in the resistance and the Nazis arrested her for hiding British soldiers. She was like a mother to me, and . . . and now she's gone. I can't stop thinking about her, and wondering where she is and what's happened to her.' Thalia went on to explain everything, talking about her fear that Tasoula was already dead, about being on a Nazi watchlist herself, and about how she clashed with her mother so could not confide in her. She even told her aunt about Peter.

'Thalia, I understand your concern about Mrs Tasoula,' Metis said. 'She's a very brave woman — Greece needs more people like her to take a stand against the occupiers. Me, I'm too old to play an active part, but I applaud those who do. Sadly, though, there's nothing you can do to help her. Just pray that they will spare her, Thalia. That's all. The Greek resistance and the Allied forces will push these Germans out of Greece one day, and you should cling to the hope that Mrs Tasoula will be here to enjoy a free Greece again. If, God forbid, she doesn't make it, take solace from the knowledge that you were close to a true heroine. Someone who did what she did so that future generations might live in peace. Pray for her, Thalia, that's all you can do.'

Her aunt was right: she would pray for Tasoula, even though prayer didn't seem like enough. At least Metis appreciated the real sacrifice that Tasoula had made for her country.

'It's just so awful, aunt. I can't get Mrs Tasoula off my mind . . . I'm worried sick about her, but I'm sure she would want me to remember why she did what she did rather than grieve over why she's being punished. I love her like a mother. If I'm honest, I love her *more* than my mother.' Tears rolled from her red-rimmed eyes.

Metis took Thalia's face in her hands, looking into her tear-filled eyes. 'Thalia, there's something you should know. Something very important. Perhaps I shouldn't be telling you this, but you're old enough now to learn the truth. Nikolaos and Desdemona Christidou are not your natural parents. They adopted you when you were just five years old. I doubt they will ever tell you, but you deserve to be told.'

Thalia's jaw dropped. She shook her head, flabbergasted. 'Is that true, *really* true?' she asked, still trying to take in what her aunt had said. 'I've always been told that I was born in Kolindros and my parents shifted to Thessaloniki when I was a young child.'

'That part is true, but your birth parents didn't shift. They still live in Kolindros.'

Thalia buried her face in her hands, needing time to think. She had so many questions, but her aunt's revelation explained a lot. Why she looked so different from Nikolaos and Desdemona; why they never showed the love and kindness that a child should expect from her parents. It explained why they always argued; why they treated her more like a slave than a daughter; why they would berate her for no apparent reason.

'My God. I can't believe it. All these years I've thought my parents didn't truly love me, and now I find out they're not my parents at all. How did all this happen?'

She listened closely as Metis explained. Thalia had been one of nine children. Her father had fallen on hard times and didn't have the money to feed and support them all, so he offered to adopt out Thalia to a childless cousin, Desdemona. She had epilepsy, so had decided not to have children of her own because of the risks that entailed.

'Since the Christidous owned a taverna, by comparison they were well off. Your birth parents didn't want to give you up, but thought that you would be better off with their cousin. Nikolaos and Desdemona promised they would give you a good life and would care for you as if you were their own child. Part of the arrangement between your father and the Christidous was that your natural parents wouldn't try to contact you. It broke their hearts, but they honoured the agreement. I know they still think of you and love you very much, but they had no choice. So, that's your story, Thalia. The Christidous adopted you. Hmmm . . . it always seemed to me that they were more interested in cheap labour than a daughter.'

Her aunt's shocking news brought back many unpleasant memories. Thalia recalled that from a very early age, her parents had tasked her with scrubbing floors, cleaning windows, washing dishes, dusting ornaments and many other jobs. Even when she was working full-time, they sometimes made her work long hours in the taverna as soon as she got home. Her beauty attracted lewd remarks and crude gestures from late-night drunkards. She had once had to fight off an intoxicated would-be Casanova by biting his lip when he tried to kiss her.

Thalia was grateful to Aunt Metis for telling her the truth. At least she now understood more about her background. She resolved to seek out her birth parents, but at the right time — not in the midst of a bloody war.

'Thanks for telling me about being adopted, aunt. I've often wondered why I don't get on with my parents . . . I mean my adoptive parents. I suppose they've done their best — and they *have* supported me — but there's always somehow been something missing. Something that's not right in our relationship. They've been cold and distant, and now I understand why. It must be hard for them to love me like their own daughter.'

'I hope I haven't upset you, Thalia, but you do deserve to be told the truth; it might as well be now. As for this Petros, I don't know him, but you must forget him. One of my friends in the First World War fell in love with a British soldier. It was towards the end of the war when Greece joined the Allies. He promised to marry her after she got pregnant, but he left soon afterwards and she never heard from him again. Imagine the shame of being pregnant and unmarried in 1918 . . . her friends and family ostracised her. No one would give her a job. No one would marry her. She committed suicide two years later . . . her illegitimate daughter was sent to an orphanage. These wartime romances never last — so my advice to you, Thalia, is simple: don't get involved with this man. It will only end in heartache. At least you're not pregnant . . . are you?'

'No, of course not. We've never even kissed. I just can't help how I feel. Anyway, he's left Greece. He escaped.'

'Well, Thalia, that's good. It may not seem like it, but it's for the best. He'll have forgotten you by now. You'll never hear from him again.'

Chapter
Twenty Two

Once Peter had finally been declared fit for active duty, the army posted him to a tank division as a gunner. A three-week gunnery course followed by two weeks of wireless training was mandatory before he could join his unit. Apart from coming first in his gunnery course, the major highlights of this stint in Cairo were being awarded the Military Medal for bravery, and a promotion to lance corporal.

The Allies' military strategists had converted the 4th Infantry Brigade into a tank brigade: the failure of British tanks to support advances made by the infantry had led to heavy casualties, hence the creation of a new division of Sherman tanks armed with 75 millimetre guns on rotating turrets and Browning machine guns. As a newcomer Peter knew nothing about these machines, but the old hands wouldn't stop moaning about them.

'The Krauts' big Tigers will bowl them over like nine-pins,' one complained. 'Couldn't punch a hole in a kerosene tin,' another lamented. Another common refrain was 'Designed by a half-wit.' The extreme risk of fire when under attack was one of the major hazards — the veterans all jokingly referred to the Shermans as the 'Ronsons' after the cigarette lighter's slogan 'It lights up first time, every time'.

After a couple of weeks of training, Peter came to realise that the criticisms were justified. Serious design flaws rendered the tanks vulnerable and easily out-manoeuvred, and their inferior firepower meant they were no match for the bigger Tigers. Still, he would be a Sherman gunner soon and he had to make the best of it.

It was difficult to keep his spirits up. Not only was he still struggling with Neil's death, but Peter also yearned for Greece. He'd felt so much at home there: more so, he had to admit, than he did in New Zealand. His three months of leave in New Zealand had only intensified his longing for Greece. He thought often of his Greek family, and of Thalia and the other dressmakers he had grown so fond of; and prayed that Tasoula and Thanasis had survived and that perhaps, by some miracle, they had already been freed. He even considered writing to Giorgos, but realised that this would not only be futile but also potentially calamitous: if intercepted, a letter from a known fugitive would cause serious trouble for his friend.

After training was complete, the army deployed Peter back to his original battalion, the 20th, now also an armoured unit and based just outside Rimini in Italy. A troop ship got him as far as Naples. It berthed alongside an American vessel, and both Kiwis and Americans disembarked at the same time.

Peter didn't care for the Americans. It wasn't that he didn't like them as individuals, but many GIs based in New Zealand during the war had caused a lot of animosity. The Bedroom Commandos, they were called by locals. Peter knew of more than one pregnant Kiwi girl who had been abandoned by an American soldier, with no money and no support from the father-to-be.

Underlying racial prejudices came to the surface, too. One of Peter's friends had been injured in the Battle of Manners Street in Wellington. The Americans, in most cases racist Southerners, had tried to bar a group of Maori soldiers from entering the Services Club. Pakeha and Maori soldiers — and civilians — stood side by side to protest at this discrimination. A brawl erupted and spilled out on to Manners Street, where the two opposing groups slugged it out for over two hours. Peter's friend had required several stitches for a knife wound to his arm.

Tensions were therefore high as the two nationalities mingled at the dockside. Both sides traded insults and hurled racist comments at each other. Trouble was looming, but just as the verbal barbs were threatening to erupt into physical violence, a booming voice rose above the din of the banter: 'Hey Yank, how are *my* wife and *your* kids getting on?'

It was a pointed jibe at the reputation the Americans had for wooing — and screwing — New Zealand soldiers' wives and girlfriends while their loved ones fought on the front lines. It proved to be a timely quip, as spontaneous laughter erupted from the Kiwi contingent. The Yanks didn't quite see the humour, but the intervention had defused a potentially ugly confrontation. The same loud voice started singing 'Hitler Has Only Got One Ball'; others joined in and the Kiwis marched off to the station to entrain for Rimini.

It was good to be back among his army friends; people who had shared similar experiences and understood what he had been through.

———————

15 December 1944 was Peter's birthday. It was also the eve of his first engagement since Crete.

The sergeant pushed his head through the small opening in Peter's tent. 'You okay, Lance Corporal? Big day tomorrow.'

'I'm fine, Sarge. I haven't tasted real warfare for a long time so I'm a bit nervous, but I'll be okay.'

'You're nervous? I'm scared shitless — don't mind admitting it. Every time it's the same: my guts are churning and I'm as jittery as hell. Anyone who says they're not frightened is either an outright liar or full of shit.'

'You're right there. Sarge, would you do me a favour? My brother was killed a while back . . . and in case the same thing happens to me, I'd like to write a letter to my family. Would you mind taking it? I'm not expecting to cop one but, you know, just in case.'

'Sure thing. Happy to, but you'd better bloody well make sure I never have to send it.'

'That's the plan, Sarge.'

Peter penned a letter to his father and siblings. He told them how much he loved them and that they shouldn't mourn if he was killed in action. *I'll just be doing my duty like all the other lads*, he wrote, *and I promise you I'll do you proud.* He asked his father to pass on his love to all his close relatives — aunts, uncles, cousins and nephews — and his best mates. He folded the letter, sealed it and kissed it for good luck, praying that it would never have to be sent.

He was ready to call it a night when he thought about Thalia. He had tried to push thoughts of the young seamstress out of his mind after he left Thessaloniki, but he couldn't let go altogether. Without exactly knowing why, he picked up his pen again and began to write. His spoken Greek was fluent, but he had never mastered the written language. Thalia would have to have it translated if she ever received it.

Dear Thalia, he wrote, *I hope you still remember me and the wonderful times we shared. I have never forgotten you, Mrs Tasoula and all the other girls, and I have very fond memories of those days despite all the hardships we faced.*

Do you remember the time we put up the warning bell? We argued about how to do it and, of course, you won. What about when you intervened to stop the German officer who came looking for lodgings? Do you remember that? You saved me from being recaptured, no doubt about it. Or the time you pretended to be my girlfriend to evade the German search patrol? I owe you a lot, Thalia, and I'll never forget your courage and bravery, nor your kindness and friendship.

Tomorrow, I go into battle. If you get this letter it's because I've been killed in action. I just wanted you to know that I think of you often.

There is so much more I want to say, but this is not the right time.

Dearest Thalia, if you receive this, I hope you have a long and happy life and think of me from time to time.

Peter 'Petros' Blunden

P.S. Please tell Mrs Tasoula I've never forgotten her and Thanasis and what they did for me. Like you, they are very brave people.

Peter read and reread the letter before sealing it. He hadn't been able to bring himself to tell Thalia how he really felt about her. It didn't seem right to do so, yet it also seemed wrong not to. If she received the letter, he would be dead, Peter reasoned, so what was the point of saying anything?

———————

The pleasant, undulating countryside around Faenza, with its colourful orchards and neatly planted vineyards, seemed an unlikely backdrop for a pitched battle. It looked far too serene and peaceful, more like a setting for an afternoon hike or a summer's picnic. But the town was strategically important. It would be a difficult location to attack: the hills, steep valleys and obscured roads favoured the German defenders over the Allied attackers. Peter surveyed the terrain to assess the level of cover available and estimate the enemy's strength. There had been little advance reconnaissance, meaning that they would be moving forward blindly. The Germans seemed to have taken advantage of the natural cover; they appeared to be well positioned along the slopes and ridges and there were sure to be tanks hidden in concealed positions.

'Jesus, Mac, the odds are stacked against us here,' he said to his good mate Mac West. 'Jerry has us well covered. We need to keep our eyes peeled or we'll be dead meat.' Mac was the driver and Peter was the gunner in their Sherman tank.

'You're bloody right there. The buggers could come at us from anywhere,' Mac said as he got ready to drive into the unknown.

The Shermans with their smaller guns were no match for the bigger Tiger tanks the Germans had. It would be welterweight against heavyweight. To have any chance of taking the town, they would have to rely on speed and surprise. Smoke shells gave the Shermans a slight advantage, but only if the burning phosphorus set the Tigers alight.

At the outset of the battle, it looked like the Germans were withdrawing. Peter's tank pushed forward, strafing hedgerows and shelling any stray German tanks as they went. But soon the Germans mounted a swift and effective counter-offensive. Battle raged for most of the day. Punch and counter-punch.

Just as the sun disappeared, Peter spotted a retreating Tiger tank. He aimed and fired. 'You beauty, Pete,' Phil Watkins — another good mate, and the tank's commander — yelled above the clatter of the rattling chain-tracks rumbling forward. 'Bullseye. Straight into the turret. Another one down!' Peter gave a thumbs-up and looked for the next target. He was pleased to have notched up a direct hit.

'This one's for you, Neil,' Peter muttered as he lined up another Tiger. But without warning, the Sherman dipped sharply and then jolted to an abrupt halt.

'What the hell? What just happened?' Mac shouted.

'Bloody bomb crater. We're stuck in a crater.' Peter had to

bellow to make himself heard above the noise of the tank and the enemy fire. 'We're sitting ducks if we can't get out.'

'Shit! What now?'

'Reverse! Reverse!' Phil shouted.

The engines strained, revving so hard that clouds of smoke pumped out from the exhaust, but the squealing tracks failed to gain traction and move the mountain of metal. The vehicle was truly stuck. Peter was debating whether to stay put and wait for help or clamber out and make a run for it, when a warhead rocked the tank, blasting a hole through its armour. 'Bazooka! Bloody bazooka!' The sound was deafening, and Peter was sure his head was about to explode.

'Out. *Out!*' Phil screamed. 'Dismount. Get the hell out of here before we go up in flames.' But there was no time. The tank tilted sharply, almost toppling over. Peter flew sideways, smashing into a metal strut and gashing his forehead. Blood spewed from the wound. He fell against the side of the hull, this time splitting his lip. Then there was nothing. Silence. No fire.

Peter wiped the blood away from his lip and forehead with the back of his hand, and felt the gash to check how deep it was. Nothing a few stitches won't fix, he thought. He looked around. He could see two of the others picking themselves up, but not Mac or Phil.

'Hey, Mac,' Peter shouted. 'You okay?' No answer. He yelled again, louder this time: 'Are you all right?'

A feeble voice, barely audible, answered back. 'I thi . . . nk so. Bashed my bloody head on the floor. Ears are ringing like bloody church bells; can hardly hear. But no broken bones, I don't think, thank God. A few cuts and bruises, that's all. It hurts like buggery, though.'

That was Mac West accounted for. 'What about you, Phil?'

'All good. Box of birds. I'm going up top to take a gander.' Phil disappeared through the commander's hatch. A few seconds later he shouted back down to the crew. 'All clear. I'm on my way——' They heard a crack, followed by a dull thud. Phil slid silently to the metal floor, crashing face down. 'Sniper!' Peter yelled.

'Bloody cuckoo!' Mac said, using the military slang. '*Bastard*.'

Peter moved over to his friend's motionless form. 'Phil!' No response. Peter shook him; still nothing. He rolled the limp body over. There was no need to check his pulse to confirm that he was dead; Phil had taken a bullet to the head, shattering his skull.

'My God. Not you, Phil. My God, surely not. Why did you have to die on me? You don't deserve this.' Peter whispered a quick prayer, then braced himself for more shelling. But none came. Everything stayed silent. It was eerie. Peter waited until the ringing in his ears subsided, then wrapped a piece of oily cloth around his wound and tied the ends together. Carefully, he crawled out of the tank, surveying the damage and scanning the battlefield in case the sniper was still hanging around.

But the Allies had pushed the Germans back. Theirs had been the last action for the day. They had taken Faenza.

Medics arrived afterwards to remove Phil's body. He would at least get a decent burial. An armoured recovery vehicle towed the tank out of the bomb crater; it was damaged but salvageable. With only one engine functioning and no intercom, it limped off towards base for repairs.

The platoon leader gave Peter temporary command of the tank's crew. They were all exhausted, and saddened by Phil's death, but also elated at the victory. The four surviving men stopped overnight in a nearby village, where other tank crews had also laid over.

'I'm off to take a shufti around town,' Mac said, after they'd settled into a local hall they had commandeered. 'No point in hanging around here.'

'Take care, Mac,' Peter warned. 'Jerry might still be in the vicinity. I don't trust the Eyeties either. Sure they welcomed us as liberators, but they would have done to the same to the Krauts if they'd held Faenza. If there are any Germans still around, the Eyeties would dob us in for a glass of Chianti.'

Half an hour later, Mac bounced back into the hall with a goofy grin plastered across his face. 'You've gotta come, Peter. You just won't believe what I've found. An abandoned vermouth factory. There are six vats of the stuff, just sitting there waiting to be drunk. Six vats of vermouth!'

Peter lifted an eyebrow. Mac was such a practical joker; this seemed like another of his pranks. 'Really, Mac? I'm not that silly. Stop pulling my leg.'

'No, Peter, it's true, I swear it. The distillery is deserted. Has been for a long time by the look of it. Anyway, no one's coming back anytime soon. Come and see for yourself.'

Peter was still unconvinced, but summoned the rest of the crew. Mac led them to the factory. The stainless steel tanks lining one wall of the cavernous building persuaded Peter that it was indeed a vermouth distillery. Cupping his hand, Peter held it under a vat tap to sample the brew. 'This is good. Bloody good. The real thing.' He apologised to Mac for doubting him.

The others tasted the caramel-brown liquid and also declared it to be excellent. Being connoisseurs of vermouth had nothing to do with it. It was alcohol — that was all that mattered. The men seized whatever they could find to drink from: a dusty jar on a window ledge, a cup with a broken handle, a jug and a silver ladle, presumably used for scooping the fortified wine into drinking vessels.

Peter tapped several times on his glass jar with an old spoon to attract attention. 'First, a toast to the memory of Phil Watkins. He was one of the best. A first-rate tank commander and a fearless soldier. He was also a wonderful friend. May he rest in peace.' Peter raised his jar. 'To Phil.'

The others raised their drinking vessels, too; one by one, they paid their tributes. Phil was remembered as 'a top bloke', 'a good joker' and 'a true-blue cobber'. In the silence that followed, the men tried their best to hide their emotions, but Peter could see tiny teardrops sneaking down from crinkled eyes. He shed a few himself.

In typical Kiwi fashion, word of the vermouth factory spread fast and before long the other crews joined them. The noise of excited chatter and glass clinking against chipped china soon filled the room. 'We could have ourselves a right old shindig here,' Mac said, as he downed another shot from his cracked cup. The roguish glint in his eyes spelled trouble. But they were in enemy territory and still at risk of a surprise attack, so Peter called a halt to the night's festivities before the vermouth could take command. The crews returned to their quarters, but not before they had filled four ten-gallon containers of vermouth for Christmas.

It took two days to repair the tank's engines and render it battle-worthy again. Peter's first foray into armoured warfare earned him a promotion to corporal and the temporary command of the tank was made permanent. Phil's death, however, took the gloss off any pride he might have felt.

───────────

Christmas passed with plenty of good cheer — and vermouth — and 1945 began with growing optimism for an imminent victory.

In the first few days of the new year, Peter found himself back on the front line. The 4th Armoured Brigade was stationed just west of Forli, ready to launch an all-out attack to take the town. At first the Germans blocked the advance. Felled saplings were strewn across the road to impede progress, and Tiger tanks, well camouflaged in alleyways and under trees, were able to wait until they could fire from close range. But even though the Germans were well entrenched and did their best to repel the Allied advance, they seemed to have lost the will to fight and put up little resistance. It must have been obvious to the enemy that they were now on the losing side.

Peter's tank was shelled once, not a direct hit but enough to rattle both it and the men inside. There seemed little likelihood of it catching fire, so Peter gave the order to move on. The battle for Forli had none of the intensity of the Faenza engagement, and they eventually took the town with few casualties. Peter's cousin, John Blunden, was one of those few. Towards the end of the action he had been fatally wounded. With Neil's passing still painful, Phil's death very fresh and raw and Tasoula's uncertain fate continuing to trouble Peter, John's demise was yet another blow.

Peter and his crew spent that night in another small village, sleeping inside the armoured vehicle to discourage looting by the locals. But it wasn't Italian looters that woke Peter; it was a British Army Service Corps truck that pulled up alongside the tank. Peter got out to investigate. The driver opened the tailboard to reveal a large haul of stolen goods: bicycles, furniture, clothing — even a small piano. And Chianti: dozens of the bulbous bottles partially sheathed in fiascos — straw baskets — and doubtless filched from a local wine merchant. A crowd gathered and the ASC driver and his mate auctioned everything off. It disgusted Peter: goods stolen from the Italians being sold back to the Italians. The Germans weren't the only ones guilty of pillaging and plundering.

Peter could do nothing to stop the illegal auction, however. These were British soldiers, well outside the jurisdiction of the New Zealand Armed Forces. And he doubted that anyone would do anything even if he did report them. It felt terribly wrong. Only a day before, Peter had been locked in a fierce battle in which his cousin had been killed, and here were a couple of crooks profiting from the misery of others.

The war was coming to an end. Everyone knew it. But Hitler refused to accept the inevitable. Madmen seldom admit defeat, so the lost war was destined to continue. Peter's role in it, however, would soon be over.

At Forli, his commander informed him that he would be among the first draft of the long-service men — the *Tongariro* draft — to be sent back to New Zealand. Peter had done his duty. He had been wounded and captured in the chaos of Crete, had escaped from Greece, had been awarded the Military Medal for bravery and had fought with distinction in the Italian campaign. The original soldiers of the 20th Battalion — the few who were left — were to be repatriated to New Zealand.

Just before the end of January 1945, after a stirring farewell to the troops from General Freyberg, Peter and the rest of the draft set off for their forward base at Bari and from there to Maadi. After a short time in Egypt, they boarded the *Tongariro* and set sail for home. Peter was exhausted and battle-weary, but relieved that he had seen out the war relatively unscathed. He wondered how his Greek friends had fared — in particular, Tasoula and Thanasis.

Had they survived?

Chapter
Twenty Three

'Stay there and don't move.' The guard shoved Tasoula in the back, pushing her into the small cell, then locked the steel door and left. There was no chair; only the floor to sit on or the walls to lean against.

Tasoula's introduction to Stein prison was harsh and humiliating; worse even than Pavlou Mela. Having stripped her of her clothes and most of her belongings, the guard now left her standing naked in this unventilated, windowless room.

Over an hour later, a mountain of a woman with short-cropped hair and a black moustache appeared with a bundle of garments. She looked Tasoula up and down, making it clear she liked what she saw, before throwing the clothes to the floor, forcing Tasoula to bend down to pick them up. Calico underwear and vest; a green woollen shirt with several patched holes; an ill-fitting, unlined jacket; a coat made from an old grey blanket that smelled of stale body odour; and canvas shoes with wooden soles. To someone whose profession was dressmaking, having to wear this outfit was degrading.

'I'll take these,' the jailer said, fingering the few possessions Tasoula had taken with her from Pavlou Mela. 'You'll have no need for them here.'

Tasoula had little of value left, but when the guard ripped the pendant from around her neck — a carved ivory cross that Thanasis had given her — her eyes filled with tears. A precious link to the son she loved had been broken. 'Oh, Thanasis,' she whispered to herself. 'What will become of us?'

———

Stein prison, the second largest in Austria, near the city of Krems an der Donau by the River Danube, was a four-storey building built in the shape of a cross with four large courtyards. It was split into two separate enclosures — the men's prison and a smaller women's section.

The guards were just as brutal as those at Pavlou Mela, and the food no better. Tasoula's bunk had been designed to sleep two, but she shared it with three others. The initial delousing, which she now accepted as standard practice, was followed by an explicit warning about the punishment awaiting those who broke camp rules. The women were told that anyone attempting to escape would be shot, and that they could expect the same punishment if they failed to carry out their allotted tasks to a satisfactory standard. There was no chance of escape, anyway; the few who did venture into no-man's-land, an unfenced area beyond the imaginary prison boundary, did so to commit suicide without having to take their own lives. The trigger-ready guards willingly obliged.

The one consolation Tasoula had left to her was that Thanasis was in the same prison. She couldn't see him or talk to him, but at least he was close. To get messages to him, she harried and badgered anyone who moved between the two compounds, and thanks to sympathetic local workers she managed to smuggle letters to him from time to time.

Tasoula was put to work straight away, in a nearby camp factory making German uniforms. She worked twelve hours a day, six days a week; Sunday was her only day off. She earned a little for the work she did, not in cash but in almost worthless coupons which she could spend only in the prison canteen.

Each day Tasoula did her best to sabotage the military costumes: sewing buttons so that they didn't line up with buttonholes; stitching hems loosely so that they would fall down; neglecting to sew pocket linings together so that keys and wallets would fall straight to the ground. She even tried cutting one sleeve shorter than the other, but that was a bit too obvious. Anything less obvious that would cause inconvenience or embarrassment, she tried. Once the uniforms had been despatched, no one would be able to identify the culprit.

The factory was housed in a flimsy, corrugated-iron building — a disused warehouse — with a bare earth floor and no windows. With no heating in winter, frozen fingers struggled with the delicate needlework while frosty breath, steaming in the chill air, shrouded the workers' faces. In the sweltering heat of summer, the lack of any ventilation meant that the stench of unwashed bodies, drenched in sweat, pervaded the workroom.

When it rained, the earthen floor became a boggy mess, miring the women in ankle-deep mud.

The building was a death trap. Now, in June 1944, American air-raids over Austria had become frequent. Any stray bomb could obliterate the rickety warehouse and most of those inside within minutes. Large circular gasoline tanks in a nearby storage yard exacerbated the danger. Often all that could be heard of the raids was a dull rumble in the distance as the bombers unleashed their lethal loads, but sometimes thunderous booms were heard much closer to the garment factory.

On 26 June, a Monday, Tasoula noticed the drone of aircraft intensifying as they hurtled towards the factory. The piercing screech of air-raid sirens added to her alarm. Leaving her workstation, she rushed to the door and looked up to see lines of silver-bodied planes glinting in the sunlight.

'Run! Run!' she shouted. 'Out of here before the whole place goes up!' The guards had already gone once they'd heard the sirens, leaving the prisoners to fend for themselves. A wave of bodies surged onto the courtyard, looking for refuge. Most couldn't actually run. Weak as the women were, some could only hobble towards safety.

The first bomb hit about a hundred metres away, spewing flames and red-hot metal as it struck an empty outbuilding.

'Over here,' Tasoula yelled, pointing to a basement door outside a large concrete storage shed. 'It's our best chance.'

The second bomb was closer; it showered them with stones and metal shards and blasted them with inferno-like heat. Those women who were strong enough scrambled for the door and jostled their way down the stairs, crowding into the small room. The American aircraft were now right overhead. More bombs dropped. Judging by the sound of the blasts, the bombs were falling right around them, presumably targeting the neighbouring fuel depot and the nearby Moosbierbaum oil refinery and chemical works. Tasoula was terrified that the building above them would collapse, entombing them in their underground shelter. But while it rocked and rattled with each explosion, it didn't crumble.

Then, suddenly, nothing. The sound of bombers faded into the distance, and the wailing air-raid sirens went quiet. The women cautiously made their way up the stairs to survey the damage. Cement blocks, metal fragments, glass, machine parts and other debris lay strewn across the ground. An upended coal wagon was precariously perched with its front wedged into a crater and its rear upright, teetering as it fought gravity. A large cable drum had been ripped from its mount and tossed several hundred metres into an open ditch. Several thick columns of heavy black smoke snaking skywards suggested a direct hit on the oil refinery. The garment factory was untouched.

Two of Tasoula's workmates hadn't made it, both too frail to reach the basement refuge in time. Their mangled bodies lay sprawled in the yard. Tasoula mouthed a silent prayer. A macabre thought crossed her mind: further bombing raids might see her Nazi-imposed death sentence carried out by an American pilot.

———

Punishment for any misdemeanour at Stein was harsh. Even the most trifling transgression — a plate dropped by mistake, or a tool broken — attracted a severe penalty. Deaths were an everyday occurrence. Firing squads were common, public hangings less so, but other time-proven techniques worked just as well. Disease and starvation, the most effective of the Nazis' extermination methods, caused most of the deaths. Tasoula witnessed others flogged or murdered by more traditional means: two men shot for stealing bread, another beaten unconscious for spilling a tray of food on a German officer, and yet another left outside to freeze to death in sub-zero temperatures, punishment for collapsing at work.

One Sunday, a rifle butt slammed into Tasoula's back and a guard pushed her towards the prison courtyard. Other female prisoners were also being herded into the square.

'What's going on?' Tasoula asked the woman next to her in the crowd.

'No idea. It won't be anything good, that much is for sure.'

A woman on Tasoula's other side pointed to a makeshift platform. 'It's happening over there,' she said. 'The word going around is that they're about to execute a prisoner for stealing. Bastards!'

'What did he take?' the first woman asked. Not that it mattered; the Germans didn't need any excuses.

'Stole a tube of toothpaste from a delivery truck,' a woman one row back whispered. 'A single tube of toothpaste.'

'Poor beggar,' the first woman said, nudging Tasoula in the side. 'He doesn't deserve to die for that, does he?'

Tasoula didn't answer. Unless it was a close personal friend, she knew better than to respond to anyone protesting against German atrocities. Stooges were everywhere.

The women watched as a man in prison garb was led to the platform. The soldiers hoisted a timber T-structure into place and attached a rope to one end: a gallows pole. A black-uniformed German officer with a megaphone then mounted the platform. A ripple of whispers spread through the crowd. No one spoke out, for fear that they would be singled out for the same punishment, but the buzz of hushed conversation was loud enough to attract the German's attention. He fired two shots into the air. 'Silence! *Silence!*' he shouted through the loudhailer. 'Quiet now, or you'll be next.'

The crowd obeyed; it was no hollow threat.

Soldiers thrust the man onto a trapdoor below the noose. It was all over in less than a minute: the order given and the trapdoor released. His body was left dangling from the timber beam as a deterrent. It was a stark reminder to Tasoula that her own death sentence was just one German signature away from being carried out. A reminder, too, that she must focus on her own survival, not the plight of others. She would do what she could to support her fellow prisoners, but she had a simple rule to follow: if she were to help others, she had to help herself first.

———————

The months passed slowly; the first year even more so. Every day was the same: more beatings, not enough food, punishing workdays and oppressive living conditions. If it could be called living.

Halfway through her second year at Stein, the camp authorities gave Tasoula a different job: making netting from dried corn leaves. The work was tedious, but at least it wasn't hard. However, it had its hazards — inflammation in both eyes, caused by dust from the dried leaves, induced such bad swelling that Tasoula was struggling to see. One eye closed altogether, and vision in the other was reduced to a narrow slit. After an appeal to her supervisor, she was granted a doctor's visit. Even this, a trip to the infirmary, provided a welcome respite from the tedium of daily life.

The doctor didn't inspire confidence. About as wide as he was tall, he had beady eyes and a glossy sheen on his face and cheeks, the result of unusually greasy skin or overactive sweat glands. With his black hair parted on the right and falling across his forehead, along with a small, clipped moustache, he might have looked like Hitler if he had been thirty kilograms lighter.

The conversation started off with all the normal pleasantries.

'Ah, I see what the problem is,' the German doctor said, after examining both eyes with an ophthalmoscope. 'What you have is prurient eye cystitis. I don't expect you to understand what that means, but it's easy to treat.'

'Thank you, doctor,' she said, relieved that it was nothing serious. 'What should I do?'

'I'll give you an ointment to rub into your eyes twice a day; but first, let's have a look at your records. What's your name again?' he asked.

'Anastassia Paschilidou. But everyone calls me Tasoula.'

The German scanned the rows of tall metal filing cabinets until he came to the drawer marked with a large 'P'. 'Paschilidou.

Paschilidou,' he said to himself as he fingered through the brown cardboard files. 'Ah, here it is. Let's see what it says.'

He pulled the folder out, sat down at his desk, and began to read. Tasoula saw his mouth tighten, his eyes narrow and a broad crease spread across his forehead. She could tell something was wrong.

'You bitch. You ungrateful, worthless whore. You deserve to be shot, not treated.'

Tasoula smiled at the irony of this statement.

'Hiding British soldiers. Sabotaging the German army. Working with the bloody resistance. People like you are vermin. Not worthy of any sympathy.'

Tasoula stayed silent. And defiant. She wasn't about to give the man satisfaction by showing any emotion. 'If that's all, doctor, I'll bid you good day,' she said, sarcastically.

'No, bitch. That's *not* all. Not at all. Stay where you are.' He picked up the black Bakelite telephone and spoke to the camp commandant. Whatever he said spelled trouble for Tasoula. And it didn't take long to find out how much trouble.

———————

'Paschilidou, Anastassia,' the voice rang out across the courtyard where the guards had assembled the women for the daily roll call. Two other names followed hers. It was the moment Tasoula had dreaded. Others before her had been called out in the same way; none had returned. Tasoula made her way forward. This was it, she was sure of it. She prayed as she approached the guard; not for herself, but for Thanasis.

The three women waited, one crying, another staring vacantly ahead, apparently resigned to her unknown fate. Tasoula stood upright, calm and impassive.

A voice behind her shouted, 'You! Burgau!', and someone gripped her by the shoulders and pushed her forward. She was led away to collect her few belongings before being taken to a small open-deck truck with metal panels on the rear and sides. There were no seats. Five other inmates were already sprawled across the hard deck; Tasoula joined them on the floor.

For most of the eight-hour drive, it rained; everyone was soaked. Tasoula had been at Stein for almost two years. Two years of abuse, humiliation and deprivation. She had no idea what was to come next.

Burgau, a sub-camp of the notorious Dachau concentration camp, housing mostly women, was about fifty kilometres west of Augsburg in Germany. It served the Kuno factory, which assembled Messerschmitt aircraft. Originally the factory had been located in Augsburg itself, but had been relocated to Scheppacher Forest near Burgau after the Americans bombed the original site.

The overcrowded forced-labour camp was surrounded by a ten-foot-high barbed wire fence, with four watchtowers — one at each corner — and fourteen wooden barracks. Inmates comprised prisoners from Nazi-occupied countries, like Tasoula, along with Polish and Hungarian Jewish women transported from Bergen-Belsen and Ravensbrück. Although the conditions at Heptapyrgion, Pavlou Mela and Stein had been atrocious, characterised by brutality, oppression and inhumanity, Burgau took barbarism to new depths.

Tasoula's only consolation — although it often didn't seem like one — was that she was still alive. Her death sentence hadn't yet been administered. Perhaps the authorities had lost her files during the various transfers, although given the German obsession with record-keeping, that seemed unlikely. Or perhaps, she reflected sardonically, her sentence was to be death by starvation.

Like most camp inmates, Tasoula was put to work at the Kuno factory assembling the mass-produced Messerschmitt Me 262. Roll call, at 4:30 a.m. six days a week, was followed by a two-kilometre walk to the factory, accompanied by armed SS guards and vicious dogs. Once there, the work was repetitive — the only things she could do to retaliate against her captors were to go slow or submit defective aircraft parts, hoping that they would pass inspection and then fail later at a critical time. She never knew if her efforts had been successful. Then, after twelve hours each day, the same long walk back to camp.

Meals consisted mainly of soup, with a thin slice of bread in the mornings, and occasionally a tiny ration of sausage or curd cheese. The soups, served twice a day, usually contained potatoes, often rotten; the other key ingredients seemed to be nettles, grass and some green slime that Tasoula never identified. Sometimes she stole a potato or some bread to supplement the subsistence diet or, more often, to give to someone more needy. Such a crime carried the death penalty, so for most it was a dangerous activity. But not for Tasoula: they couldn't execute her twice.

Tasoula had been emaciated when she arrived at Burgau, but with an even less nourishing diet and longer workdays, she lost yet more weight. Soon she was struggling to walk to the factory and back, but she pushed herself to make the journey and do the work. Those who couldn't continue simply disappeared; there one day, gone the next. The one thing that kept her going was hope: that she would live another day, then another, and would eventually be reunited with Thanasis.

One memorable day, Tasoula's spirits were briefly lifted. An old friend and former resistance colleague, Mrs Despina Paraskevaides, arrived at the camp after being transferred from Pavlou Mela; the next day, Mrs Apidopoulos, whose five-year sentence had been commuted to three, was due to be released — a rare occurrence at Burgau and one that brought some cheer. There was little joy in the reunion with Mrs Paraskevaides, as the German court had also given her a death sentence for hiding Allied soldiers, but it did provide an opportunity to get news from Thessaloniki.

'I'm so sorry they arrested you, too, Despina,' Tasoula said to Mrs Paraskevaides. 'When you survived the purge that netted Thanasis and me, I thought you must be safe.'

'Not so, sadly. Collaborators are everywhere. A woman I considered a close friend — someone I trusted — betrayed me. She told the Nazis everything. Even told them about the food I stole to feed the soldiers. So here I am. People you think you can trust, you find you can't. What's happened to our country when Greeks would stoop so low as to betray one of their own?'

She sighed, running her hands through her straggly black hair. There was no warmth in her saddened eyes, the eyes of a woman who had lost faith in human decency. Once the life and soul of every party — Tasoula remembered her vivacity well — her zest for life had now been crushed.

'What of you, Tasoula?'

'I'm okay,' she said, immediately realising that she looked anything but. 'I get by. I just try to make it through every day and pray that I will live through the next. We get little news in here, but from the snippets I do pick up I hear that the war is going badly for the Nazis. It surely must end soon — the thought of that keeps me going. And, of course, Thanasis. What word of Thessaloniki?'

'It's bad, I'm afraid. The Germans are getting smarter, and Greek resolve is getting weaker. Every day there are more arrests. The worse the war is going for the Nazis, the more vicious they become. They have devised new tactics — mostly bribery and privileges, or blackmail — to persuade Greeks to give up their own. It's tragic, but it's happening. More and more of our underground associates are being rounded up, and there's scant information about what happens to them.'

Tasoula's face clouded over. She thought about all the brave people who had risked their lives for Greece. What was happening to them now?

'Of your close friends, the Andreous are still free but no longer hiding any soldiers. They have little to do with the resistance now — I can't blame them, really. Veroni Margariti is also safe as far as I'm aware, but I haven't seen her in ages. The Nazis arrested Father Andreas, Mrs Angelidou and Jan Frère, the Frenchman. I'm not sure about Mihail Xanthopoulos but most of our other colleagues are in prison.'

'It *can't* last much longer,' Tasoula said, attempting to reassure herself. But she knew it was her who would not last much longer. 'And what of Petros Blunden? Did he get away?' Mrs Paraskevaides had hidden Peter several times when it wasn't safe for him to stay at Tasoula's. 'The Gestapo pigs told me they had captured him, but I don't believe it.'

'I heard Petros escaped out of Greece,' said Mrs Paraskevaides, 'but that was third-hand information from a friend of my cousin's.'

'I hope you're right about Petros. He's such a determined man — I'm sure he would have made it. And Thalia? Thalia Christidou? What of her?'

'Thalia came looking for you after they arrested you. Very distraught she was. I ran into her on Enou Place, and she asked what I knew. All I could tell her was that they had imprisoned you and Thanasis. Apparently she spent days asking everyone in the area for information. But I haven't seen her since.'

'Ah, dear Thalia. She visited me at Heptapyrgion; she was always the most loyal of the girls. I hope she's safe and away from Thessaloniki. The Germans were after her, too, when they raided our house and took us away. She was on their list.'

'When I saw her, she said she was working in Giannitsa, but I know nothing more than that.'

Dropping her head into her hands, Tasoula prayed that Thalia was safe. She thought again about some of her dearest friends who would now be awaiting execution — or be dead already.

While waiting to be released, Mrs Apidopoulos had been listening intently to the conversation. She interrupted. 'I've just had a thought. Listening to you two talk about your Thessalonikan friends has given me an idea. I'm leaving tomorrow, so why don't I take some letters with me? I'm sure I can smuggle them out and pass them on to one of your contacts.'

'It's dangerous. Far too dangerous,' Tasoula said. 'I won't have you taking the risk.'

'What's the world coming to if I can't help a friend? I'll take the letters and that's that.'

Tasoula protested for a while longer, but Mrs Apidopoulos would have none of it. Tasoula had to admit that the opportunity to get word to her family and friends was too good to pass up. She couldn't write to Thanasis, of course, but wrote one letter to her sister Katina and another to Thalia, with instructions to both to circulate the information to her close friends.

Dear Thalia, her second letter read. *I have been praying for your safety every night, so I hope God has answered my prayers.*

I'm as well as can be expected. I'm in the Burgau concentration camp and life here is pretty grim. I don't know if anyone has told you, but the judge sentenced me to death. Nothing has happened so far, but don't be surprised if you hear the worst. Don't worry about me, Thalia, I'm not afraid to die. I did what I did for Greece and if I have to pay the ultimate price for that, then I'll die knowing I did what I could. I'd do exactly the same again.

Don't mourn for me, girl, just remember the good times we had together. But I won't bore you with my problems. How are you, dear girl? I hope you're okay and well away from Thessaloniki. It's not safe there anymore.

Have you heard anything about Petros? Did he get away? My friend here told me she thought he had. I hope so. He's a good man and I'm sure he'll return to fight the Nazis again.

I only have this small scrap of paper so I can't say any more. I may never see you again, but I want you to know that I love you like a daughter. Think of me when you can. Stay safe, Thalia, and be careful.
With love,
Mrs Tasoula
P.S. My friend will give this to your parents as I can't think of any other way to get it to you.

Tasoula felt her eyes welling up as she folded the note, but she wouldn't allow herself to cry. It was a simple task for her to sew her letters, along with several others, into the hem of Mrs Apidopoulos's dress. She also put a false lining along the inside hem so that the Germans wouldn't feel the papers hidden there if they searched her.

———————

As time passed, Tasoula could tell that the war was coming to an end, despite the constant stream of German propaganda saying otherwise. She noticed a distinct change in the attitudes of the guards. Some seemed more amiable, doubtless wanting to be regarded more favourably when the end finally came; others had become more brutal, taking out their frustrations at the impending defeat on the prisoners. Word had reached the camp that the Russians were forging ahead through Austria on their way to Germany itself. But everyone somehow knew that there would be no easy victory for the Allies and no reprieve for the prisoners until Hitler had finally been crushed. Tasoula hoped she could hold on long enough.

One persistent rumour added to her concerns. Himmler had apparently signed a decree that amounted to a death warrant for the Burgau inmates: 'No prisoners are to be rescued alive,' he had allegedly ordered. As the end of the war became increasingly imminent, Hitler seemed determined to eliminate every trace of the atrocities the Nazis had committed in their infamous death camps. Tasoula might escape the hangman's noose but still die, as part of the systematic extermination of concentration-camp prisoners.

Camp gossip also had it that Hitler had directed all captives, including prisoners-of-war, to be used as human shields to slow the Allied advance. While there was no way of knowing if this was true, it was completely believable that a fanatical Hitler would stop at nothing in the hopeless pursuit of an impossible victory. Tasoula thought of Peter; and prayed that if they had captured him, he wouldn't be among the POWs caught up in this mad plan.

———————

'Who did you give our address to, Thalia?' demanded Desdemona, holding up an envelope with Thalia's name on it.

'No one, Mamá. Not a soul. I promise.'

Out of duty, Thalia had called in to see her adoptive mother on one of her irregular visits to Thessaloniki. Their relationship had almost completely broken down after Thalia had learned that she'd been adopted. There was no cordial greeting when Thalia turned up, just this immediate accusation that she had disclosed the Christidous's address to someone.

'Well, you must have. How would someone be able to deliver a letter to you at this address if you didn't tell them where we lived?'

'I *told* you. I've not given your address to anyone. Now give me the letter. It's for me — no one else.' Thalia went to grab the envelope, but Desdemona pulled it away.

'If this has anything to do with these resistance people you're involved with, I'm taking it straight to the authorities. I don't want to be mixed up in any of that nonsense. We have to get along with these Germans, not fight them.'

Thalia didn't recognise the handwriting, so had no idea who the letter was from. What she did know was that if it *was* somehow linked to the resistance and the Germans got hold of it, they would immediately arrest anyone mentioned in it. Naturally, she would be the first. She was already on a Nazi watchlist, and a letter addressed to her from an underground contact would give the Nazis all the evidence they needed.

'Please give it to me, Mamá,' she pleaded. 'I'm sure it has nothing to do with the resistance.'

'I don't believe you, Thalia. The woman who delivered it wouldn't give her name. Wouldn't tell me who sent it. Just that it was very confidential and must be given to you and you alone. Why would she be so secretive if it's not to do with those people?'

Thalia didn't have a clue as to the sender of the letter or the reason for the secrecy, but she was coming to the same conclusion as her adoptive mother. It had to have something to do with the resistance. She *had* to get hold of it before Desdemona opened it.

'Now *give* it to me, Mamá. It's mine!' She snatched the letter from Desdemona's hand, tearing the corner of the envelope as she wrenched it from her grasp. Saying a curt goodbye, she left.

As soon as she was away from the house, she ripped open the letter, and let out a jubilant cry when she saw Tasoula's handwriting. Tasoula was alive! She had to be. After reading the contents, however, her mood darkened somewhat. She felt both joy and despair: joy that Tasoula had survived, despair that she was still under threat of execution and was in a concentration camp.

She also felt something else. For the first time in her life, someone had told her they loved her. 'I love you, too, Mrs Tasoula,' she said out loud. When she stopped crying, she rushed off to tell Fifi the news.

Chapter
Twenty Four

Tasoula was now close to the end. She could hardly bear to look at herself in the shard of grimy mirror crudely fixed to the wall of her overcrowded hut. Scabs covered most of her face; ugly red blotches, probably infected, and suppurating sores infested the rest of her body. She could feel things crawling through her greasy locks. The lack of adequate nourishment had caused bouts of bloody diarrhoea and, at times, the loss of vision and hearing. In the small mirror fragment she could see that her arms were as thin as spindles; and her sunken eyes threatened to disappear into their sockets. She didn't need a mirror to tell her that her ribcage was pushing through her gaunt skin; she could feel that with her hands.

She couldn't have weighed much more than thirty kilograms, less than half her normal weight. But she was alive. Barely, but still alive. If she wanted to see Thanasis again, she just *had* to hold on.

Some time in April 1945 — Tasoula had lost track of days and dates — she opened her eyes one morning to make out the blurry image of a young soldier standing over her. He carefully dabbed her face with a damp cloth to help rouse her from semi-consciousness. The German guards had already abandoned the camp; if Tasoula had been capable of walking, she might have walked free. Instead she lay on her wooden bunk, so weak and exhausted that she was unable to move.

'I'm George Christofer, an American GI,' the young man said in Greek. 'You're in safe hands now. And you are?'

'Tas . . Tas . . oula Paschilidou,' she croaked, struggling to pronounce her own name. 'Have you found the others? How come you speak Greek?' she asked, confused.

'I'm a Greek American, so I understand the language. My parents are from Athens. I'm so pleased to meet you, Tasoula. Are there other Greeks here?'

'There are thirty-nine of us,' she wheezed, before collapsing.

A Red Cross ambulance transferred Tasoula to Hindenburg barracks in Augsburg for medical treatment. It took three weeks for her to gain some strength; another three to gain weight. Even though the food was nourishing and plentiful, her stomach wasn't able to cope with either the quantity or the rich flavours.

Within a few weeks, the Americans told her they had rescued Thanasis from Stein prison. Despite her weakness she wrote to him straight away, confident that the US Army would deliver the letter. She even began to think about a life after war. But things would never be the same again. Three years as a condemned prisoner in the most horrific conditions had destroyed her mentally as well as physically. There was no way back. Her once-smiling eyes were now dull and lifeless; spontaneous pre-war laughter had given way to mirthless post-war despair. She might have escaped the death penalty, but she was still serving a life sentence.

The only thing that cheered Tasoula up was a reply from Thanasis.

Dearest Mamá, his letter read. *Thank you for your letter and thank God the war is over. I'm pleased that you're being looked after by the Americans. They promised they would find you, and I rejoiced when I heard you were safe. I've been so worried about you, so this news came as an enormous relief. I am being treated very well. The GIs even take me out in their jeep when they're collecting supplies or driving to another unit.*

I can't wait to see you, Mamá, although I fear a reunion will have to wait for a while yet. Life at Stein got worse after you left. We all knew that the war was going badly for the Germans, and the guards retaliated in the most brutal way. Many more beatings, and a lot more deaths. But the most terrible thing happened just as we were about to be released. As the Russian troops advanced, the SS got ready to abandon the prison.

I'll never forget the day — 6 April, a Friday. Word went around the camp that the war had ended. And the prison director let us all go. Every prisoner at Stein.

Mamá, you wouldn't believe the joy. Everyone sang and danced and shouted. It was incredible. After all these years, the Allies had defeated the Germans. The guards opened our cells and we all piled out, excited and eager to get away.

But then the bloodbath started. A hail of bullets greeted us as we entered the courtyard. The prison director — the courageous man who had let us out — had been executed by an SS officer. He and his men were now in charge.

The carnage was worse than anything I have ever seen. Mamá, you wouldn't believe it. They slaughtered dozens of inmates in cold blood. The SS guards herded all those who attempted to escape into the central yard and mowed them down. It went on for hours.

My friend Mimis and I ran back to our cells and stayed there. We couldn't bear to watch. When the gunfire stopped, boots came stomping up the stairs. We were sure our time had come.

Fortunately a higher-ranking officer had taken control; he ordered the guards to lock us in. I looked out the window and saw dead bodies — there would have been more than a hundred — littered around the prison yard. We learned later that they murdered over two hundred prisoners.

The following day, the SS forced many of the inmates to bury the corpses in several mass graves and clean the courtyard of blood and human remains. Luckily Mimis and I weren't given this gruesome task.

Mamá, I'm only thankful that you weren't there to witness such a terrible tragedy. I shall never forget what happened. I never want to see anything like that again.

As I say, the American soldiers are treating me well and I desperately hope that we will be together again soon.

Your loving son, Thanasis

Tasoula wept. Yet she wasn't surprised at what Thanasis had described. The Nazis had ended the war the same way they had started the occupation of Greece — with a mindless atrocity. She wondered how many of her friends at Stein had been butchered by the Germans in this last act of madness. But at least Thanasis was safe.

Chapter
Twenty Five

Life back in New Zealand wasn't what Peter had expected. After a couple of civic receptions for returned servicemen — one in Christchurch and one in Oxford — everyone seemed to have forgotten the war. It felt as if they didn't want to be reminded. People who had lost close relatives and best friends were understanding, but they were the only ones who were.

The country had changed. Those who hadn't served seemed eager to avoid those who had. Pre-war friendships, so close before 1939, weren't quite the same; uneasy pauses punctuated what would previously have been free-flowing conversations. Those who had volunteered often looked sideways at conscripts. Front-liners regarded military pen-pushers as malingerers. Those who had been on active duty throughout their time at war sometimes looked down at POWs, even those like Peter who had had the courage to escape, insinuating that somehow they were lesser soldiers.

Wives and girlfriends who before the war had been flirtatious and vivacious became strangely reserved. Bedroom encounters while their partners were fighting on the front lines had made them anxious to avoid the accusing stares of those who knew the truth. Prejudices that hadn't existed before the war were plainly evident after it.

Rising prices and everyday small-talk began to assume more importance than acknowledging the sacrifices of men who had survived one of the greatest wars in history. Peter guessed this was because New Zealand hadn't experienced the wartime hardships that Britain, Greece and most of Europe had. Apart from some rationing, fuel shortages and war reporting, life had carried on pretty much as normal.

Peter couldn't settle down. Restless yet listless, he missed the companionship of the men he'd served with and the predictable routine of army life. He sought the company of other returned servicemen; only they truly understood what he had been through.

If Peter was honest with himself, he was disappointed with New Zealand and its people. He had fought with distinction while those around him perished, earned a Military Medal for bravery, suffered the indignity of capture, and showed courage and determination to escape and re-join the war. Yet no one at home seemed to care. This wasn't what he had expected when he'd lined up against the enemy in Crete and Italy. Truth be told, he didn't know what he had expected, but it wasn't this. He had dreamed of resuming a normal life, but the reality was very different.

Peter also yearned for Greece. He missed the country,

its people, and its way of life; he fretted about Tasoula and Thanasis and wondered whether they had survived the war. The answer came in the form of a surprising letter, simply addressed to:

Peter Blunden
Soldier
New Zealand

How it had found its way to him was remarkable — a tribute to the army's Postal Service. Peter recognised the handwriting straight away and tore the note from the envelope. It was written in English; Thanasis must have translated for Tasoula. With a slight shock, he realised at once that this meant both of them had survived.

Dear Petros, he read. *I hope this letter gets to you. I didn't know where I should send it. How are you? Are you back in New Zealand? Did you get away safely from Thessaloniki? We have received no news of you at all, nor anything of the other English soldiers. The Germans told me they captured you, but I didn't believe them.*

You were always too smart for them, so I'm sure you escaped and made it to Turkey. I hope so. Thanasis and I often think about you and pray that you are safe.

We are okay. Well, that's not really true. We have survived the war but, Petros, we have suffered the most horrific punishment. The Gestapo arrested Thanasis and me two days after you left and put us in Heptapyrgion prison — you remember, that big castle on the hill — and then sent us to Pavlou Mela concentration camp. They sentenced me to death and Thanasis to five years' hard labour. Petros, it was the most terrible time of our lives. Thank God you left when you did. I'll never forgive the Germans for what they did to us. But I regret nothing I did — and would do it all again.

There's so much more to tell you and I'll explain everything in another letter.

Petros, please write and tell us you're okay. We've been worried about you. Please write back.

Love,

Mrs Tasoula and Thanasis

P.S. Thalia is well and sends her kindest regards.

Tears dripped down Peter's cheeks as he put the letter down: tears of guilt because his presence there had led to their arrest; tears of sadness at what they had been through.

He wrote back the same day, reassuring Tasoula that he had indeed escaped and had returned to New Zealand. He told her a little about his escapades, and stressed that she and Thanasis had been in his thoughts ever since he'd left Thessaloniki. After signing off to them both, he added another line:

P.S. Please pass on my best wishes to Thalia, too. Tell her I often think of her.

Just as he was about to lick the seal on the envelope, he stopped and pulled the letter out again, adding four more words to the postscript '. . . *and the other girls.*' He hoped that the full stop he had inked on the original P.S. wouldn't be too obvious; characteristically, he didn't want Tasoula or Thalia to think he was being too forward. Memories of Thalia rekindled emotions he had mostly suppressed for almost three years. It wasn't that she hadn't been on his mind, but the immediacy of war had left little time to dwell on anything but the conflict.

———————

Two months later, he received a reply from Tasoula. She was back in Thessaloniki, trying to resurrect her shattered life. In passing she mentioned Thalia and someone called Lyke; it was clear this Lyke must be Thalia's boyfriend. A hollow sensation arose in Peter's gut, followed by a flash of anger. He had never felt this way before: like a jilted lover. Jealous. The realisation that Thalia was with another man — and probably happy — hit him hard. It also made him even more reluctant to reveal his true feelings.

It was Mac West, from the tank crew in Italy, who prompted Peter to act. The two had been friends before the war, and their shared experiences drew them even closer after it. Neither had a job, and both were skint. A borrowed packhorse and a couple of guns were all they needed to head for the wild and go deer-stalking. It was a chance to escape the disappointment they both felt about living in a country that had changed so much.

During one of their many campfire chats, Mac asked Peter why he often seemed so morose. 'You're always brooding, Peter. You're good to be with, and I like your company, but it's obvious you have something on your mind.'

'Ahh, it's nothing, Mac. I miss Greece and I miss the people there, that's all. I never realised how much I miss it. I was only there for ten months . . . but in many ways it seems more like home than here. I love the people — they're brave, resilient and very generous, even though they endured the most unimaginable hardships during the war. The Germans never broke their spirit. So yes, I'm really missing Greece.'

'And?' Mac asked.

'And nothing. That's it.'

'Don't bullshit me, Peter. I know you well enough to realise there's something else. Something's troubling you. Just give me a heads up — perhaps I can help.'

'There's nothing you can do, Mac. Nothing at all.'

'Sometimes just having a yarn helps, Peter.'

Peter scratched his forehead and rubbed his eyes; it was what he did when something was disturbing him. Well, he had to get it off his chest sometime and he might as well offload to Mac as anyone else. So he told Mac everything. About his attraction to Thalia. How she twice intervened when German soldiers were about to search his room. How she'd pretended to be his girlfriend to evade a German patrol. He even told Mac that Paddy had advised him to forget Thalia because nothing would ever come of it. And that shyness and self-doubt was preventing him from telling her how much he cared for her.

'So that's it, Mac. That's everything. I can't get her off my mind. But I'm sure she's in love with someone else — a chap called Lyke. So now there's no hope.'

Mac was an unlikely confidante — a brusque backwoodsman who had worn the same checked shirt, stained oilskin jacket and grease-marked wide-brimmed Akubra hat ever since they'd been back in New Zealand. Someone more at home with a beer in his hand at the local pub or gutting and skinning a deer than counselling a love-struck returned soldier. Yet now, his emotional sensitivity surprised Peter.

'Bullshit, Peter. There's *always* hope. Don't be a bloody fool. If you love this lassie, you've gotta tell her. Jesus Christ, after what you've been through, telling some woman that you love her should be a piece of cake. Get off your arse and write to this Greek goddess. We'll post it as soon as we get back to town.'

Peter hadn't said the word 'love', but Mac was right. He *did* love Thalia; he always had. He suddenly realised that he couldn't live out the rest of his life without knowing whether she felt the same way.

That night, he wrote two letters: one to Tasoula and the other to Thalia. He addressed them both to Tasoula though, as he couldn't remember Thalia's address. She didn't speak English anyway, and his written Greek was hopeless. Thanasis would have to translate.

At the end of his letter to Tasoula, after asking after her, Thanasis and all their old friends, he wrote:

I have a special favour to ask of you, Mrs Tasoula. Thalia Christidou has been on my mind a lot lately and I've enclosed a letter for her that I'd like Thanasis to translate.

He read and reread the letter to Thalia before folding Mrs Tasoula's letter and slipping the note for Thalia inside.

Dearest Thalia, it read. *I hope you're well and that Greece is returning to normal after such a devastating war. I hope you still remember me and all the good times we enjoyed together.*

I miss Greece very much — and I miss you very much. This will come as a shock, but I've come to realise that I've fallen in love with you, Thalia. In fact, I've been in love with you for a long time, but I was too shy to say anything.

I understand you may not feel the same way about me, but I can't go on without telling you. You may already have a boyfriend, perhaps even a fiancé, and, if so, I will have at least told you I love you.

Thalia, I would very much like to marry you. Nothing would make me happier. I'm sorry I can't be there in person to ask for your hand, but please don't doubt my sincerity or commitment.

Don't think badly of me for asking and I won't think any less of you if you say no. I will always remember you with fondness, regardless of your answer. I anxiously await your reply.

Yours sincerely

Peter 'Petros' Blunden

———————

After three failed attempts to post the letter, Peter was ready to give up. Fear of rejection was behind it; he would rather not know than be rebuffed. On the third attempt he got as far as the Post Office, but a sudden worry that a marriage proposal coming out of the blue would upset Thalia made him slip the envelope back into his jacket pocket, promising himself that he would rewrite it.

When Mac asked about the letter, Peter told his friend he had chickened out.

'For Christ's sake, Peter, you've been shot at by Krauts,

jumped from a bloody train and done a runner through Greece — and you're too bloody frightened to post a bloody letter! What's got into you, man? Hey, what's the worst that can happen? She says no, that's what. And, if she has any sense, that's exactly what she will say! Here, give me the bloody thing. I'll do it.' He snatched the envelope from Peter, turned and walked off.

'Give it back, Mac. Let me have it,' Peter called after him, but half-heartedly. Inwardly he was relieved: Mac had made the decision for him. All he could do now was wait.

Chapter
Twenty Six

In Thessaloniki, Tasoula was trying her best to create a new life for herself. It was difficult. Her concentration camp demons wouldn't leave her alone. Nightmares plagued her every night and nothing she did would erase them. She washed several times a day, just because she could. In captivity, a communal shower once a fortnight — for a few minutes only and without soap — was all the guards had allowed. And she refused to waste even a scrap of food; anything she didn't eat one day, she added to the following day's meal. She instinctively shuddered whenever a strange voice called her name, with a sudden fear that it would be her execution call.

Business had picked up a little after the war, and Tasoula now had sufficient work for six dressmakers. Tasoula wanted Thalia to come back, but the younger woman refused because others needed the job more than she did. Work from friends and acquaintances was enough for Thalia to get by. They saw each other often, though, and Thalia became even closer to her mother figure.

But the bad outweighed the good. For most, life in post-war Greece was almost as grim as it had been during the occupation. While the Germans had gone — and their departure brought great joy — the economy had collapsed and Greece sat poised on the brink of civil war. Those who had collaborated with the Nazis were at best ostracised, and at worst punished mercilessly through the ruthless rough-justice system administered by resistance fighters and those who had been betrayed.

Tasoula did have some pity for people who had traded information for food or money, to stave off starvation and provide for their families, but none for those who had done it to curry favour with the invaders or protect their pre-war wealth. Collaborators didn't always willingly collaborate, however. Some naïve Greeks had been coerced into betrayal through trickery; others had been told that close relatives would be killed if they withheld what they knew.

When Peter's letter arrived, Tasoula was anxious for some good news for a change. Two notes had been slipped into the envelope, both in English; Thanasis would have to translate. He did this for the first, writing the Greek underneath the English, and gave it to his mother. She smiled when she learned that Peter missed Greece and its people. She and Thanasis missed him, too. He had fitted in so well when he was with them. She thought back over the years since Peter had left. Unlike many of Tasoula's friends, they had all survived the war despite their suffering. All had faced adversity in different ways, but survived nonetheless.

Thanasis started on the second letter. His eyebrows lifted when he began reading, then he pursed his lips and whistled softly. When he had finished translating, he passed the letter to his mother without saying a word. After reading the letter, Tasoula was elated. Of course she knew of Thalia's affection for Peter — and now it was evident that Peter adored Thalia. The attraction was mutual. She remembered the lingering looks that Peter had directed at Thalia, and hers in return; the backward glances whenever they passed each other, and Thalia's blushes when Peter smiled at her. She recalled how Peter seemed to go out of his way to be around Thalia.

There was only one problem: Thalia was going steady with a local boy, Lyke, and they were about to become engaged. Tasoula respected Lyke; he would be a good match for her former seamstress. But she also sensed that Thalia's feelings for Lyke might not be as strong as his for her. This was just a hunch, though, and she didn't want to break up their relationship. Besides, Peter lived on the other side of the world and marrying him would mean Thalia leaving her homeland — and her childhood sweetheart — for someone in a distant country.

Still, Peter had asked her to pass on a letter to Thalia, so that's what she would do. Tasoula sent a message to her friend, urging her to come to the house as soon as possible.

———

When the young woman arrived, Tasoula wasted no time in getting to the point of her visit. 'Please sit, Thalia. I have some astonishing news for you.' Thalia was nervous. What could be so important that Tasoula would summon her to the house with such urgency? She sat, fidgeting: clasping her hands tightly together just as she had done in that first interview for the dressmaking job.

'I have a letter for you, from Petros,' Tasoula said, then paused. Should she tell Thalia about Peter's proposal, or give her the translated note to read for herself? She considered for a second or two, then decided. 'Thalia, you must read this letter now. It's very important.'

Frowning slightly, Thalia's hand trembled as she took the folded note. A letter from Petros? What could he want? Her fingers lost their grip and she dropped the letter, watching as it fluttered to the floor. Her hands still shaking, she picked it up again — then read it, unable to believe its contents. She read it a second time to make sure she understood what Peter was asking.

Thalia's mouth fell open. A thousand thoughts were racing through her mind. Old memories came flooding back, memories of the good times she had shared with Peter. Of the intensity of her feelings for him. Of the nervous embarrassment when they had gazed at each other. Of the laughter they had shared.

When she finally spoke, all she could say was: 'What? Petros? Me?'

Tasoula wasn't sure what emotions had Thalia in their grip. Disbelief? Or was it hesitation? Or uncertainty? Or indignation at the unsolicited proposal? She replied with a calmness she did not feel. 'Yes, Thalia, Petros has asked you to marry him. It's a lot to take in, and it's a long time since you've seen him, but he's a decent man and his proposal will be genuine.'

Shocked, Thalia shook her head disbelievingly. She couldn't comprehend the full significance of Peter's request. 'I . . . I'm not sure what to think, Mrs Tasoula. It has been years since he left. And he's so far away. I was so much younger then. I did have strong feelings for Petros, I admit that, but was I just a young girl infatuated with a brave soldier? I don't know. I really don't understand what I feel or what to say.'

Thalia paused, then gathered herself. 'What do I do, Mrs Tasoula? Lyke has asked me to marry him, and I've sort of accepted. I've told him I need more time, but I've said nothing to suggest I won't say yes. Now this? What am I to do?'

Thalia closed her eyes, trying to think; trying to make sense of this unexpected news. She was torn. If she were to be honest with herself, she was still in love with Peter — always had been — but she also had a strong sense of loyalty towards Lyke, who had been there for her and supported her through the tyranny of Hitler's regime. They had known each other since their schooldays. He was a good person; he didn't deserve to be discarded like an old toy she'd become bored with.

And what would Peter be like now? Had the war changed him? What did she know of him apart from what she'd learned in the few months he had spent with Mrs Tasoula? Even now she wasn't completely sure where New Zealand was.

'I'm so confused, Mrs Tasoula. I've never told Lyke I love him, but I know he thinks I do. What should I do?'

Tasoula wasn't sure how to respond. Lyke would make a caring husband and good father, but the feelings Thalia harboured for Peter were intense. She temporised. 'My dear Thalia, I can't tell you what to do; you must make up your own mind. All I can say is that Petros is an honourable man, a decent person who won't let you down, and he would not have taken this decision lightly. And we both remember how much you cared for him when he was living here. I discouraged you then because I thought you would never hear from him again after he left — I didn't want to see you hurt. Besides, if the Germans had thought you were in a relationship with an Allied soldier, your life would have been in grave danger.'

'Oh Mrs Tasoula, I'm . . . just so confused.'

'I understand, Thalia. I really do. It's a big decision, but it's one you must make for yourself. It's clear that Petros hasn't forgotten you. After all this time — and after he has returned to his family and home country — he still cares about you and wants to marry you. But Lyke is also a good man. He's handsome and kind, and many young women would be proud to carry his surname. He has no shortage of admirers, yet he chose you. The only advice I can offer is to let your heart decide. You don't want to go through the rest of your life regretting the choice you make. Follow your heart, Thalia. That's all I can tell you.'

Thalia sighed. It thrilled her that Peter felt the way he did, but it also troubled her that she must now choose between two men who loved her.

Chapter
Twenty Seven

This was the hardest decision Thalia had ever had to make. Lyke was her steady boyfriend; about to become her fiancé. She liked him a lot, respected him for being caring and supportive — but did she love him? She couldn't be sure. She had fallen in love with Peter once, but that was over three years ago, and she had only been seventeen at the time. Had it just been a wartime infatuation, prompted by the unusual times they lived in? She was now twenty, and so much more mature. How did she feel now?

Tasoula had told her to follow her heart, but her heart wasn't giving her any directions. She was still torn between the local boy she knew and trusted and the foreigner she had once fallen for during the turbulence of war. Sleep proved impossible. Some nights, she decided on Lyke; on others, she chose Peter.

She sought the advice of her best friend, Fifi. Perhaps she could help her make up her mind. But it was no good.

'Thalia, please don't ask me that — I can't tell you what to do. This is a decision for you and you alone. Petros is a wonderful man, handsome and caring, and if he had asked me to marry him I would have said yes in a heartbeat. But it's not me he wants. He's in love with *you*. Thalia, you'll make the right choice, I'm sure of that, but only you can make it.'

'Fifi, I'm so unsure. I know what you say is right, but I can't decide. I don't want to let Lyke down . . . and this is a decision for the rest of my life. The simple answer would be to say yes to Lyke and no to a man I haven't seen for years and lives so far away.'

'It's not about what's easy or convenient, Thalia. It's about what will make you happy. But if you decide in favour of Lyke, please tell Petros I'm available,' Fifi joked. Thalia laughed, but deep inside the thought of her best friend with Peter prompted a twinge of jealousy.

The answer to her dilemma didn't come in a flash; it was a gradual realisation. Yes, she liked Lyke — liked him a lot — but the more she thought about it, the more she realised that he was a wonderful friend and loyal boyfriend but *not* the person she wanted to spend the rest of her life with. She couldn't be sure if Peter was, but there was something special about him; something that set him apart from anyone else she had ever known. Lyke would be the safe option, but Thalia had never been afraid to venture into the unknown.

In the end, she made a spur-of-the-moment decision. Some would call it foolhardy, but Thalia had always been impetuous. Before she changed her mind, she rushed off to tell Tasoula. It would be Peter.

Thalia kissed Tasoula on both cheeks, then they both sat down at the dining room table.

'I've made up my mind, Mrs Tasoula. I'm accepting Petros's proposal. I'm going to marry him. I'm so excited, Mrs Tasoula. This is the first time I've ever felt this way.'

Tasoula smiled, as if she expected this answer. Thalia registered the knowing look. 'You don't seem surprised, Mrs Tasoula. You look as if you already knew.'

'I've always known, Thalia. So no, I'm not surprised. And, yes, I'm excited for you. It's wonderful news and I'm so happy. Petros will make a good husband, you'll see.'

Tasoula wrapped her arms around Thalia and hugged her. She felt the wetness of Thalia's tears against her cheek. She pulled her even closer. 'I love you, Thalia. I love you like a daughter, and all I've ever wanted is for you to be happy. Now, girl, write that letter, and post it straight away.'

Using a pen and notepad that Tasoula fetched from the dining room bureau, Thalia wrote, the tears still trickling down her face.

Dear Petros

I acknowledge receipt of your kind marriage proposal and thank you for your interest in me. It is with pleasure that I can inform you—

She stopped, scribbled over the words, and screwed the paper up into a crumpled ball. It was far too formal. If this was the man she was going to marry, the letter had to convey some emotion.

Dearest Petros

Thank you so much for your letter and marriage proposal. I accept. With all my heart, I accept. I'm so happy, I haven't stopped singing and dancing and smiling for days. Petros, I've never stopped thinking about you since I left Mrs Tasoula's. I was in love with you then, but too shy to admit it. At the time it seemed like an impossible dream. With the war on and you living so far away, I convinced myself that nothing would ever come of it, so I kept my feelings to myself.

My dearest Petros, I'm so excited and can't wait to tell my friends and family this wonderful news. I love you, Petros — I'm not sure where Nea Zilandia is, but I'll travel anywhere in the world to be with you.

Your loving Thalia

PS. Please tell me what I need to do. I realise I'll require papers to leave Greece, but what else must I do?

She debated whether to put 'XXXX' at the end, but decided against it because they had never actually kissed.

Thanasis was a little embarrassed at having to translate such an intimate letter. When he finished, his cheeks still a little pink, Thalia sealed the envelope and rushed off to post it.

When she told them what she'd done, Thalia's friends and family weren't as thrilled as she was. In fact, they weren't thrilled at all.

'I forbid it,' her adoptive mother said sternly. 'Nothing good will come of it, mark my words. He'll abandon you when he tires of you. Nothing's surer. We know what a bitch you can be sometimes.'

A surge of anger coursed through Thalia. Desdemona had

criticised and belittled her all her life. But she steeled herself to say nothing.

'You have no family there and he'll leave you with no money and no way to get home,' continued Desdemona. 'And what about Lyke? What will I tell my friends when you break off the engagement? And his family? I'm very close to them. What will they think?' Unsurprisingly, she seemed more concerned about the damage to her reputation that a broken engagement would cause than about Thalia's happiness.

'Petros would never leave me destitute in a faraway country. Never. Besides, Mamá, I'm not actually engaged to Lyke; I haven't given him an answer yet.'

'Nonsense. Everyone knows you're going to marry Lyke. His mother and I are already planning the wedding.'

Although tempted to respond, Thalia ignored this remark.

'Thalia, I forbid it and that's final.'

'But you can't. I'm of age. I'm old enough to make my own decisions, and I have. I'm marrying Petros and that's that.' At this, Desdemona stormed out, cursing Thalia under her breath.

Thalia's cousin was also actively discouraging. 'Thalia, you can't do this. You're leaving your home in Greece, and your own people, for what? To marry a foreigner you haven't seen for *years*. For all you know, he might be a criminal. It's madness. Utter madness. And what will happen if he doesn't like you? He'll sell you to some other man, that's what. You'll be a slave. Imagine that — being sold to some stranger for a few drachmas! You can't do it. You *mustn't* do it. If you go, we'll never hear from you again.' Thalia started to protest, but again realised it would be pointless.

Somewhat to her surprise, Thanasis gave her no encouragement either. 'You'll be living in a mud hut, Thalia, with no running water and no modern conveniences. This is a fact,' he said with authority. 'The doctors there practise voodoo and the only way to get anywhere is by horse and cart. Think about it, Thalia. How could you bear to live like that after all the comforts we have here?'

Thalia didn't know where Thanasis had got these 'facts' from, but she *did* know they weren't true. And as for the 'comforts' of Greece, few of these were evident in the current economic crisis.

'Nonsense, Thanasis. You're mistaken. Petros told me that New Zealand has one of the highest standards of living in the world and a first-class health system. Most homes have a car, and there are trains, planes and ferries as well. New Zealand is really safe, too. The most dangerous thing is the occasional earthquake — and God knows, we get enough of them here. Petros described the mountains and the lakes and the vast native forests. It sounds like a wonderful place.'

Although Thalia didn't convince Thanasis, he didn't pursue the argument.

All her friends bar Fifi had similar sentiments. 'It's so far away,' one said. 'We'll never see you again.' Another, echoing Thanasis's beliefs, told her: 'It's such a primitive country. You'll be forced to live like a beggar.' Thalia smiled at that; many in Greece lived in abject poverty, but of course her friend didn't mention that.

Thalia appreciated that her friends and relatives were well-intentioned; they were saying the wrong things for the right reasons. Thalia understood why they didn't want her to leave for a country so far away, a country they knew nothing about. Thalia herself only knew what she'd read about New Zealand in books at the local library, and what Peter had told her.

The negative comments exacerbated her own doubts. What if they were right? What if she didn't like it there? What if Peter had changed? Or had changed his mind? After all, it had been over three years since they had last seen each other. Lyke, on the other hand, was dependable and reliable; she knew what she would get with him. He would look after her and provide for her.

But Thalia was headstrong, independent and determined. She would let no one tell her what to do. She had always yearned for adventure, and going to New Zealand would give her that.

Fifi, of course, gave her full support. She had known Peter for almost as long as Thalia, and had no doubts about his sincerity. Nor about his commitment to care for her friend.

'You must go, Thalia. It's a long way to a strange country, but Petros won't let you down. He'll take care of you, I'm sure of that. This is your chance to get out of Greece and all its troubles, and start a new life in a new country. You'll regret it if you don't.'

Fifi was right; there was little to stay for. Greece was in turmoil. Tensions between the Communists and the monarchists were escalating, and the political and economic instability was tearing the country apart. This was her chance — possibly her only chance — to be with a man she now realised she loved. She was going to New Zealand; nothing would stop her. And while she was nervous and apprehensive, she was also excited.

Peter checked the mail every day, sometimes twice a day, anxiously waiting for Thalia's response. Three weeks passed; nothing. Then another three, and still nothing. Why hadn't she responded? Perhaps she hadn't received his letter, or maybe she had and wasn't interested. Or had she just ignored it? As each day went by, he became more and more convinced that Thalia must have rejected his proposal. That she didn't share the same affection for him as he did for her.

Finally, twelve weeks and three days after he had posted his letters, an envelope arrived, addressed in Thanasis's familiar handwriting. Peter looked at it for several minutes, afraid to open it in case it contained bad news. Holding his breath, he slipped his forefinger under the top of the flap and tore it open, then unfolded the note inside and began to read.

He wasn't normally a man who displayed his emotions, but there was nothing normal about this day — acceptance of a marriage proposal wasn't an everyday occurrence. Anyone passing might have thought they were watching a madman, pumping his fists and flapping his arms as if he had just won two thousand pounds in the Art Union lottery. It felt like he had.

Chapter
Twenty Eight

The next few weeks were a blur for Thalia. The response she received from Peter was full of elation. He told her that the New Zealand government would pay for her passage to New Zealand as part of its war brides programme. He gave her a list of things to do to prepare for her trip: a passport to organise, official approvals to request, clothes to pack, notices to be given, travel authorisations to complete and documents to sign. Dozens of documents. Forms for the New Zealand authorities, health certificates, visa and residency applications, proof of identity papers, consent forms. Thalia had never signed so much paperwork.

Then there were the inevitably sad farewells. As Thalia had no idea when she would be leaving, she had to say her goodbyes in advance. Army personnel would pick her up — no day or date had been given — and take care of all her transport arrangements. For weeks, nothing. Thalia began to despair, worried that Peter had changed his mind. She had written to him but received no reply. This wasn't unusual; mail deliveries in post-war Greece were erratic, and sometimes it seemed that more letters were lost or destroyed than delivered. But nevertheless, it was worrying.

One lunchtime, Thalia and Fifi were sitting at an outside table at the local kafenion discussing her concerns when they saw a US army jeep turn into the street. The driver slowed near their café, both soldiers in the front seats looking around. 'That will be for me,' Thalia half-joked, but her smile disappeared as the jeep did the same at the end of the road.

'Don't worry, Thalia, your turn will come.' Fifi did her best to reassure her friend, but Thalia's gloomy eyes told her that she wouldn't be easily consoled. Before Thalia could reply, the same jeep turned back onto the street and pulled up alongside their outdoor table. It had driven around the block.

'Thalia Christidou?' the GI asked tentatively. Thalia replied in Greek, 'Yes, that's me.'

The soldier beckoned her over and pointed to a name typed on a form. It was hers. Thalia nodded. 'Thalia Christidou, please come with me. We were told we would find you here,' the soldier said in English. 'I have orders to pick you up and transport you to the army base.'

Thalia didn't understand, but if she went to Tasoula's, then Thanasis would make sense of everything. But deep down, she knew this was it. Gripping the door of the jeep as if to make sure it didn't leave without her, she turned to ask Fifi to write Tasoula's address on a scrap of paper. This she handed to the driver, who then drove the two girls to Adrianoupolis Street.

Luckily Thanasis was home; there was little time. Thalia was due to leave for Thessaloniki airport at 7 p.m. that day.

Now, on Tasoula's doorstep, faced with the imminent prospect of living on the other side of the world, Thalia panicked. 'I can't do it, Fifi. I just can't do it.'

Startled, neither Fifi nor Tasoula said anything. The two GIs looked on, perplexed at this exchange in a language they didn't speak.

'Tell them, Thanasis. Tell them I'm not going.' All of a sudden, the thought of leaving Fifi, Tasoula and all her friends overwhelmed her. But Thanasis said nothing either. Then Tasoula moved towards Thalia. Fifi put her arm around her friend's shoulders, drawing her close while Thalia sobbed.

'Ask the soldiers to wait in the jeep, please, Thanasis,' Tasoula said.

Between them, Tasoula and Fifi tried to comfort the distraught Thalia. 'You must go, Thalia. Your life is with Petros now. Think about why you decided to marry him in the first place. Remember how excited you were when you accepted his proposal. You were excited because you're in love with Petros and wanted to make a home for yourself in a new country. Nothing has changed. You're still in love and you can still find happiness in New Zealand. You must go, Thalia.'

'Mrs Tasoula's right, Thalia,' Fifi chimed in. 'Nothing has changed — it's just nerves, that's all. The thought of leaving your country and your friends. It's not surprising that you're anxious, but you have a new life ahead of you. Soon, you'll forget all this. It will be a distant memory.'

'I'll *never* forget. I won't ever forget you, or Mrs Tasoula,'

Thalia said angrily through her tears. Fifi was talking as if their friendship meant nothing.

'That's not what I meant, Thalia. We'll never forget you either, but you'll soon forget your last-minute nerves. Now get yourself together and be on your way.'

'I . . . I suppose, but—'

'Enough, Thalia. It's time to go. Petros will be waiting for you.'

Thalia took a minute to compose herself. Wiping her tears away with the sleeve of her dress, she straightened her shoulders, took a deep breath and counted to ten, as she always did when she was stressed or upset.

'You're right. Both of you. I'm going. I accepted Petros's proposal, and I don't want to spend the rest of my life wondering what might have been.'

She looked at Fifi and then at Tasoula. Her eyes welled up once more; Tasoula could see the tears forming. 'Best you go now, Thalia, before we *all* start crying.'

Thalia smiled at that, albeit a little wistfully. She hugged the other two women and Thanasis, told them she loved them, and promised she would come back to Greece someday. As she left, the three waved goodbye, though Thalia could hardly see them through the trickle of tears. The GIs took her to pick up the one suitcase she was permitted to take.

———

The next few weeks passed quickly. On 14 July 1946, Thalia flew from Thessaloniki to Athens — the first time she had ever been on a plane — and was transferred to a hotel. It was the first time she had ever stayed in one of those, too. Just over two weeks later, she took her second-ever flight, from Athens to Cairo. Thalia had seen nothing like Cairo — a chaotic, overcrowded, crazy and dynamic city full of all nationalities. It both excited and repelled her.

After a week in Cairo, British soldiers took her to the Ismalia transit camp to wait for a ship to New Zealand. Finally, on 22 September, she walked up the gangway of the RMS *Rangitata* carrying her small suitcase containing the sum total of her personal possessions. On board, a steward showed her to a dormitory-style cabin she would share with seventeen other war brides, all bound for Australia and New Zealand.

From the moment she unpacked her few clothes, home-sickness engulfed her. Now that she was away from friends and family, she felt isolated, unwanted, alone and desperately depressed. She had made the biggest mistake of her life, and now there was no way back. She had abandoned a country she loved, friends she loved, a culture she loved, and Lyke, a boyfriend she might have grown to love. And for what? For a country she knew little about — and had previously thought was near England — and a man she hadn't seen for over four years and had never even kissed. How could she be so stupid?

For five days, Thalia refused to leave the cabin, taking meals in the room. For most of those five days, lying face down on her bunk, she cried. No one could shake her from her misery; three days of rough seas only added to it. To make matters worse, the only people she could converse with were Maria and Angeliki, two girls from Crete, who tried their best to cheer her up.

'Come on, Thalia. Snap out of it. It's no good crying,' Maria said, trying to console her. 'What's done is done. We're all in the same boat. There's no turning back now, so we have to make the most of it. I miss home just as much as you do, but I'm on my way to a new life. A chance to start again. Everything will turn out okay — you'll see.'

Thalia grunted. She wasn't convinced. 'But Greece is—'

'Stop it, Thalia,' Angeliki said, raising an open palm to halt the self-pity. 'Greece is our past. It's our future we must think about now. And, like it or not, our future is in New Zealand. You can't keep going on like this. Face it, Thalia — you've made a decision, and that's that.'

Her new friends were right, but Thalia still couldn't shake off her feeling of hopelessness. 'I suppose . . . ,' she said, with little enthusiasm. 'Do you think we'll ever go back to Greece again?'

'Of course. We'll go back and visit all our old friends. Of course we will.' They all knew that returning to Greece was unlikely, nigh-on impossible, but the comforting words helped.

'Look, in a few days we'll be in Colombo — that's in Ceylon, where they produce all the tea — and you're coming ashore with us, whether you want to or not. Even if I have to drag you from your bunk and force you off the ship.'

Unwillingly cheered by their determination, Thalia felt a glimmer of enthusiasm for the first time since boarding the *Rangitata*.

That day in Colombo proved to be the turning point. Led by the other two, Thalia visited Victoria Park, the massive Galle Face Green, Wolvendaal Church and all the other top attractions. She even managed a boat trip on Beira Lake. But it was the city itself that captivated her. The sights, the smells, the unfamiliar people, the colourful clothes and the uncontrolled chaos were unlike anything she had ever experienced before. It opened her eyes to a strange and exotic culture that she had not known existed. Soon, she was looking forward to Fremantle and planning what to do there. Her natural exuberance shone through anew and she joined in all the social activities on board.

The month-long voyage soon passed, and on 22 October they neared Wellington. As the ship cruised through the Wellington heads, passengers lined every vantage point, an undercurrent of excitement coursing through them. The soldiers returning to loved ones; the sons — and even some daughters — eager to see parents for the first time in years; and the war brides like Thalia, waiting to be reunited with their future husbands.

Thalia marvelled at the panoramic views as they unfolded. The hills dotted with a myriad of houses on large, uncluttered tracts of land — not packed together as they were in Thessaloniki. A long, tree-lined boulevard to the left, the tall buildings of the city itself in front, and the dozens of small craft alongside escorting them in. This was New Zealand, and she loved it already. She was dressed to the nines for the occasion, in a tailored dress, a smart double-breasted coat and a white beret.

Nervous, even slightly frightened, Thalia scanned the swarm of faces lining the dockside. She was worried that Peter might not be there, that he might have left her stranded and destitute in a foreign country with a language she didn't understand. She cupped her hands over her eyes to shield them from the morning sun. Perhaps that would give her a better view.

But there was no familiar face. Around her, soldiers and girls waved their arms and screamed as they spotted loved ones or waiting relatives. She pushed further forward. Still no sign of Peter. 'I think he's abandoned me,' she said to Maria, who had already spotted her beau and was waving to him.

'Nonsense, Thalia. He'll be here. You'll see. There are just so many people.'

'But what if he isn't?' She spoke to empty air; Maria was already making her way to the gangway. Thalia wailed, convinced that she had been forsaken. Moving right up to the railing, she gripped the wooden handrail so hard that her knuckles turned white. Peter wasn't there. He wasn't coming. She was alone.

Then, at the back of the crowd, she saw a fedora hat bobbling above the throng, and a lofty figure politely but firmly pushing his way through the mass of people. At first she didn't recognise the man, but as his tall, imposing frame drew closer, she realised it was Peter. Relief surged through her. She had never seen him looking so dapper — double-breasted gaberdine overcoat, black felt hat and plain blue tie.

'Petros! *Petros!*' she yelled, waving her hands above her head. 'Petros!'

Peter gave no sign that he had seen or heard her. He looked to his left, then his right, casting around for a familiar face. But it didn't matter that he hadn't noticed her yet. He was here. He had come. She was about to move away from the railing when she saw him waving back. He had seen her, after all. They were both flapping their arms, smiling so much it almost hurt.

It seemed to take forever to disembark, but when Thalia's turn came, she jostled her way through the departing passengers. Her Cretan friend was already locked in a passionate embrace. And there, right beside the gangway, was Peter — the man Thalia was about to marry.

'Petros!' She gaped at him, almost in disbelief. 'Petros.'

The reunion was suddenly awkward. They stood facing each other, neither certain what to say. Peter reached across the space between them. He pressed both hands against Thalia's cheeks, then gently tilted her head back until their eyes locked.

'Petros, I'm so—'

Peter put a finger to his lips. No words were needed.

They kissed for the first time.

Peter Blunden and Thalia Christidou

Author's Note

The Dressmaker & The Hidden Soldier is based on a true story. Inevitably, where facts or circumstances could not have been known or could not be validated, or where information was sketchy and records incomplete, some fictionalisation of certain details has been necessary, but the core facts of the story are documented and verifiable.

I've drawn extensively on the 64-page memoir that Peter Blunden wrote after the war and a short passage he wrote on Thalia's behalf. While thorough, his account of his wartime experiences is far too modest and I hope I have given his daring exploits the recognition they deserve. The additional information provided by their children, Nora and Pepe, enabled me to better understand their personalities and character traits.

Thanasis self-published his memoirs in a book titled *Fighting Without Weapons* and that proved to be a very important source of information on life in wartime Greece, Peter's time with his family, and the events leading up to Tasoula's subsequent arrest and incarceration. His account of his mother's trial and her time at Heptapyrgion, Pavlou Mela, Stein and Burgau painted a clear picture of her terrible ordeal. Various post-war newspaper reports — in both New Zealand and Greece — were also extremely helpful, as was an interview given by Peter.

Thalia's story was the most difficult to piece together, and I have tried to portray the harshness of life in Nazi-occupied Greece through her eyes. Little is known about Thalia's adoptive parents, save that Thalia had a difficult relationship with them and an upbringing that was strict, demanding and largely loveless. Nikolaos and Desdemona were not their real names, and their characters as depicted are fictitious.

Paddy Minogue, John Haycroft, Mac West, Uncle Giorgos, the Frères, Yarnee Mavrodos, Mrs Koula Angelidou, Father Andreas Papandreou, Mihail Xanthopoulos, Lyke, Fifi, Pauline and Madam Lapper were all real people, and I have done my best, with the limited information available, to describe their characters and personalities. George Christofer, the American GI who rescued Tasoula at the end of the war, was also a real person. Remarkably, he and Tasoula reconnected in 1973 when George, by then ex-mayor of San Francisco and head of the American Economic Mission, visited Greece. Others, like Nugget Carmichael, Ted Anderson and Phil Watkins, were also real people but their actual names are not known.

As part of my research for this book, I visited Thessaloniki and saw for myself the locations of some of these terrible events.

The block in which Tasoula's house was located has been demolished to make way for architecturally soulless apartment buildings, a pharmacy and a café. However, it is easy to envisage her large imposing home and imagine the events that took place there. Enou Place is now a playground — in need of serious care and maintenance — and cheerful groups of squealing children have replaced the menacing gangs of German soldiers.

I visited Heptapyrgion prison. It was a very emotional experience, and I was overcome when I thought of Tasoula being imprisoned in such a barbaric place. The description I have given it in this book is far too kind. It's beyond dreadful, and the reality of Tasoula and others like her being locked in its tiny lightless cells secured by heavy iron doors — malnourished and under constant threat of torture or execution — sickened me. Not since I visited Auschwitz and Dachau have I felt so revulsed.

Pavlou Mela is now a derelict site and plans have been approved to create a metropolitan park.

I also went to the Thessaloniki War Museum and the Jewish Museum, both of which gave me a much better understanding of the horrors of life in Hitler's Greece.

In addition to the memoirs of Peter, Thalia and Thanasis, I also relied on eyewitness accounts of others who had experienced life in Heptapyrgion, Pavlou Mela, Stein and Burgau to describe the conditions they had to endure. The first-hand accounts of reprisal killings on Toumba Mound were blood-chilling.

This book does not purport to be an accurate record of the

events as they happened. In his memoir Peter didn't always record the precise timing of his various experiences, so I have tried to reconstruct the timelines based on the dates of known incidents. Further, some of Peter's descriptions of his exploits are brief — all recorded matter-of-factly with characteristic modesty — and often details are limited, so I have had to expand on these to create a more cohesive account of what happened. The dialogue is, of course, fictitious: no one could know what was actually said at that time, but I have tried to incorporate the sort of language and expressions the characters might have used. For Peter and Thalia, this was based on the descriptions of their personalities provided by Nora and Pepe.

As I worked on their story, I started to truly appreciate the extent of the oppression and persecution that Peter and Thalia and their Greek resistance friends suffered during the Nazi occupation, and the danger Peter faced during his escape and his time back on the front lines. Like many of my generation, I have never experienced war or deprivation and it is therefore difficult to fully understand the enormity of this bloody and brutal conflict. All I know is that we owe Peter, Thalia, Tasoula, Thanasis and their ilk an immense debt of gratitude for the sacrifices they made to enable us to live such a tolerant and liberal lifestyle. I hope you enjoyed reading their story as much as I enjoyed writing it.

Acknowledgements

Particular thanks and recognition go to Nora Nicholson and Pepe Johnston, the daughters of Peter and Thalia, and the rest of the Blunden family. That they trusted in me to tell their parents' remarkable story is both humbling and flattering. It has been a privilege to work on such an intensely personal account of their parents' wartime exploits and I hope I have justified their faith in me. Nora's and Pepe's contribution to the finished book is significant; their input, co-operation and enthusiasm have very much shaped the way I developed the story.

Thanasis also deserves praise. Although I have never met him, his self-published book gave me a terrifying insight into the fate of resistance fighters who were arrested by the Nazis and forced to endure the horrific conditions in the concentration camps. He and his mother were ordinary people who, like many of their countrymen and women, displayed extraordinary courage in the face of a tyrannical occupier. As Churchill once said, 'It's not that Greeks fight like heroes; it's that heroes fight like Greeks.'

Teresa McIntyre, my editor, made an invaluable contribution to the telling of the story. Sometimes, as a writer, you can get so engrossed in the story that you assume too much of the reader: that they understand more of the background than you should reasonably expect of them or, worse, you give them too much irrelevant information that detracts from the storytelling. Teresa's sharp eye and judicious editing has filled in some important gaps, corrected many errors and removed unnecessary or repetitive material. The book is much more readable as a result of her influence, and I have very much enjoyed working with her. Any mistakes, inaccuracies or omissions are my fault, not hers.

Jenny Hellen, Abba Renshaw, Leonie Freeman and the team at Allen and Unwin have, as always, been helpful and supportive. That they had enough confidence in me to let me loose on this book, with only the briefest of plot outlines and a single draft preview chapter, was not only gratifying but also challenging. For their sake, I hope the book is a success. Angel McNamara is another who made an important contribution to the book. Her meticulous research provided valuable information on conditions in occupied Greece and background on the resistance movement.

My wife, Anemarie, also deserves recognition for her patience and tolerance as I worked on the manuscript — often at nights, over weekends and during holidays. Her belief in me has always been unwavering.

If you liked *The Dressmaker & the Hidden Soldier*, you'll love *The Note Through the Wire* — an extraordinary true story of a love that emerged, against all odds, between two young people from opposite sides of the globe as they fought for freedom during World War II.

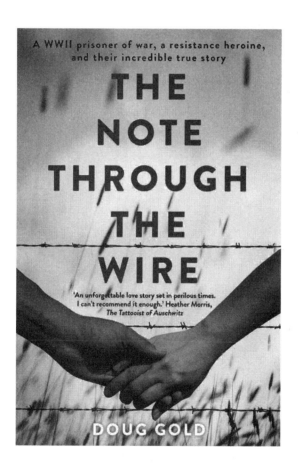

A WWII prisoner of war, a resistance heroine, and their incredible true story

THE NOTE THROUGH THE WIRE

'An unforgettable love story set in perilous times. I can't recommend it enough.' Heather Morris, *The Tattooist of Auschwitz*

DOUG GOLD